Also available ~~from~~ **and Carina Press**

Chasing Justice

Coming Soon

Killer Secrets

HUNTING
THE TRUTH

—

Kathleen Donnelly

carina
press

carina
press®

Recycling programs
for this product may
not exist in your area.

ISBN-13: 978-1-335-47591-6

Hunting the Truth

For questions and comments about the quality of this book,
please contact us at CustomerService@Harlequin.com.

Carina Press
22 Adelaide St. West, 41st Floor
Toronto, Ontario M5H 4E3, Canada
www.CarinaPress.com

Printed in U.S.A.

For my aunt June and uncle Maury, thank you for your love and always encouraging my dreams.

And for my husband, Jeff,
your love and support mean the world to me.

HUNTING
THE TRUTH

Chapter One

Pinecone Junction, Colorado

Maya sat on the edge of her bed, soaked in sweat. A chill swept over her. Shivering, she stood and walked across her room, bare feet freezing on the cold floor, and grabbed an old Marine sweatshirt from her dresser. Socks too. The clock radio said it was 0400. When she lay back down, she didn't pull the covers over her—she wouldn't be able to go back to sleep.

Juniper, Maya's U.S. Forest Service law enforcement K-9, snored on the other side of the room in her crate, curled up in a little ball. The Malinois had become used to Maya waking up early or in the middle of the night and slept soundly through her nightmares. Part of Maya wanted to wake Juniper up and have her climb into bed with her, but she didn't want to disturb the dog or start a bad habit she'd regret later—especially since Juniper was likely to shred the comforter.

Listening to Juniper's snores, Maya turned on the lamp by her bed. She pulled a journal out of her nightstand and wrote down the details of the nightmare. Her Veterans Affairs therapist had recommended this exercise, but Maya also thought her memories could help her investigation. Her hands shook as she tried to scribble down the notes. Hopefully, she could decipher them later.

In the first part of my dream, I was camping with Nana and Mom. We ate s'mores and then played tag. Afterwards we all snuggled up in our sleeping bags. I was happy, content and felt safe. Then the second part of the dream began. The nightmare. I was back at the house where Mom and I lived. Mom was grabbing me by the shoulders and telling me to run and hide so the bad people wouldn't find me. I remember being so scared as I went to the closet and concealed myself. Smoke started drifting in and I knew I was trapped. I was trying so hard not to cough and give away my location. I heard the gunshot that killed my mom. That memory startled me awake.

Maya closed her journal and put it back on her nightstand, her hand still shaking from the adrenaline the dream created. She picked up her cell phone and went to contacts and her favorite list, which only had two numbers—Pops, her grandfather and the local sheriff for Western River County, and Josh Colten, the chief deputy sheriff.

Josh had become a close friend. They had kissed, once. And since then, Maya had avoided ever kissing Josh again. Not that she didn't want to. She just couldn't trust herself to be in a relationship right now. She suspected Josh understood this and was being patient. That only drove Maya crazier because it proved he was a good guy. But it also made her wonder at times if *he* had decided they should just be friends. It was easier to not ask. She didn't know which would be more difficult emotionally—a relationship or just remaining friends.

No matter what their status, Maya knew she could call Josh at any time if she needed something. She thought about doing that now but hesitated. Josh would help her sort through her nightmares, but it was four in the morning. Maya didn't want to be that crazy girl who called at all hours.

She set her phone back down. Noticing that Juniper was now awake, she got off the bed and unlatched the crate door. Juniper came out stretching and yawning while Maya rubbed her ears and then massaged down her back. Juniper responded with a tail wag and little groan, making Maya smile. She didn't know what she'd do without Juniper.

Juniper and Maya had completed their K-9 certification for the U.S. Forest Service over the summer, making them an official team. Maya was a U.S. Forest Service Law Enforcement officer for the Pino Grande National Forest in Colorado. She and Juniper had teamed up when Juniper's first handler and Maya's good friend, Doug, was killed. Maya had been resistant at first about the commitment of working another K-9, but now she was happy she'd accepted the job. She couldn't ask for a better partner.

"Come on," she said to Juniper. "If we're going to be up this early, let's at least get some coffee."

Juniper grunted and followed her out to the kitchen. Maya worked on getting the coffee started. Juniper strolled over to the couch, her golden eyes glancing back to see if climbing up would be allowed.

"No, you stay off the couch. Your bed is over there," Maya said, pointing to the dog bed in the middle of the living room. "You can go back to sleep there with your teddy bear. I know you're not a morning dog."

Juniper's pointy ears drooped and she gave Maya a look that mixed pathetic with annoyed. Then she trudged over to her bed, lay down and stretched out. She gently picked up and held an old teddy bear in her mouth. It was the one toy Juniper hadn't destroyed. Maya didn't want Juniper to have too much freedom in the house—you didn't want a working dog to enjoy staying home more than their job—but if she let Juniper go back to sleep, she could have a cup of coffee before they went for their walk in the chilly fall morning.

She turned around, staring across her kitchen, which opened to the living room. A large evidence board sat near the couch. When she had first started focusing on this new investigation, some of her nightmares from serving in Afghanistan had gone away, but they'd been replaced by new nightmares. This investigation was personal, and Maya desperately wanted answers.

Copies of crime scene photos and notes were pinned up. She had copied them from the homicide book along with all the reports to study during her free time. She'd never take the real pictures or reports home and compromise the investigation. In fact, she knew she had to work on this investigation on her own time, but luckily a good friend of hers was the investigator for the CBI—the Colorado Bureau of Investigation. Because of the family connections with this investigation, the state had taken over.

Her friend, Lucas Tucker, had shared what he could knowing it could get him into trouble if anyone found out, but he knew that she was intent on solving the crimes. It also helped that he was a fellow Marine and Maya had served with him in Afghanistan. Maya and her military K-9 Zinger had saved his life when Zinger found an IED before Lucas stepped on it. He always said he owed her. She didn't really agree because she thought she was just doing her job, but she would take any and all information that Lucas would give her.

She had turned the pictures over, so she didn't have to look at them. Seeing the photos of her loved ones would only trigger more nightmares.

But Maya knew what horrific sights lurked behind each photo. This was personal because the victims were her mother, Zoey, and her grandmother, Nana. Maya swore she would figure out who took them from her and why. She had reopened the investigation by looking into evidence Pops had marked and the CBI had gathered at the crime scenes. Even though Nana's death appeared to be a suicide, a police officer treated every scene like a homicide and Pops had done just that. When he had arrived home and found Nana, he had secured the scene and made sure the evidence was not contaminated. Maya didn't know how he had managed. Her grandfather was a strong man. She could barely stand to look at the pictures.

Packed in an evidence bag were cigarette butts that Pops found behind some trees the night Nana died. Trees were good spots to watch the intended victim while staying hidden. Someone had spied on Nana, but no one had investigated what Pops found. It didn't matter if you were the sheriff. If the coroner and investigators thought it was a suicide, that's what it was ruled and that was the end of the investigation. Only Pops and Maya were alike—Pops hadn't given up. He couldn't use department funding or deputies, but he had continued to investigate on his own. Maya started helping him a few months ago and she wanted DNA run on the cigarettes.

That's when Maya found out Lucas had taken on a job with the CBI. She'd called him up and explained the situation. He had agreed to have the cigarettes tested for DNA before she'd left for certification in July. Now it was late September and the changing leaves outside only reminded Maya of how much time had passed with no results yet. She knew the lab was backlogged and cold cases didn't receive priority, but she kept hoping that Lucas would call soon. If the cigarettes had matching DNA, then maybe the gun could be explained.

Maya, Pops and Josh had all gone through different scenarios with the gun. How had the same gun been used to kill Maya's mother and Nana? Had Nana kept the gun all these years? Josh had even asked the difficult question that Maya and Pops didn't want to think about—could Nana have killed Zoey?

Zoey had been found with a heroin needle in her arm and a gunshot wound to the head. The gun was never found—until Nana's death. The same weapon had killed both. Investigators suspected that maybe Nana had killed Zoey, hidden the gun and then years later taken her own life out of guilt. Perhaps she was angry that her daughter was using drugs again and putting Maya in jeopardy.

But Maya and Pops's answer was always no. No way would Nana do such a thing. And no way would she ever take her own life. It was frustrating at times because there were more questions than answers.

Hearing the coffeepot sputter and hiss as steam escaped, Maya opened a cabinet and went to grab a mug. As her hand touched the smooth handle, Juniper leapt off her dog bed, barking and growling. She hurtled herself over to the far window near the evidence board and pushed her nose against the glass, continuing her snarling and barking.

The mug fell to the floor, shattering into pieces.

Maya grabbed her shotgun that sat by the front door.

"Juniper. Come," she ordered. She didn't want the dog to be an easy target at the window. Juniper hesitated and then came over to Maya, who told her to heel and then immediately went to the back door in her bedroom. That door opened out to a porch and Maya made sure it was locked.

A tingle Maya acquired from being in Afghanistan and from her time as a law enforcement officer swept over her. The sensation came from someone watching you, and she had felt that a lot recently. Sometimes Juniper would bark. Other times she wouldn't, making Maya wonder if she was paranoid and projecting her emotions onto her dog. Or maybe Juniper only saw rabbits outside and barked at those, but Maya didn't want to disregard her instincts. Or her dog's.

She hadn't told Pops or Josh. She didn't want them to worry.

Maya kept Juniper by her side and stayed in the hallway for cover. She listened for any noise, but there was only silence. Peering around the wall, she strained to peek out the windows, but with the lamps on inside and the darkness outside, it was difficult to see. If only she'd shut off the lights when Juniper had started barking.

"Come on, Juniper. Let's check outside."

After tugging on a pair of jeans, she secured Juniper's tracking harness and snapped on the leash. She grabbed her jacket and hooked on her duty belt with her Glock. That would be easier to handle than a shotgun.

The pair stepped out into the cool morning. The first

hints of sunlight silhouetted some large fir trees. Juniper trembled by Maya's side, waiting for her handler to give her a command. Maya stayed still and listened.

Outside the cabin was acres of forest. Not easy to clear as she could go for miles searching for someone and there were plenty of hiding places.

A black raven squawked in a tree. The creek that flowed behind the cabin gurgled and bubbled, running slow this time of year. Nothing unusual, yet Maya unholstered her Glock.

She and Juniper stepped off the front porch. *I'm tired of being the prey. It's time to figure out if someone is watching me.*

Letting out the long tracking leash, Maya cast Juniper in different directions. "Seek. Go find 'em."

Juniper stuck her nose to the ground and began working back and forth, looking for a scent. Maya directed her dog toward the end of the cabin and the window where Juniper first barked, keeping them close to the cabin wall. Juniper didn't seem to be finding a scent to track. Maya kept an eye on her dog, watching for a change in body language. Together they crept toward the corner of the cabin.

Step by step, Maya worked to control her breathing. She had her Glock in hand and, despite the adrenaline, held it steady. Juniper crept with her, at times sticking her nose up in the air and at other times pushing it to the ground. Then Juniper's tail came down. Her body was tense, but not tight and rigid like when she had caught a suspect's odor. Maya didn't see any signs of shoeprints, but she continued to follow her dog. Maybe Maya was imagining this. Maybe Nana's case and the thought of someone watching her family was creating delusions.

They came up to the corner and paused. Then Maya and Juniper stepped around in unison, Maya with her gun pointed and Juniper growling.

Three pairs of eyes stared back at them.

A mother fox and her two kits sat across the stream, paws still wet from crossing. They were probably spooked from Maya and Juniper sneaking up on them. The mother fox had a dead rabbit in her mouth.

"Juniper," Maya said, exasperated. "Come here. Sit."

She holstered her gun. Juniper paused and stared at Maya and then at the intruders. She let out a low whine and ducked her head down.

"Come. Here. Now," Maya said in a stern voice.

Juniper sighed and turned around, coming back to sit by her side.

"You all go on now and have your breakfast. And stay away from the neighbor's chickens. Help yourself to more rabbits so Juniper has less to chase."

The foxes scampered off into the trees.

Maya and Juniper headed back in. She had a broken coffee mug to clean up and a nasty headache starting. As she opened the door, a gentle breeze picked up, bringing with it a slight smell of cigarette smoke. Juniper stuck her nose up in the air. Maya studied her dog's reaction. They could go out and try tracking again, but just as quickly as the scent started, it left.

Am I imagining things like the smell of cigarettes? It could be scent from a car passing by on the road. Maya noticed that Juniper had quit air scenting and shoved her nose toward the door, wanting in, ready for her breakfast. If Juniper didn't show interest, then it probably was a passing car.

Get your act together, Thompson. Stop imagining

things that aren't there. Maya and Juniper went back
inside, but as she shut the door behind her, she took one
last look outside, hoping she wasn't losing her mind.

He watched Maya and her K-9 head back into the cabin.
She was vulnerable living alone out here in the middle
of nowhere, except for the dog. If it weren't for the dog,
he'd have already finished the job he came to do.

He slunk back into the trees toward the road and took
another long drag off the cigarette he'd lit, enjoying the
nicotine hitting his system. He was grateful for the distraction of the fox family. If they hadn't been there, the
dog might have found his trail. He was careful where
he watched from, hopefully far enough away that Maya
wouldn't cast the dog in the right area to catch his scent,
but police dogs were good. Eric Torres knew this from
personal experience.

He walked back to the road and climbed into his truck,
taking another drag from the cigarette. Smoking was
his bad habit, but it seemed the least of his worries right
now. *Habits.* People were funny and trying to figure
out the habits of others was difficult, but Eric was fine
with long surveillances. He'd done it for years as a cop
and even though he'd left the profession, or rather been
forced out, it was easy to get back into doing something
like this. Especially when it gave him a chance to watch
Maya and plot how to get to her. Although he'd been
watching her enough to know that she was tough, and
this wouldn't be an easy task.

He'd used binoculars to peer through the window
before Maya woke up. The evidence board was looking more in depth. She had turned the pictures around.

They bothered her. It was a weakness and maybe something he could use.

But he'd seen her notes written up on the board. The one that worried him the most was the one that read, *Cigarettes found at each scene. Check with Lucas on DNA.* Last night, she'd added another note: *Who was watching Mom and Nana? And why?*

And why was circled in bright red dry-erase marker. Maya was getting closer to the truth—*she's investigating, and I can't let her do that.*

He had to stop her.

Eric needed to figure out what made Maya tick and how to best approach her. Taking another drag off the cigarette as he drove away, Eric wondered, what weaknesses did Maya have other than the pictures? What could he use to get her attention and get her to give him what he wanted? If she didn't, she'd be joining her mother and grandmother in the cemetery.

So far, the few things he could see that meant the world to her and could be used to get his way were the dog, the deputy sheriff, who obviously had intentions other than helping with the investigation, and her grandfather, the local sheriff. Going after a sheriff was way too risky. But the dog and her deputy friend—those two were good possibilities. He'd have to think it all over and list out the pros and cons of each one.

Not much stopped him from getting his way.

Chapter Two

A few hours and four cups of coffee later, Maya and Juniper got in the patrol car and headed down the mountain toward Fort Collins. Exhaustion washed over her. The caffeine didn't seem to be helping. Juniper, on the other hand, shredded her current blanket in her K-9 compartment and then curled up and went back to sleep.

Maya came out of the mountains and down toward the front range. The drive took about an hour, but she had decided it was worth it to go once a week to the veterans' support group. Her boss, the patrol captain, Todd Davis, had agreed to give her every Tuesday off so she could do this. Josh often came with her and then they'd have lunch afterward. Sometimes they'd attend an AA meeting too. Maya knew she had a ton of support, but that didn't always make things easier. Sometimes it even made it harder.

As she turned onto Highway 287, her cell phone chirped. Josh.

"Hey there," Maya said, putting the phone on speaker. "How's it going?"

"Good," Josh said. "Sorry I couldn't go today."

"No worries. I'm going to the support group and then to do a little shopping in Fort Collins. Might take Juniper on a jog on the Poudre Trail since she has enough energy to shred blankets."

Josh laughed. "Maybe you should quit giving her things to rip up."

"And take away all her fun? I couldn't be that mean."

"You sound tired. Did you sleep okay?"

Maya hesitated. *How the heck did he know that just by talking to me? I thought I sounded all right. I don't want him to know how I just about shot a fox family because I thought they were intruders.*

"Yeah, I'm sleeping pretty good," she eventually answered.

"I don't believe you."

"Would I lie to a law enforcement officer?" she asked, mixing a bit of humor and sarcasm.

"I don't know, would you?" Josh said.

She laughed and then said, "Will you be done with the mountain of paperwork Pops gave you by dinner? I was thinking I could grab some food at the Black Bear Café, and we could eat it at my cabin."

"Sounds like a plan."

"Great. I'll call you when I get back from down in the valley."

"I look forward to it," Josh said.

They both hesitated. Maya knew that in most relationships this would be her opportunity to say something important that showed she cared for Josh. Something simple like, *I can't wait to see you tonight.* Or even going further and telling him *I love you.*

But instead, Maya said, "Me too. Talk soon."

Then she hung up.

"What's wrong with me?" she muttered.

Juniper answered with a grunt.

"I don't need your opinion."

A few miles later, Maya and Juniper arrived at the building for the support group. She parked next to a blue Jeep that belonged to one of the group members, Kendra. Maya and Kendra had sort of become friends, although Maya had a hard time with any type of close relationship ever since she'd returned home. But Kendra had just moved to Colorado after discharging from the Air Force and was searching for a job in law enforcement, so Maya had agreed to have dinner sometime with Kendra and discuss different agencies in the area. As a Forest Service officer, Maya worked with several sheriff departments since the forest boundaries were in multiple counties.

"Hey there," Kendra said to Maya as they each stepped out of their vehicles. "How's it going?"

"Good, thanks," Maya said. She opened the door to Juniper's special compartment and made sure she had water. Juniper tried to push past her, wanting to come out, but Maya gently restricted her.

"We'll go on a run after I get done here, girly," Maya said, making sure that the climate control settings were good and Juniper would be comfortable until the session was over.

"You should bring her in sometime," Kendra said.

"Yeah, Juniper would like that, but not everyone loves dogs. Not to mention, she's a patrol dog, not a therapy dog."

"True. So hey, you want to do lunch after this? Then I'm going to go get another tattoo. It's going to be the Air Force emblem with the years I served. You should get one," Kendra said. "I'm getting it here on my other arm next to the skull and crossbones."

"I'm so sorry, I can't today," Maya said. "I have some errands to run, and Juniper really needs to get out for a hike. Maybe the next meeting? At least for lunch. I'm not ready for a tattoo yet," she added, thinking about the one design she had considered—a tribute to her fallen military K-9, Zinger.

"Sure, that works. And you should bring your boy toy too. What's his name?"

"Uh, Josh. He's not my boy toy."

"Girl, you're crazy if you don't throw yourself at him."

"It's not like that," Maya said. "We're just friends."

"Yeah, right," Kendra said, as Maya shut the door to Juniper's compartment. They started to walk across the parking lot. "Maybe you should talk about your denial issues today at group."

"I'll think about it," Maya said with a grin. Kendra did have a point. About Josh—not about denial issues. Well…maybe she had a point there too.

The pair walked into the room and each grabbed a cup of coffee. Maya poured extra creamer into hers. Then she took a seat in the support group circle. Kendra plopped down next to her and was filling her in on her last disastrous date and applications she had out to other police departments.

Maya scooted back in her chair and started to tune Kendra out. She liked Kendra, but the feeling of someone watching her plagued her. *Have I become that paranoid? Maybe it's from the dreams I've been having. Should I talk to Dr. Meyers about this? Or could someone really be watching me? If so, why? What do they want?*

Maya crossed her arms, pulling them in tight. The dreams happened daily and like the one she'd had the previous night, they often started with good memories and then changed to the night her mother died...

When she was four, almost five years old, she had believed she was the best at keeping secrets and playing games. When she played hide-and-seek, no one ever found her. She had listened in on conversations between her mother and her nana without them knowing.

As Maya sat at the old wood kitchen table eating her macaroni and cheese with hot dogs, she hid her latest secret. She had pulled out the small pieces of meat and carefully covered and concealed the hot dog slices in the napkin on her lap for her new friend, Gunner. Maya didn't have many friends except for her grandparents, Pops and Nana. So, when she met the giant German shepherd owned by their neighbors, she felt an instant connection. She loved his big pointy ears and the way he would chase his toys. Maya didn't even mind all the slobber.

Then she heard Gunner bark frantically outside. Simultaneously, someone pounded on the front door.

"What the heck?" Maya's mom muttered, marching over to the front door in the living room.

Where Maya sat at the kitchen table, she couldn't quite see out the window that overlooked the porch. Her mom opened the door, blocking Maya's view there too. Wondering if maybe Nana and Pops were stopping by for a surprise visit, Maya slipped off her chair and trotted around the table over to the window. She pushed back the white curtain, peering outside. There was a man standing there. He had dark curly hair and squinty eyes that reminded Maya of a rattlesnake she'd recently seen. Her nana had told her to stay away from rattlesnakes because they would strike and were poisonous.

There was a gun in a holster in the back of his pants. Guns were dangerous. Her mother and Nana had told her so. Pops, a deputy who took bad people to jail, had told her to be careful with firearms and that only people who wore a star on their shirt like him were allowed to have weapons. He promised he would teach her to shoot when she grew up, but for now she needed to know guns were dangerous and not toys. So why did this man have a gun? Did her mom know about it?

Maya snuck over to the couch that faced the front door. She hunkered behind it, hoping hiding would make her feel safer. Her mom and the man had started to argue and then escalated to yelling. She heard her mother sob, but then the door had slammed shut.

The bad man was gone—

"Hey, are you listening?" Kendra asked.

"What? Uh, yeah. I was listening."

"You're not a good liar," Kendra said. Maya was worried she'd hurt her feelings but saw Kendra smile.

"Sorry about that," Maya said. "Just have a lot on my mind."

"No worries," Kendra said. "Here's the good doctor now. Let's see if he can cure us today."

Maya shrugged, not certain what to say. There wasn't a cure for PTSD, only learning to manage it better. Things like mindfulness and AA helped Maya, but she had a long way to go. Kendra seemed to cope by trying to be flippant. *To each their own, I guess.*

Chapter Three

Dr. Meyers, a tall man with thick glasses and a goatee, came into the room and took a seat. Maya liked Dr. Meyers. He understood her and the other veterans because he'd served himself. He came from a military family starting with his grandfather, who was a Tuskegee Airman, and had served in Desert Storm and Iraq. When he got out of the military, he said he'd realized that helping other veterans recover from their traumas helped him as well. Maya didn't know how he did it, but she knew he cared.

"Morning," Dr. Meyers said.

Some of the others in the group mumbled an answer. A few veterans were talkative, but most, like Maya, preferred to stay quiet. Dr. Meyers never seemed to mind or push any of them.

"Let's talk about something that keeps troubling you and we'll see how we might be able to help," Dr. Meyers said. "I know this can be difficult, but it's important to share with the group so we can support you through it. We've all seen difficult things. It's part of being a combat soldier. Or maybe there's something that's happened in civilian life. Whatever it is, this is a safe place to share. Who wants to go first?"

There was silence, and then an older gentleman spoke up. Gray haired, he was about the age of Pops and, like Pops, had served in Vietnam toward the end of the war.

"I have this event that haunts me," the man started. He paused for a second. "I was out on patrol with my unit. We'd all smoked a shitload of weed just trying to survive each day. Ya know?"

Several people murmured in response. Maya stayed quiet. Alcohol was her form of weed, but she knew plenty of soldiers who had smoked it. She didn't judge— they all had to deal somehow.

"So, it was a pretty normal patrol," the man continued. "We came to this village we suspected were harboring Viet Cong and the next thing we knew, we were being shot at. The guy next to me, his head exploded. There was no chance of saving him. I went nuts. I pulled the trigger 'til the clip was out. Then it was silent. It was all over as quick as it started. Then I heard this sobbing. It was a little kid. A girl. She was hiding from us."

Maya took a deep breath. Her chest tightened. She fought to breathe. Dr. Meyers was saying something back to the man, but she couldn't hear.

I'd hidden.

She'd been the only witness. Why couldn't she remember more details from that night? Her muscles tightened like when she was hiding in the closet. She could taste the mac and cheese and smell…smoke.

She closed her eyes. Dr. Meyers was saying something, but if she could keep remembering, she could bring a killer to justice. Memories started snapping together like a jigsaw puzzle.

Her mom had turned around and grabbed Maya by

the shoulders. "You are the best at hide-and-seek. Do it now and don't let the bad people find you."

"What? Is the scary man back? Should I call Pops?"

"Just hide. Promise me you'll stay where they can't find you."

"Okay." Tears had streamed down Maya's face.

"I love you, baby. I love you." Maya's mom gave her a big hug and then pushed her away. "Go. Now."

Maya turned and ran down the hallway. She had a secret place where her mom had never found her when they played—the closet. There were lots of items in the back that Maya could slip behind, including jackets and a vacuum big enough to conceal her feet and legs. She squeezed herself into the small space. She thought she could hear Gunner barking again outside.

Did the bad man come back? If Maya could get to a phone, she could call Pops. But there was no way she could get to the phone without leaving the closet and being in plain view. If there was one thing she'd learned from being the best at hide-and-seek, it was that you never took the risk of being seen.

She had heard her mother yelling, so she curled up in a ball against the closet wall, clenching her fists and holding back sobs. She had been so scared, but her mom had told her to hide.

BANG.

Maya's breathing quickened. She gulped rapid, shallow breaths. She rubbed her sweaty palms on her jeans, struggling to keep remembering.

"Maya? Maya? Are you okay?" Dr. Meyers's voice interrupted her memory as Kendra nudged her. Maya found herself back in the support group room. Everyone stared at her.

"Uh. Yeah…yeah, I'm good."

"Is there anything you want to share with the group?"

"I just… I don't know."

"It's okay, Maya. You don't have to go until you're ready."

Maya's heart pounded. She'd never really shared with the group, but maybe this was a time to do it. Maybe if she opened up, some more memories would come back to her. Memories that would help her nail the people responsible for killing her mother and Nana.

"I'm ready," Maya heard herself saying. She could tell by the expression on Dr. Meyers's face, he was surprised but also pleased.

The words spilled out. Maya wanted to stop them, but she couldn't. She told the group about the night her mother died. How she hid. How she was the only witness, and how she was remembering things. In pieces, like snapshots.

"As I investigate, I keep having more memories. If I can just remember, I can bring closure to my mother's murder and maybe figure out who killed my grandmother. I know their deaths are connected." Maya paused, not wanting to share much about the gun. It would look bad for her grandmother, and she knew in her heart that Nana didn't kill her mother. "I'm waiting on DNA evidence to prove that, but if I could recall something important, like any small detail about the person who showed up at the door the day my mother died, that would help our investigation. It's frustrating to be a witness and not be able to help."

Maya stared around at the group, expecting some sort of judgment like she was crazy. Her hands shook. She clasped them together on her lap. Many of the group members nodded with understanding looks on their faces. Even Kendra seemed more serious, as if Maya had touched on a memory for her too.

"So that's it. That's my trauma. Or at least one of them," Maya said.

"Thank you for sharing, Maya," Dr. Meyers said. "I know that was difficult, but by sharing you can heal and move forward. You were also a child. Don't be too hard on yourself in regard to the memories."

"Yeah. Right. Okay."

"We are out of time for today," Dr. Meyers said. "I'll see you all next week, but know that if you need anything, you can reach out at any time."

Maya stood. Kendra came up next to her and wrapped her in a hug. Not knowing how to react, Maya awkwardly returned the gesture.

"Thanks for sharing all that about your mom. I understand how awful that is. My mom was murdered when I was a kid too." Much to Maya's relief, Kendra released her and stepped back.

"Really?" Maya asked. Kendra had never mentioned it before, although the violent death of a parent wasn't really something you told people about. "Did they catch the killer?"

"It was my old man. Typical domestic thing."

"I'm sorry to hear that," Maya said.

"The thing is, I'd love to talk more with you about it. I mean, I haven't met too many people who lost a parent to violence growing up. It's what inspired me to get into law enforcement. I want justice for all the mothers out there who get the crap beat out of them, ya know? I know you can't do lunch, but I could come up to Pinecone Junction tonight and do dinner."

"I can't. I'm so sorry. Josh and I are having dinner tonight."

"I hope you get dessert with dinner, if you know what I mean," Kendra said with a wink.

"There's the Kendra I know and love," Maya said, willing her face to not turn red at the mention of Josh and dessert. She started rubbing her necklace, a nervous habit that had started years ago. "I better get going. Check on Juniper, get my errands done. The day is going by fast."

"Sounds good." Kendra leaned in closer toward Maya and squinted. "I love your necklace. It's pretty cool. Where did you get it?"

Realizing that she was still fingering the necklace, Maya let go of it. Nana had given it to her, and she wore it for good luck. It was a key engraved with her birthdate and her mother's birthdate. It meant a lot to her, but otherwise it was just a plain-looking necklace. No diamonds or anything flashy. "It was a gift from my nana. It belonged to my mother."

"I'm glad you have it," Kendra said.

"Me too," said Maya. "See you next week."

She headed out the door into the bright sunshine. She was ready to escape, get her errands done and exercise Juniper, then get back up to her cabin where she could sort through her thoughts. Maybe she'd share some of her memories with Josh at dinner and get his opinion.

A tall guy with dark hair stood next to Maya's patrol vehicle. He was talking to Juniper through the window and flashed a smile in her direction, a small dimple appearing as he grinned. Maya loved that dimple. She allowed herself a small smile and tried to ignore how happy she was seeing Josh standing there. Her heart rate quickened. *Good grief, this is like a schoolgirl crush. Get over it...*

Maya didn't know why Josh had this effect on her. Yes, he was good-looking to say the least, but she'd worked with plenty of guys in the military and many of them were handsome too. But none of them brought up these intense feelings. They were more like brothers to her.

She'd give anything for a drink right now. Something to calm her nerves. But Maya knew that would be the worst thing she could do. She'd managed three months now without a drink and had the AA chip to prove it. Take it day by day. That was the advice Josh had given her. He'd told her that the cravings would also start dying down, but at the moment, Maya just wanted to escape. If only Nana were here. They'd talk about Josh. Nana would give her good advice.

A wave of sadness only increased Maya's craving. How could so many feelings hit a person at once? She just wanted to make them all go away.

As Maya headed over to her vehicle, Kendra caught up to her and gave her a light punch in the arm. "Go have some fun, Thompson."

Snapping out of her trance, Maya said, "Uh, yeah. Okay."

"Hey, Kendra," Josh said as the pair approached.

"Hi, Josh. You have an opening yet on the department for me?"

"Actually, we might," Josh said, handing Kendra his card. "Give me a call. I'll get you more information and we can start the application and interview process."

"Thanks," Kendra said, "I'll be in touch." She turned toward Maya and gave a wink. "Enjoy the scenery on your walk today."

Maya shook her head and finally had to laugh. "Okay, I will. See you next week. And maybe see you up at the station for an interview."

As Kendra waved bye and headed to her car, Josh said, "She sure talks about the scenery a lot."

"I think she really likes Colorado..." Maya said, stifling a laugh. "What are you doing here? I thought Pops had you buried in paperwork."

"I finished early."

"Really?"

"Okay, maybe not, but your grandfather told me to finish later and come meet you."

"He told you that, huh?"

"You sound like you don't believe me," Josh said, pretending to be hurt.

"I don't know. That doesn't sound like Pops..." Maya stopped herself. Why was she arguing? Josh had made the time to come see her and Juniper. She should be more appreciative.

"If my paperwork is worrying you, I could always head back and finish it."

"No, no, it's not worrying me." Maya stared into Josh's dark chocolate-brown eyes. To her relief she saw that he seemed more amused than hurt. *I've never met someone who understands me this well.* She unlocked her vehicle and said hi to Juniper. Turning back to Josh, she said, "You want to go for a walk along the Poudre River?"

"Actually, I have some good news for you first."

"Really? What?"

"I found your mom's friend, Denise Douglas. She lives here in Fort Collins. Want to go see if she's home? See if she remembers anything?"

"Yes," Maya said. Denise and Maya's mother were best friends in high school. In fact, her mother, Zoey, had convinced Denise to run away with her. Maya suspected Denise could fill in some holes in their information about her mother's activities up in Montana that might help them find her killer, but they'd had a hard time locating Denise. Josh had volunteered to take on that task. She couldn't believe that Denise was right here in Fort Collins. She was limited on what she could do with the investigation, but one thing she could do was talk with witnesses. "Do you have her address?"

"I do. How about I ride with you?" Josh said, opening the passenger door and climbing into the front seat.

"I would love that," Maya said. She locked gazes with Josh. "Thank you so much for continuing to pursue this lead and finding Mom's friend. It really means a lot to me."

"Of course," Josh said. "Hopefully she'll have some good information that we can pass on to Lucas."

Maya headed around to the driver's side of her patrol vehicle, trying not to get too excited about meeting her mom's friend. She might not even be home. Maya slid into the front seat and opened the partition between the cab and Juniper. Juniper poked her head through, her pointy ears flipping forward as she licked Josh on the cheek.

"Getting fresh with me, huh, girl?" Josh laughed and scratched Juniper behind the ears.

Maya started the car as Josh gave her the address to Denise's house. Would Denise be able to provide information to unanswered questions? Maybe something that would explain why her mother was murdered? Maya could only hope those answers were minutes away.

Chapter Four

They pulled up to a nice house on the west side of town. The neighborhood showed the growth the Colorado Front Range had experienced over the last decade. Two-story houses sat side by side not too far from an old farm that clashed country with urban living. Each house had a manicured front lawn, backyards with swing sets and toys and flowerbeds that were starting to be cut back for the fall. A few dogs barked from surrounding houses and Juniper started to bark back.

"Quiet," Maya said, getting a pathetic "what did I do wrong" look back from Juniper. She still needed to burn off some energy today and Maya hoped they had time to get out on the trail.

Josh double-checked the address with his notes. "This is the right house."

Maya took in the two-story home painted a light cream color with a dark red trim. A wave of sadness hit her. If her mother hadn't been murdered, maybe they would have had a home like this. What would it have been like to have a mother to meet up with and share hopes and dreams with? Maya was so grateful for Nana, but she realized how much grief she still had over losing her mother.

"You okay?" Josh asked.

"Yeah, I just hope she's home." Maya opened the door and stepped out of her vehicle, shoving her emotions aside for the time being. He never judged her, and she appreciated that. It was just hard for Maya to open up.

They started up the walk to the front door. Josh was behind her and gently put a hand on her back. Maya flashed him a smile, knowing he was there to support her.

She rang the doorbell, both of them staying off to the side—a habit from being law enforcement officers. A dog started yapping inside. Maya guessed it was probably a small dog based on the bark. She was about ready to ring the doorbell again when she heard footsteps approaching the front door and then it opened.

A middle-aged lady with the first signs of gray in her light brown hair, reading glasses hanging around her neck and a kind expression, stared back at them. Her expression shifted from kind to surprised and then she went sheet-white like she'd seen a ghost.

"Denise Douglas?" Maya asked.

"Who's asking?" Denise snapped back.

Maya hesitated. She knew from pictures and from what everyone said that she was the spitting image of her mother. Seeing Maya standing on her front step was probably a shock for Denise. "Denise, I'm U.S. Forest Service Officer Maya Thompson. I think you knew my mother, Zoey?"

Denise didn't answer. She locked her gaze onto Maya and then to Josh. "What do you want?"

"I'd love a few minutes of your time to talk about my mother and what you knew about her. From what we know, you went to Montana with her when you were in high school."

"I don't have anything to tell you. That was a long time ago."

"Ma'am." Josh spoke up. "Zoey's homicide case has been reopened and the CBI is investigating. We're just helping them out. If we could have a few minutes of your time, we'd really appreciate it."

"I said, I don't have anything to tell you. Now, if you would please leave, I would appreciate it. My daughter will be home from school soon and I don't need her or my neighbors seeing two officers standing on the front porch."

Denise was about ready to close the door, but Maya stuck her hand out, blocking it from shutting.

"Please," she pleaded. "You were my mom's best friend. Anything you can remember would help."

"I think you have the wrong information. I barely remember your mother from high school. Now please leave."

Maya stepped back, allowing Denise to shut the door. Disappointment filled her and she took a deep breath.

"It was worth a try," Josh said. "How about we still get Juniper out on that walk?"

Arriving at the river trail parking lot, Juniper began circling in the back and barking in excitement.

"She definitely needs to get some energy out," Josh said.

"She's been rambunctious," Maya said as she exited the vehicle, thinking about Juniper barking earlier at the foxes. "It'll be good to be back on duty tomorrow. She doesn't do well with days off. She needs to work."

She pulled out Juniper's off-duty collar and leash from behind the seat. The excited yips continued. Maya opened the door to the specialized K-9 compartment. The area was outfitted with rubber mats, temperature control and Juniper's blanket, which was now in confetti-size pieces. She knew she shouldn't give Juniper a blanket, but since the dog hadn't actually eaten any of the shredded parts so far, she figured she could still provide Juniper some comfort.

Maya waited until Juniper calmed down before opening the door. Josh stood out of the way of the fur missile ready to launch. Juniper's front paws danced up and down in anticipation as Maya secured the collar. Then Juniper came flying out, landing gracefully and shaking her whole body. She saw Josh and went to jump up on him, but Maya caught her in time and had Juniper sit and settle. When Maya was satisfied the dog was listening, she allowed Josh to pet her and then they started their walk.

The river was running low, and rocks jutted up from the streambed. A low gurgling sound came from the water. Maya loved September in Colorado. The river seemed peaceful, unlike spring, when it came alive with deep water and strong rapids from the snowmelt. The leaves were changing up in the high country and while the days could still be warm, the nights were cool and crisp.

"Thanks for driving all the way down here to tell me about Denise and go with me to talk to her," Maya said.

"You're welcome. I wish she would have talked with us more."

"I do too, but I'm sure it was also a shock to her to have us show up out of the blue on her doorstep. I just want justice and to find some sort of closure."

"I know, but we also have to remember that sometimes we don't find a suspect and even if we did, what is closure?"

"I'm not going to give up on this investigation," Maya said.

"I would be shocked if you did. That's one of the many things I like about you: you don't give up. Not to mention I enjoy spending time with you and this seemed like a good reason to get out of paperwork and join you and Juniper today."

Maya's heart rate quickened. She focused on the trail ahead. "I'm always glad to see you too. So how did you talk Pops into letting you come down here? I know he likes paperwork being finished and he must have given you a stack since you're the chief deputy."

Josh sighed. "I do have a stack of paperwork, but I told your grandfather about finding Denise and that you were already down here. He told me to finish the paperwork later."

Maya pulled Juniper up at an area near some ponds. A flock of Canada geese swam out in the middle of the water. Their summer goslings were following behind, looking like gawky teenagers. Juniper perked her ears up and focused her eyes in their direction while Maya studied Josh's face. She could tell he was holding back on something.

Lightly touching his arm, Maya said, "I'm glad Pops let you out of the office for the afternoon. But I think there's something more you want to tell me. What is it?"

Josh took a deep breath. "I haven't talked with your grandfather about this yet, but I've been contacted by some state investigators. They're being cryptic, but I can tell they're looking for information about what your grandfather knew about Doug and the drug trafficking before they talk with him. I don't know what's next. My guess is that the sheriff's committee will be meeting to discuss if they will ask him to step down or continue his duties. I just felt like I had to talk to you about it and tell you that I've had to answer questions. I wish I could somehow protect your grandfather, but I have to be honest with the investigators."

"I know. I understand."

Maya let her hand drop back down from Josh's arm, although what she really wanted was to step closer and feel his arms wrap around her. She needed Josh to tell her everything would be okay, but the reality was that Pops was in trouble if investigators could prove that he'd withheld information. To make it worse, it was because of Maya's friend and Juniper's former handler, Doug. Doug had told Pops about drug trafficking in the national forest and his involvement, but had asked Pops to stay quiet and let him turn himself in. Pops had agreed but then, as the saying went, the shit hit the fan and Doug and several other people died. The state was now investigating a law enforcement code of ethics charge against Pops. He could go to prison.

As Maya gathered her thoughts, a man came up the trail in the distance and sat down on a bench close to the ponds. He pulled a pack of cigarettes out of his pocket and lit one up. The smell of the smoke wafted in their direction, taking Maya back to that morning. Had she smelled smoke at her cabin? Should she tell Josh about her feeling that someone was watching her? That the feeling had started when they reopened the investigation? Or was she just on edge because cigarettes were found at both crime scenes along with the added stress of Pops being in trouble?

As the smell of smoke continued wafting toward them, Maya closed her eyes.

She had been hiding in the closet. She had covered her ears after the loud bang, but they continued to ring. She couldn't help herself—she had to see what was going on.

She had carefully opened the door just a crack, taking care not to make any noise. Her mom had sat slumped in a chair, staring straight ahead. There was a shadow, but Maya couldn't see who it was. The shadow was doing something to her mom and Maya was so scared. She'd gone back inside the closet and back to hiding, pushing herself back into the corner.

As her ears stopped ringing, Maya heard footsteps coming down the hallway. Big feet that made a loud clunking noise. She pulled jackets around herself, shivering in fear. The closet door opened, and Maya held her breath, squishing her eyes closed. The smell of cigarettes permeated the closet. Then the door had shut, and she had breathed a sigh of relief.

The footsteps had retreated.

"Maya?"

Dark had surrounded her.

"Maya?"

Silence.

Except someone was talking to her.

Josh.

Maya snapped out of her trance.

"Hey, you okay?" Josh stood closer now. Concern crossed his face. Maya could smell his musky cologne rather than cigarette smoke.

"Sorry. Yeah, I'm good… I'm having these memories come back. About the night my mom was murdered. It's like they're all hitting me at once."

Juniper stood and pushed her head into Maya's palm. She returned the dog's love with a scratch on the head. Josh took another step closer, and to Maya's surprise, he reached out and then wrapped her in his arms. At first she hesitated, but this was what she'd wanted just a few seconds ago. She allowed herself to lean into him and rested her head against his chest, his cotton shirt soft against her cheek. She felt safe for a moment.

Juniper, annoyed, shoved her pointy nose in between them and pushed her way into the hug. Maya took the opportunity to pull back from Josh. What was she doing? She didn't need anyone protecting her. She didn't need someone to make her feel safe. She was tough and could handle these memories on her own.

As Maya stepped back, she saw the man on the bench squashing the cigarette under his foot and then staring in their direction. Was he watching them? Was she really becoming this paranoid? Juniper stuck her nose up, air scenting of the breeze. Her hackles came up and a low rumble started in her throat, her gaze intent on the man as well.

"What's up with her?" Josh asked.

"I don't know." Maya took a firm hold of the leash. Juniper was a loving and friendly dog, but she was still trained to apprehend criminals. If Juniper didn't like someone, she could flip that switch. Maya didn't need her biting a civilian. But she also trusted Juniper with her life and Juniper was wary of the man. Was she reading Maya's body language and feeling her paranoia? Maybe, but Maya always trusted her dog.

"Do you think that man is following us? Or acting strange?" Maya asked as the man stood and started walking in the opposite direction.

"No, I don't think so. Wish he wouldn't smoke out here with it being so dry, but at least he picked up the butt and took it with him. Why? Is there something you're not telling me?"

"No." Maya glanced down and petted Juniper. She was a horrible liar. She wanted to tell Josh about the feeling someone was watching her, but that would only make him worry about her. She didn't need that right now. That would complicate her life, not help it. "No, everything's good. I just was wondering why Juniper was reacting, that's all."

Josh shrugged. Maya could tell he didn't totally believe her. "Well, she's a working dog. She wants to keep you safe."

"And she needs to get some energy out."

Maya was about ready to say they should keep going, but her cell phone rang. Grateful for the interruption, she looked at who was calling. It was her friend Lucas from the CBI. Maybe this was the break in the case they needed.

It wasn't smart to have sat down on the bench where they could see him. Eric knew that, but then again, why should he worry? He was just an average citizen out for a walk and smoke. He'd started following them keeping a good distance, but then they'd stopped to talk and that had presented a dilemma. Luckily, the bench had been there, and he'd been able to pretend to watch the geese on the pond.

He'd thought there was going to be a problem when

the dog started growling and staring at him. The dog had probably smelled his scent, and even though she'd been distracted this morning by the foxes, she knew who he was and was aware of him. Luckily, Maya and the deputy decided to continue their walk.

Eric was done with surveillance for today. After a few weeks of doing this, he had Maya's schedule down well. She was predictable minus the fact that she patrolled over a million acres of forest. He didn't always know where she was headed, but being an ex-cop, he knew how to listen in on dispatch and could create a call that would draw her out. But he still had the problem of the dog and the deputy.

The dog would be out on patrol with Maya. He would have to get Maya away from the patrol vehicle, but he still had to be careful. K-9 handlers had a special remote on their duty belt. They could hit a button and the door would open for the dog to come help an officer in trouble. And then there was the deputy. He couldn't keep his eyes off Maya and seemed to always be her backup, protecting her. That created a problem too.

Eric liked challenges, though. Everything about this was a challenge and he would figure out a way to solve it. Until then, he had someone to go see. Someone Eric could get information out of—even if it took a little bit of persuasion.

Chapter Five

Maya answered the phone, hoping Lucas had good news. "Hey there, what's up?"

"How are you doing, Tree Cop?"

She laughed at the nickname that Forest Service officers were given since they worked out with the trees. Although Maya wanted to get past the pleasantries and get to why he was calling, she knew Lucas was doing a favor for her, and she needed to have patience. Not to mention he'd always had her back when they were in the Marines. "I'm doing well, thanks."

"And Juniper?"

"She's good too," Maya said, squeezing the phone tighter. Josh reached out and took Juniper's leash so Maya could pace. *Dang, he knows me too well.* Her anxiety was killing her. Juniper tilted her head, staring at Maya, wondering what was going on.

"Well, I have some good news for you," Lucas said.

"What is it? Does the DNA match?"

"Yep."

"Yes?" Maya continued pacing. Josh took Juniper off the trail as another couple walked by. The geese continued swimming around the pond. Some fluffy clouds floated by overhead. Everything was so normal and yet, at this moment, Maya knew her world had just changed.

"The DNA from the cigarettes found at both scenes match, so you have a connection between these two crimes. I love my job."

"Lucas, you're the best."

"Feel free to call me anytime and tell me that."

Maya laughed and gave Josh a thumbs-up. He returned her smile and Juniper let out a yip.

"Sounds like even Juniper is happy," Lucas said.

"You got that right. Is there a match in the system? Any names coming up?"

"That's the only bummer. I'm not getting a match in Colorado, but I'll send the results to CODIS tomorrow."

"Okay." Maya stopped pacing and closed her eyes. CODIS was the Combined DNA Index System run by the FBI. It was a national database to help link suspects in crimes that crossed state lines. CODIS was probably a long shot, but worth it.

"We'll figure this out, Maya. Don't worry. Gotta run."

"Thanks, Lucas. Bye." Maya hit the end button on the phone and grinned at Josh.

"Good news, I take it?" Josh asked, handing Juniper's leash back.

"Yes." Maya filled him in on what Lucas had told her as they continued their walk. A warm breeze picked up and rustled the cottonwood tree leaves that were turning a light gold.

The couple that had passed them were now out of sight, so Maya let Juniper's leash out and allowed her the freedom to run back and forth. Juniper loved to explore and take in all the scents around her. She attempted to pounce on a grasshopper, but the bug managed to escape. Maya and Josh picked up their pace to help expend some of Juniper's energy.

"This is good news," Maya said. "This is what we've been waiting for. It's actual evidence that connects my mother's death and Nana's. There were cigarettes at my mother's murder scene. Pops made the CBI investigators collect the other cigarettes outside his house the night Nana died. He wanted the investigators to look into it more because he knew Nana didn't smoke, but they wouldn't. They had tunnel vision with Nana's death being self-inflicted.

"Now we know there was definitely another person at both scenes and they could have had the gun all these years. Finally, something that explains both of their deaths that makes sense—the same person killed them. Now we just need to figure out who that person is and their motive."

"I understand and I agree…" Josh said.

Maya could tell he was holding back. "But…" she prompted.

"I just don't want you to get your hopes up and then find out there's no match in CODIS, that's all."

Maya sighed. Josh was right. She knew it. "You're right, but it just feels like this could move the case forward. I can't wait to tell Pops."

"I know and I hope too that this is the big break we've all been waiting for. Time will tell. Ready to head back?"

"Yeah, I'll drop you back off to get your car. I need to head to the store and then I'll meet you with dinner at my cabin."

Maya whistled and caught Juniper's attention as she was all the way out on her leash. Juniper was staring at

something in the bushes and ignoring her. Maya shortened the leash and put some pressure on it, but Juniper
still didn't want to budge.

"What the heck?" Maya asked. She went closer to
the bush and saw what had grabbed Juniper's attention.
A large bull snake was lying in the shade, but seeing
Juniper, it had coiled up. Bull snakes weren't venom-
ous, but they mimicked rattlesnakes and a bite could
still cause problems. "Juniper, pfui," Maya said, using
a stern tone and the strong command for "no." *Man,
she's testing me lately.*

"What is it?" Josh asked, coming up behind Maya.

"Bull snake. I don't need her getting bit. Juniper,
come."

"That's a big one," Josh muttered.

"Probably about six feet long when it's not coiled up."

Juniper finally listened and left the snake alone, coming back over to Maya. They all watched the snake un-
coil, but it kept its head lifted staring at them, making
sure they wouldn't be a threat.

Dark, snake-like eyes.

Maya could still remember the man that day at the
door when she was a kid. Like a snake, the man had
looked like he was ready to strike. He had scared her
mom, Maya knew that much. She thought she vaguely
remembered the smell of cigarettes too. Maybe the DNA
would lead to him. Maybe the man was like a snake and
had struck back at Maya's mom and Nana. But the big
question was, why? What did they have or know that it
made it worth killing them?

Maya finished her errands, glad that Juniper was finally asleep in the back. Although that was a catch-22

because by the time they got back to Pinecone Junction, Juniper might have more energy to burn. If that was the case, then maybe after dinner, Maya could work Juniper on the odor wall she'd built out of cinder blocks. The wall was up against one side of her cabin and was a great exercise for working narcotics odors and keeping a strong indication.

They would practice with it to make sure Juniper stayed independent from Maya and wasn't trying to cue off her. Maya even placed distractions on the wall like socks or other toys. When it came to narcotics detection, she needed Juniper to be one hundred percent and not waver off the scent. Maya thought of the foxes that morning. Maybe they needed to find some sort of distraction that would mimic an animal when tracking. Juniper's training never stopped. Maya trained almost every day to keep her dog sharp.

But she had her own distraction that evening—Josh. Maya had picked up dinner for both of them from the Black Bear Café on her way home. Josh texted that he'd be at her cabin waiting for her and Juniper. Maya was happy to spend time with him and have him as a friend, but there was a side of her that wanted more too. Was she ready for a commitment like that? While she knew she was doing better learning to manage her PTSD, there was still a part of her that felt broken. A piece that no one would want—not even Josh. She was afraid of scaring Josh away, but the flip side was she didn't know if she could handle having a relationship either. Things definitely seemed complicated.

As she pulled down her driveway, she saw not just Josh's patrol vehicle parked at her place, but also Pops's sheriff's vehicle.

"What's he doing here?" Maya asked Juniper.

Juniper yawned and gave a squeak in response.

"It's not like I'm not happy to see him. Didn't mean to give you that idea. But he usually doesn't just drop on by without calling first, so that makes me worry."

Maya checked her cell phone making sure she hadn't missed any calls. *Nothing.* As she pulled into her parking spot, she saw Josh and Pops sitting on her camping chairs on the porch. Neither of them looked comfortable.

"Maybe I should invest in some nicer porch chairs," Maya said to Juniper, who gave a bark.

Maya climbed out of the vehicle, grabbing the food off the front seat. "Hey there," she said to the guys. "Pops, I didn't know you'd be here. I picked up dinner for Josh and me, but there's plenty to go around."

"No, I'm good," he said, standing and stretching.

He stepped off the porch, and Maya could still see a slight hitch in his gait left over from when he was shot taking down a drug ring last summer. The same drug trafficking ring that was responsible for the investigation into Pops's ethics. He had been shot in his thigh and broken his fibula. He'd made a good recovery, but now the doctor kept talking to him about knee replacements. Maya knew he was considering it and that worried her. Pops had always pushed off medical care, so he must be in pain to actually think about surgery.

Maya opened Juniper's door and let her out. Juniper ran over to Pops but didn't jump on him. It was like she knew she had to be a little more careful.

"There's my girl," Pops said, scratching Juniper and petting on her. Juniper returned the love by leaning up against him.

"She really loves you," Maya said with a smile. She glanced back at Josh, who was leaning against one of the cabin's log support beams. He had his hands in his pockets and didn't look happy. Something was up.

"So, anyone going to tell me what's going on?" Maya asked.

"Let's get your groceries and dinner inside," Pops said, grabbing bags out of the front seat of Maya's vehicle.

"Pops, I can get that."

"No, no. I have it."

Maya watched him limp as he went inside her front door toward the kitchen. Josh stepped down from the porch to help grab the rest of the bags and their dinner so Maya could get Juniper.

"What's going on?" she asked him.

"I'll let him tell you," Josh said.

"Great," Maya muttered. "Now what?"

She whistled and Juniper came running back over. Maya had built an outdoor dog run over the summer and thought that would be the best place for Juniper at the moment. She locked the gate and ignored Juniper's sad face at being left behind. The dog would rather be with them, but first Maya wanted to hear what Pops had to say without any distractions.

She bounded up the steps as Juniper gave indignant whines and barks, then went through her front door. Her cozy cabin seemed cramped with both Pops and Josh inside of it.

"So, what's going on?" she asked.

"Why don't you sit down?" Pops asked, pointing toward the kitchen table and chairs.

"No, I just want to know now what's going on."

"Well, I'm going to sit down," Pops said, ambling over to the table and sitting down in one of the wooden chairs.

Maya knew better than to argue with him. With a sigh, she strode over to the table, and plopped down in the seat next to him. Josh followed behind her. "Okay, we're all sitting down. Pops, you're scaring me. What's going on? Are you sick? In trouble?"

Pops stared down at the table. Maya worked to give him time, and just when she thought she couldn't handle it anymore, Pops spoke up. "You remember after Doug died, I mentioned I might be under investigation?"

Maya nodded, thinking about her conversation in confidence with Josh only a little bit ago. The investigation must be moving forward. Someone must have talked with Pops today.

"Well, I am," Pops said. "Under investigation, that is."

Maya looked back and forth between Pops and Josh and their somber expressions.

"What does that mean? What's next?" she asked. She knew that it could mean Pops would be arrested, charged and could serve prison time if convicted. Maya pushed those thoughts aside and started to rub her necklace.

"I could lose my job. That would be the best-case scenario. I could also go to prison and serve time."

Maya slumped back in her chair. *Can this really be happening? I knew it was a possibility, but I was hoping that somehow Pops wouldn't be prosecuted and that his case would be dismissed.*

"Pops, you can't go to prison. They wouldn't do that, would they?" Maya looked back and forth between Josh and Pops. Josh stared at the table and Pops looked out the window.

She had seen her grandfather as so strong and in-destructible growing up. He'd been the one who'd al-ways saved her, including the night her mother died. Maya had stayed hidden in that closet, scared to death when dark smoke from a fire started wafting under the doorway. The smell reminded her a little bit of a campfire. Her eyes started to sting, and her lungs were burning, making it hard to breathe. She'd tried to stay quiet, but the smoke overwhelmed her, and she let out a few coughs.

Then, the door had opened and there was Pops. He'd grabbed her and carried her outside, telling her not to look at her mother. Flames were starting to engulf the house, but Maya knew in that moment she was safe with Pops. He'd do anything to protect her.

Maybe it was time for her to return the favor.

"Maya? You okay?" Pops asked.

"Yeah, I'm good. I just… I've started remembering things from the night Mom was murdered. I was think-ing about how scared I was, and you were the one there to save me. You've always saved me, Pops. It's time I helped you. What can I do?"

Pops took Maya's hand in his. "Just stand by my side. You're still my little girl in so many ways. I was devastated when I ran in the house that night and saw your mom. My only daughter, dead."

He choked back some tears and then continued, "But I managed to find you and you were still okay. I was so grateful for that. You were like a second chance for me and Nana. You kept us going when we lost your mother and I'm so proud of you, Maya. Keep investi-gating their deaths. I don't know how much I can help you right now, but keep going and find the person who took them from us."

Maya wrapped her fingers around Pops's hand. "Of course. I can do that."

Josh stayed quiet and continued staring at the table. He looked back up at Maya. "And I'll help. Whatever you need, I'm here for both of you."

"Thanks. I appreciate that," Maya said. She paused for a minute, thinking about the Colorado law that said if a sheriff was arrested, the coroner would be in charge. "So, Pops, if you have to step down as sheriff, would Doc Clark take your place?"

"Yes and no. Technically yes, but I've already discussed it with Doc, and Josh would essentially take over. Doc doesn't have a background in law enforcement, so Josh has agreed to oversee things if that should happen."

"Okay," Maya said. "What's next?"

"Next is I'm heading home and you two can have your date," Pops said, pushing his chair back. "I have horses to feed and I'm ready to relax in my recliner for the night."

Outside, Juniper heard the chair scraping on the wooden floor and started barking again.

"It's not a date," Maya said, glancing at Josh. "We're just friends. Having dinner."

Josh stayed quiet.

"Well, whatever you want to call it, dinner, date, I'm still heading home. You two enjoy your time together," Pops said, starting toward the door. "And if you don't let poor Juniper in with you, she's going to have a heart attack. It'll be easier for her to calm down if I'm gone."

"Pops," Maya said. He paused and turned toward her. "I love you."

"I love you too, Maya," he said with a smile, and then he headed out the door, pausing to turn around and look at Josh. "You have that interview set up for tomorrow? For the possible new deputy?"

"I do. She should be there at 0900 sharp. Are you going to sit in?"

"Planning on it, but why don't you run the interview? You know, to get some practice with it as chief deputy," Pops said.

"Sure, I can do that," Josh said. "But as long as you are still here, you're still the sheriff."

"Okay, I'll make sure I sit in, but it's good for you to start running more in the department," Pops said, continuing down the stairs. He climbed in his vehicle and drove off with a wave out the window.

"Is that Kendra you're talking about?" Maya asked.

"It is. We really need one more swing shift deputy and your grandfather liked her resume. I called her. She was excited and I figured we could schedule it tomorrow. Always takes a while to go through the rest of the tests once you do the initial interview. You know how it is."

"I do. That's great," Maya said. "Hopefully, it works out."

Chapter Six

Maya let Juniper out of her run and brought her back in the cabin. She pulled out her at-home dog bed that had duct tape holding it together thanks to Juniper ripping it up in small strips. A Maligator, that's what Maya called her, since it seemed patrol K-9s were more of a cross between a Malinois and alligator.

Maya placed the bed in the middle of the living room, telling Juniper to stay in place on it. "Place" was something she had been working on with Juniper so that she could hang out in the house, but not be running around destroying things. Juniper was doing well with it.

The Malinois went over to the bed, did a couple circles and then curled up, keeping her back to Maya and Josh just to let them know she wasn't happy about being left out in her run.

"So, what's your thoughts on all of this?" Maya asked Josh. "Do you think the sheriff's committee will make Pops step down right away?"

Josh sat back down at the table and leaned forward, rubbing his forehead with his hands. "I'll do anything for your grandfather. Whatever he needs. He gave me a second chance, but when I moved here, I wasn't expecting that second chance to turn into possibly being an interim sheriff. And I have no idea on the sheriff's committee. My guess is that they will figure that out sometime this week."

"I think you'd do well. As sheriff, that is, but I know that's a big responsibility."

"It is a big responsibility. Sometimes, I still feel like I'm barely over losing my partner. I'm not sure I'm ready to run a department and some of the guys don't trust me. It's hard to be a leader without trust."

"You'll figure it out," Maya said. She reached out and put her hand on his. "You're a good cop and your prior experience makes you stronger and better able to deal with department crap because you understand both sides."

Maya knew Josh's story about losing his partner when he was a cop in Chicago. Josh had made a mistake any cop could have, but it cost his partner his life and caused Josh to spiral out of control and into his own drug and alcohol addiction. He had gone to rehab and been sober for almost two years now, but she understood that some ghosts haunted you even after you faced them.

Maya squeezed his hand. He stared at her and interlaced his fingers with hers. Her heart pounded as she stared back at him. What was she doing?

She gently pulled her hand away. "Are you hungry?" she asked.

"Not really," Josh said.

"We should eat something anyway," Maya said, getting up to get away from being so close to Josh. She pulled the food out of the bag and started to plate everything to reheat it in the microwave. "Maybe we can look over the evidence in Nana's case again tonight. And my mom's case."

"Maya, we've been over that so many times. Maybe we should just leave it alone. At least for tonight. Relax a little bit."

"Yeah, you're probably right."

Josh brought their food over and they both picked at their sandwiches. Josh finally pushed his plate back and stared Maya in the eyes. A smile flickered across his face, bringing out Maya's favorite dimple.

"What?"

"Neither of us is hungry right now. I'll put the food in the fridge for later," Josh said, standing up. As he went over to the fridge, he turned on the radio. A Chris LeDoux song came on. "I think we should relax tonight. Or at least try. As much as either of us can."

"What do you suggest?"

"How about a dance?" Josh said, holding out his hand to her. "I mean, Chris LeDoux—you can't turn that down."

"I'm impressed you know Chris LeDoux." Maya smiled, taking Josh's hand. "Not bad for a city slicker."

"Thanks."

"I haven't danced in a long time. I might be a bit rusty."

Juniper lifted her head and turned around, although she stayed on her dog bed.

"We should be careful. We could have someone interrupt our dance," Maya said, nodding toward Juniper watching them.

"I'll take my chances," Josh said, as they stepped together.

Maya and Josh found their rhythm and even added in a few spins. She found herself enjoying the time with Josh. It had been a long time since she had danced with anyone, and for a moment, Maya forgot everything that was going on. It seemed like a small sliver of time where she could find joy and everything seemed so perfect, but Maya knew that nothing was ever perfect and eventually the song would end.

They were about ready to get a little closer dancing when Juniper leapt off her bed, lunging toward the window, barking and growling.

"What the heck?" Josh said.

Maya dropped his hand and went over to the front door, where she grabbed the shotgun. "Get away from the window in case there's someone out there."

"What are you talking about?" Josh had a confused look on his face.

Maya called Juniper over and the dog came, nails clicking on the floor. "Just get away from the window and I'll tell you."

She retreated with Juniper and her shotgun back to the hallway that led to her bedroom. Josh followed them. *This morning it was just foxes. Why do I keep feeling like someone is out there? I think I'm losing my mind.*

"What's going on?" Josh asked, starting to look irritated. "Do I need to get some deputies up here?"

"Yes. No. I don't know," she answered, setting the shotgun down and leaning back against the wall. Juniper came over and pushed her head into Maya's hand. She started scratching Juniper behind the ears.

"What aren't you telling me?"

"I just… It's that…" Maya didn't even know where to start. "I think I'm just dealing with some paranoia. From PTSD and as an addict. You know how it is. But I feel like someone is watching me and Juniper keeps barking at the window like that."

"I know that paranoia can happen, and I've experienced it, but I've never thought someone was watching me. Maybe you should trust your instincts. Maybe someone is watching you."

"I know. This isn't normal." Maya sighed and rubbed her temples.

"I can go out with you and Juniper and clear the area. I would be happy to stay here tonight if it would make you feel better. I can sleep on the couch."

"No." Maya stepped out from behind the wall and back into the living room. Juniper came with her and didn't react again. "I think I'm even making Juniper jumpy, but we'll be fine. I mean, this morning I actually went out and cleared the area around the cabin and it was just a fox family out hunting. I'm sure I'm not being watched. I bet the foxes are back or even a black bear looking for food for hibernation. I'm just overreacting."

"Hey, it's okay. You don't have to make any excuses to me, but if you would sleep better, I really don't mind the couch."

Maya smiled. "Thanks, I appreciate it, but it's getting late, and I have an early morning patrol tomorrow. And my couch sucks."

"I'm only a phone call away. Let me know if you need anything. And you've always said Dr. Meyers is open to phone calls too. Maybe you should have a private session with him. I mean if you think it would help."

"Thanks," Maya said. "I'll be fine."

Josh walked over to the kitchen and grabbed his leftovers from the fridge. "Just in case I get hungry."

Maya and Juniper went with him to the front door and watched as he headed out to his patrol car. There was a part of her that wanted him to stay. And another part of her that was relieved he was leaving.

Chapter Seven

The next morning, Maya was up early. Sleep continued to elude her. After taking her cup of coffee, she let Juniper out and headed out on her porch to enjoy the morning. The sun was just starting to rise, with only a sliver of light shining through the clouds. Maya sat down in one of her camping chairs and sipped the coffee while Juniper ran around.

Juniper hadn't barked or rushed at any windows overnight, and Maya felt like whatever was bugging her was gone. Whatever. Or whoever. She'd tried sleeping but ended up tossing and turning. Dreams came and went mixed with memories of her mother and Nana. In some ways, Maya couldn't even remember what her mother looked like. Although, based on pictures, all she had to do was look in the mirror. She wished she could remember her better.

Maya took another sip of coffee as the sun moved up a little bit more and started hitting the peaks off to the west. Soon those peaks would be covered with snow, and it would be too cold to sit outside on her porch.

Her cell phone buzzed inside, and Maya whistled at Juniper to come. Juniper bounded up on the porch, tongue hanging out, happy to have had her early-morning romp. "Come on, let's go inside. We have to get ready for work."

Maya opened the door to the cabin and Juniper followed her in. Maya headed toward Juniper's crate and the dog slunk over to the couch again, glancing back with her golden eyes.

"No, you have to kennel."

Juniper sighed and turned around. She sat and stared at Maya.

"Seriously. Kennel." Maya pointed to the crate.

Juniper took a few steps and then stared at Maya again.

"Are you acting out because I'm not sleeping well?"

Juniper took the moment to look hopeful, like maybe Maya would change her mind.

"No, you need to kennel. I have to get ready for work, but it won't take long."

With another heavy sigh, Juniper went in the crate. She had a pathetic look on her face.

"Just a few minutes," Maya said.

She went over to her phone on the kitchen counter and checked it. There was a text from Lucas: DNA has been submitted to CODIS. Will let you know when I hear anything.

Thanks, Maya texted back. She set her phone back on the counter. Hopefully CODIS would give them something. If this person was from out of state, then CODIS would give them a better chance to find them.

Maya headed into her bedroom, showered and dressed in her Forest Service Law Enforcement officer uniform for work. She finished by putting on the bulletproof vest and pulling her long hair back into a tight bun. What would today bring? Being a law enforcement officer meant you never knew. You could have a day of paperwork, or you could pull over a dangerous felon and do a high-risk arrest. Maya loved all the different parts of her job. Well, maybe not the paperwork.

After walking back out of the bedroom, she let Juniper out of her crate. Juniper went from looking pathetic to jumping around on her hind legs and bouncing on and off Maya.

"Good thing I have this vest on," Maya said, as Juniper's front paws hit her.

They went out the front door and Maya stopped again. She swore she smelled cigarettes, but then the odor faded. Juniper was waiting by the door to her compartment in the vehicle. Maya opened it up and thought about calling Dr. Meyers. Maybe she really was losing it.

Twenty minutes later, they pulled up to her office, which was both a Forest Service visitor center and her home base. Juniper ran circles in the back. Maya knew that she needed to get more energy out of the dog today. She was probably acting up because Maya had so many emotions running through her with the investigations going on.

As she was ready to get out of the car and get Juniper settled, her phone rang again. This time it was her boss, Todd Davis, the patrol captain for her region.

"Hello, sir," Maya said.

"Thompson," Todd said, in his typical short, to-the-point manner. "I need you to look into something."

Maya liked her boss. He was fair and had had her back when she needed it the most last summer after her friend Doug died. "What's that, sir?"

"We're getting reports that there's someone setting booby traps in your area, near Deer Valley Pass."

"Booby traps?" Maya said. "What kind?"

"Trip wire. If someone triggers it, a ball of sharp sticks will swing at them. Luckily, the first person who found and triggered one of these was able to get out of the way. But I need you to go out on some foot patrols and see if there's any more traps out there. I'll text you the coordinates."

"Yes, sir. I can do that."

"Be careful, Thompson. Do you know how to disarm one of these if you find one?"

"I have some basic training from the military. I'm not an expert, though," Maya answered.

"If you need assistance, just call. We can figure out someone who can come and help you."

"Will do."

"Thanks, Thompson."

The line went dead. Maya stepped out of her vehicle and let Juniper out as a text came through from Todd. She would map out the coordinates and then plan her day. She opened up Juniper's door and the dog bounded out.

Maya worked on some obedience in the parking lot. She asked Juniper to do a variety of exercises including a down-stay and then come. When Juniper settled down, they went into her office, and she pulled out some paper maps. You never depended on phone GPS in the wilderness. Not only would you most likely lose service, but the directions to most places could also be inaccurate. Just the other day, Maya had helped some tourists who were trying to get back to their bed-and-breakfast. They had routes pulled up on their phone and three hours later, they were still on roads that didn't go anywhere near their destination. Maya had helped them get to the main road and back to town.

As she circled the locations on the map where she'd be headed, Juniper's tail started thumping hard on the wooden floor. She ran over to the door and sat, waiting expectantly. Only Josh brought that behavior out in her dog, but just in case there was someone else there, Maya called Juniper back over as the door opened.

Josh stepped in, dressed in his dark blue sheriff's uniform and carrying coffee and doughnuts. "Morning."

"Morning," Maya said.

"How are you doing?" He set the doughnuts and coffee down on Maya's desk. "Here's your coffee with enough cream to pretty much make it more of a latte."

"Thanks," Maya said.

"Did Juniper have any more reactions last night? Did you feel like anyone was watching you?" Josh asked as he peered in the doughnut bag and raised an eyebrow.

"No, it was fine. I'm glad you didn't have to suffer on my couch. What's wrong with the doughnuts?"

"I asked the coffee shop barista for two chocolate doughnuts. She added in extra doughnuts with powdered sugar, and she put her phone number on my coffee cup."

Maya started giggling and let it turn into a full-on laugh. "Well, she probably hasn't thought about the fact you wear dark uniforms and white powdered sugar doughnuts will only raise your dry-cleaning bill. You going to call her?"

"What? No. Why?"

"Just wondering," Maya said, taking the chocolate doughnut Josh held out to her. They each took a seat and she was grateful for more coffee.

"Kendra should be arriving soon," she asked in between bites.

Josh peeked at his watch and said, "Yeah, I'll have to get going here in a minute. Hope she works out. I've been filling in on some of the shifts and I'm ready for a break."

"The joys of a small department," Maya said.

"Yeah, no kidding. What's on your schedule today?"

"Oh, you know, a typical day. Someone has been setting booby traps near Deer Valley Pass. I'm going to head up there and try to see if I can find any more and dismantle them."

"Be careful," Josh said, finishing up his doughnut. "Radio me if you need anything."

"Thanks," Maya said. "You know, I think I went camping with my mom and Nana up near Deer Valley Pass. I can't totally remember it, except for roasting hot dogs over the fire. I think we had s'mores too. I know I went with Nana up there before I left for boot camp. If you hike back in, there's a beautiful waterfall and even a Forest Service fire tower. Anyway, it's funny what triggers memories and I think I've had more than usual. It's a weird thing—a few months ago I drank like crazy to forget. Now that I'm three months into recovery, I'm hoping to remember. But the biggest thing I keep remembering is the smell of cigarette smoke. And I keep thinking I smell it when I'm at my cabin, but I'm not sure I really do. Is that weird?"

Josh reached over and took Maya's hand. In the past Maya would have pulled away, but today, she needed the connection and reassurance. She responded by interlacing her fingers with his. "What if you *are* smelling cigarettes? You need to be careful. Think about it. We found cigarette butts at both your mother's and nana's crime scenes. I'd feel better if you weren't alone up there. I know you want to have your space, but how about I bring dinner tonight? If Juniper reacts again or if you smell cigarettes, then I can help you check it out. That way we know for sure if it's memories coming back or if someone like a neighbor kid is out smoking near your house. Sound good?"

"It does. Thank you," Maya said, gently giving his hand a squeeze before she let go. "I'm going to get a few more things together and then I'll stop in to say hi to Kendra before I head out for the day. I also want to see how Pops is doing this morning and say hi to him too. Once I'm out into the wilderness, I won't be back in town until this evening."

"I'll see you in a few minutes then," Josh said, standing. Juniper came over and leaned into him, wanting to be petted. He scratched her behind the ears and then headed to the door, his tall frame taking up most of the doorway. "Catch ya later."

The door shut behind him and suddenly Maya's office felt empty. She ate her last bite of doughnut and stood to gather some important items she'd need to be out in the forest all day, including water and nonperishable food. She had a pack in her patrol vehicle that included essentials like a compass and rain slicker. She made sure she had Juniper's portable water bowl and some extra food just in case they spent more time out there than expected. She took a quick glance at her phone hoping that a miracle would happen and Lucas would have already had a hit in CODIS, but her screen was blank. No missed calls or texts.

"Let's go," Maya said to Juniper.

Chapter Eight

Maya arrived at the Western River County Sheriff's office and found a visitor spot. She backed in; it was always better to be prepared to leave quickly. It was a habit from the military days and now law enforcement. It was one she'd never stop.

She made sure Juniper's climate control system was working and then headed into the front office. The sheriff's office was a bit outdated, but it seemed like home. It hadn't changed much from when Maya was a little girl, but Pops had decided recently that he would allocate some funds to updating the place. When that would happen, she wasn't sure. Or if it would with Pops being under investigation.

The front desk deputy nodded at her. She went through a door and down a hallway toward the interview room. She heard Pops and Josh talking and they didn't sound happy.

Maya knocked on the door. "Come on in," Pops said. When Maya entered, he added, "Hey there. Your friend doesn't happen to be up front, by any chance? You see her on your way in?"

Maya glanced at her watch. No wonder Pops and Josh

didn't look happy. It was 0915. Kendra was late. Nobody liked that, but maybe there was a good explanation.

"I didn't see her," Maya said. "In fact, I came by to say hi to her before I head out on patrol. Want me to call her?"

"I've called her a couple times," Josh said. "No answer."

Maya walked over to the old table in the middle of the room and pulled out a chair with worn gray fabric. She took a seat and unlocked her phone. "I'll try her really quick." She found the contact for Kendra and hit send. It rang over and over and then went to voice mail. "Maybe she's out of range."

"Or maybe she's blowing off this interview," Pops said. He drummed his fingers on the table. "We really need another deputy, but it's hard to find good officers who want to live up here."

"I'm sorry, Pops," Maya said. "I thought she'd show. I'll give her grief next week at our next meeting. If I hear of anyone else who might be interested in the job, I'll let you know."

"Thanks," Pops said.

Josh stood. "I'll walk you out."

"Sounds good," Maya said.

As she went out through the door, her shoulder radio went off. "FS 28."

Dispatch. Maya pushed the button, thinking this could be a busy day. "This is FS 28. Copy."

"FS 28, we need immediate response up the canyon at the Big Gulch pull-out. Have a distraught Forest Service employee who says she found a deceased female. Can you respond?"

"Copy," Maya said again.

"I'll go with you," Josh said.

"Thanks." Maya started to walk down the hall and then stopped. She hit her shoulder radio again. "This is FS 28. Is the RP a researcher with the Forest Service?"

"I'll ask," said the dispatcher.

"Why are you asking that about the reporting party?" Josh asked Maya.

"I had a researcher who stopped by last week. She had multiple things stolen out of her vehicle, including all her cash and a tree borer."

"What's a tree borer?"

Maya shrugged. "I'm not a forester, but I know it's a very sharp tool. Researchers use it to get wood from the core of the trees without damaging the tree, but this is not my area of expertise. If it's the same person, then she just moved here. I feel for her if she had her truck broken into and found a dead body all in her first few weeks of work."

Her radio crackled and the dispatcher came back on. "FS 28, the RP is the researcher you met last week."

"Copy," Maya said. "Tell the RP to stay in her vehicle at the trailhead, keep her doors locked, and if she feels in danger to leave the area and call you. We can always meet her in another location. Deputy A1 is responding with me."

"I always feel like a steak sauce when you use my badge number," Josh said. "Can't you just say chief deputy or deputy? Or even Alpha One?"

"Takes too long," Maya said, with a grin.

Dispatch responded that they'd received all the communications, and then Josh and Maya headed out the door.

"Be safe," Pops said to them.

"Always," Maya said back.

Chapter Nine

Maya ran hot with the lights on and Juniper in the back howling. She loved to howl with the siren while driving fast. Josh was right behind them along with another deputy. Even going as fast as possible, their response time was about forty-five minutes from the sheriff's office to the Big Gulch trailhead. The terrain in that area was rough, but it was a popular spot to hike and camp. The researcher had probably been working in that region.

Maya spotted the researcher's white vehicle with the brown U.S. Forest Service logo on the side of the doors. She parked next to it and Josh pulled up alongside. Juniper turned in circles in the back.

"You wait here, girly," Maya said. "If we need you, I promise I'll get you."

Juniper responded with a few loud indignant barks, but then settled back down as Maya stepped out of her vehicle.

The researcher rolled down the truck window as Maya and Josh approached. Maya couldn't remember her name, but knew she had moved to Colorado to study drought, pine beetle kill and how that could impact wildfires.

"Hi, good to see you again. I'm Officer Thompson,

along with Deputy Josh Colten," Maya said, hoping the researcher would give her name to Josh.

"Hi, I'm Sofia." She wiped away tears, her hand shaking.

"It's okay, Sofia. I know what you saw was difficult. If you want to tell us where the body is, we'll take a look. You can stay here."

"You don't understand," Sofia said. "It's not just difficult, it's horrific. I've seen dead people. I've seen horrible things in my life, but this, this somehow is the most horrible sight of all. I don't know if I will ever get this out of my mind."

"I understand. Does it look like the person slipped off the cliff above the trail? Do you need some water?" Maya hoped to get Sofia calmed down. She and Josh needed to get to the scene, but they also needed to gather information first.

"No, I don't need water," Sofia said. "And no, this was no accident. Go look at that scene down there and you'll see."

Maya and Josh glanced at each other. If this wasn't an accident, then the suspect could still be in the area, in which case it was good to have Juniper. Although she'd have to be careful that dog hair didn't end up in the crime scene or her friend and investigator Miranda would give her a hard time. But first they needed to see the scene. What some civilians thought was a murder sometimes could be an accident or even a self-inflicted death.

"You can stay in your truck. We have another deputy here to help us out. He will make sure you stay safe. We can't let you leave right now. We might need to ask you some more questions."

"If the other deputy stays with me, then I guess I'm okay, but I'm not staying here alone."

Maya had an uneasy feeling developing. That sixth sense that she'd developed in Afghanistan and her short time in law enforcement. Maybe there was more to this than she and Josh realized.

"We understand." Maya tried to use a soothing tone as she turned to Josh. "Let's call medical just in case this person is still alive when we get there."

Sofia let out another sob. "There's no way this person is still alive. No way."

"Okay," Maya said. "It's okay. Let's get you some water. We'll go check it out and then come back."

"Ma'am." Josh spoke up. "We do need to ask you a couple questions. Can you help us out?"

Sofia nodded and took a small sip of water.

"Okay," Josh said. "Thank you. Did you touch the body?"

"No. I ran away as soon as I realized what I was seeing."

"Did you see anyone else in the area?" Maya asked.

"I didn't, but I felt like someone was watching me. I know that probably makes me sound crazy or something, but it was true. I ran back to my truck as fast as I could."

"It doesn't make you sound crazy at all," Maya said, thinking about her own feelings that someone was watching her. "One last question—did you go the same way in as you came back out?"

"Yes, I was headed down this trail to collect samples from some pine trees. Instead I saw... I saw a horrible sight and I ran back up the same trail."

"Thank you, Sofia," Maya said, and then she pointed

in the direction of the other deputy. "We're going to secure the scene, but the deputy over there will stay here and make sure you are okay. If you can stay for now, that would be great in case we have any more questions, and if you're up to it, we'd love to have you fill out a statement."

"Okay," Sofia said, taking another drink of water. "Okay."

Josh went over to his deputy and spoke to him. Maya decided to get Juniper. If Sofia felt like there was someone in the area, having Juniper with them would help. She would detect anyone lurking around before Maya and Josh ever could.

Maya let Juniper out and put on her combo tracking harness and vest. She grabbed the thirty-foot-long leather lead in case they started a track. Josh came back over and they followed the path Sofia had pointed them down. Maya kept Juniper by her side still on a short leash with Josh following behind them.

The trail was steep going down and they had to navigate around boulders and step over tree roots that jutted up. Maya slipped a couple times on the loose soil and pinecones that littered the trail. She could hear Josh doing the same thing. They came to a flat area and even though they had been going downhill, her calves still burned. Sometimes going downhill was harder than uphill.

A buzzing noise seemed to echo throughout the stand of trees they approached. Maya realized the sound was flies. As she turned a corner in the path, the sound became stronger, and she could see why. She stopped in place.

She'd seen death before. As a veteran of Afghanistan, Maya had seen many things that she'd like to forget, but she had to admit, this was bad. Not something she expected to find at home. She heard Josh pull up behind her and suck in his breath.

"This is horrible," Maya said.

"That's an understatement," Josh said. "I've never seen anything like this. Not even working with some of the gang units in Chicago."

"I have. Sort of like this. In Afghanistan, but I've tried to forget those memories."

"I can see why you want to forget," Josh said.

Maya closed her eyes and grounded herself for a moment. She didn't need this to cause a flashback. Juniper whined and Maya reopened her eyes, taking in the scene in front of her. A body was strung up between two large ponderosa pine trees. Thick rope wrapped around each wrist, cutting into the skin. The person had been beaten to death to the point Maya couldn't even tell if the deceased was male or female. She was guessing female since the person was short with long dark hair, but that was an assumption. She had to keep an open mind.

Juniper air scented, but she also seemed disturbed by the scene and didn't want to go any closer.

"I think Sofia was right," Josh said. "There's no need to call medical except to help transport the body to the coroner's office. I can see why she said it was so bad. I'll see if I have radio service here and call in the crime scene techs and the coroner."

"Sounds good," Maya agreed as she took in more of her surroundings. Careful to create a crime scene perimeter, she walked around so she could look at the body at a different angle. Besides the obvious beating, a large amount of blood pooled underneath the deceased's feet. There had to be another murder weapon and Maya planned to let Juniper do an evidence search to see what they could find.

She continued to walk around the body taking in details and determining where they should run the crime scene tape. The biggest problem with a forest crime scene was the size. They might tape off an area around the body, but the crime scene in a national forest could literally be miles. Juniper might be able to help with some tracking and an evidence search.

Maya had a better view of the person's arms as she slowly stepped around.

Tattoos.

Long dark hair.

She paused. She'd seen those tattoos yesterday. In her therapy group. And there was a fresh one on the person's bicep.

The Air Force emblem with years served.

She gasped.

"What's wrong?" Josh asked.

"Josh, I think this is Kendra."

"What?"

"Come over here. Take a look at the body from this angle."

Josh followed Maya's instructions and stepped over beside her. "Holy shit," he said. "I think you're right."

"I guess we know why she didn't show this morning," Maya said. "But who would do such a horrible thing to her, and why?"

Josh stayed silent for a minute and then said, "I don't know, but we can't ID her for sure until the coroner comes. If that's her, then there's a lot of questions to answer."

"You can say that again," Maya muttered. She reached down and petted Juniper, trying to calm her nerves. How could she have just lost another friend? Who would have done this? Maya wanted answers.

Eric slunk back into the stand of trees. He was a good distance away and hoped he was far enough back and had the wind direction in his favor to not have the dog catch his scent. The deputy and Maya had arrived on scene. He should have known Maya would be dispatched out to this with the sheriff's office. This was Forest Service land. The FBI could even be called in, and that would not be a good thing for him.

He had talked with Kendra early this morning. He needed information, and from what he had found, she was the one who could give it to him. Eric was still debating the best way to get Maya alone when she would be the most vulnerable. That might make things easier, although the more he watched her, the more he realized his task ahead of him would not be easy.

But with his informant now dead, he knew that he had no time to wait.

Eric needed to get out of the area—he'd seen enough to know that soon the trail would be shut down and the crime scene would be swarming with techs and deputies. At least he knew where Maya would be for now. Maybe he could get her alone at her cabin tonight, but every time he'd come closer, the dog had noticed him and started barking.

He had to get rid of the dog. He needed Maya on her own so he could control her.

Yes, it was time to go back to get his vehicle stowed off the side of the road and get to where he was camping out. He had to think through some new plans. Getting to Maya needed to happen sooner rather than later.

Eric turned and as he walked back toward the trail, he stepped on a branch.

The twig snapped underneath his boot. Crap. He had to get out of here.

The Malinois whipped around growling. Eric sprinted off and as he dashed up the hill, already breathing hard in the thin, high-altitude air, he heard Maya say, "Let's go get 'em."

Chapter Ten

Juniper put her nose to the ground and at first seemed to have a hard time catching a scent. Maya took her toward the area where she thought she heard the twig snap and started casting her out. Juniper followed her direction, making a louder noise, sniffing and sucking in air. Maya could see she hadn't caught a scent yet and continued to cast the dog out in different directions, looking for any signs of a human being in the area recently. If Maya saw a footprint or a snapped branch, she could help her dog pick up the track. They could also place a piece of sterile gauze over the shoeprint to not only help preserve it for Miranda to get a cast of it later, but the cloth could become a scent article to use with Juniper. Maya kept packages of sterile gauze in her BDU pockets just in case.

She and Juniper continued to work the area. Maya was concerned that they were tracking at a difficult point in the day because as it warmed up, the scent would dissipate.

Just as Maya was worried that they wouldn't find a solid trail, Juniper's body tensed. Her tail poked straight up in the air and her body language switched to an intensity that Maya knew well. Her dog was in odor.

Maya let Juniper work out the scent and then followed her as the dog took off, putting slack in the leash
so Juniper didn't yank her off her feet. Maya scrambled
to keep up, slipping on some of the loose rocks in the
area. She and Juniper headed off in the opposite direction of the trail they had used to come down to the
crime scene.

"This is Deputy A1. I need immediate response to
Big Gulch including medical, coroner and crime scene,"
Josh said.

Hearing Josh's call, Maya knew it wouldn't be long
before there were more deputies, firefighters, search and
rescue volunteers and the coroner. They really needed to
have someone secure the scene, but with Juniper in hot
pursuit, the priority had changed to finding the suspect.

Josh was behind Maya as her backup officer. He
would cover her so she could watch and work her dog
without worrying about the suspect ambushing them.
They'd been practicing some scenarios like this since
Maya returned from certification, so they were all a
better team. Josh fell into place behind them and followed her and Juniper off toward a stand of pine trees.

Juniper came into a small area in the middle of the
trees and Maya pulled her up.

"Footprints," she said to Josh.

"Got it," he said, placing a marker.

Maya stopped Juniper for a second and took the
gauze out of her pocket and handed it to Josh. "Let's
put this gauze over these shoeprints and see if they can
be used for a scent article later on."

This area would now be part of the crime scene and
hopefully Miranda could get a good shoe imprint to
use for when they caught this killer. She gave Juni-

per the command to keep tracking. Juniper took off on another trail in the opposite direction of the trailhead parking area.

"Where does this trail go?" Josh asked.

"It wraps back around to Little Gulch Meadow. There's a parking area there too, but it's a lot smaller so most people drive to Big Gulch."

"How far?"

"About a half mile."

Maya continued jogging to keep up with her dog. Juniper had a solid scent and her nose stayed on the ground. Maya was always amazed at what the dogs could do when it came to tracking. Juniper was following the "hottest" scent, or last scent left along with any ground disturbance. For this type of work, she didn't need a scent article.

They continued on the trail that wove around and started an uphill ascent. Juniper didn't seem tired at all, but Maya's lungs burned as her respiration increased. Josh was huffing and puffing behind her. Maybe their morning coffee and doughnut habit was catching up with them. They continued climbing uphill. At least this part of the trail wasn't as rough as the previous one.

She could hear someone ahead of them running. Another branch snapped, and Maya heard a person swear.

We're getting close. We can catch this suspect.

Adrenaline fueled Maya as she and Juniper continued on the trail. Tree branches smacked Maya in the face, and she tried to warn Josh, but words were hard to get out as her breathing elevated. Juniper picked up her pace even more while her body language showed that her full attention was on this one track.

We're going to catch this killer. We're going to get justice for Kendra.

Juniper followed her nose, tail staying straight up in the air. When she was on an odor, she often kept her tail up even when she was tired. When she was sniffing the scent of another animal or distracted, her tail would droop.

As they approached the top of the trail, a vehicle started and pulled away.

Damn it. That's probably our suspect escaping.

They arrived at the small parking area, if you could even call it that. It was more of a pull-off with maybe room for one or two vehicles at the most.

The area was empty.

Maya pulled up Juniper. They'd lost Josh behind them. Maya doubled over, a stitch starting in her side, and fought to catch her breath. Juniper put her nose under Maya's face and stared at her, asking if she was okay.

"I'm good, girly," Maya said, still trying to catch her breath.

Josh came up behind her and placed his hand on her back. "You okay?" he asked.

"Yeah." Maya gulped in more air. "Just need to start jogging on trails so I can get in better shape. You good?"

"I am," Josh said, also breathing hard. "I think I should join you jogging."

"Let me see if she can find the scent trail here again," Maya said. She caught Juniper's attention and started casting the dog out in the area where she last had the scent.

Juniper tracked over to the front part of the pull-off and her tail dropped a bit. She began working back and forth, sucking in air and at times putting her nose up to try to catch the odor by air scenting.

"I think she's lost the track," Maya said, watching her dog weave back and forth searching for the scent.

"I bet the person had a car stashed here."

"I heard it leave when we approached this area. I think Juniper has lost the scent for now."

"I'll look around and see if there's any good tire tracks or shoe prints that we can match to the other ones," Josh said, examining the area.

"Sounds good," Maya said. "I need to get Juniper some water, so once you mark anything you find, we can head back to the vehicles. If we walk along the road, it's not that far."

"Okay." Josh slowly walked around, careful where he stepped so he didn't contaminate anything. "I have some good tire tread marks here and there's an oil leak that looks fresh. I'll put some markers down and I'll have a deputy mark this area off with crime scene tape. Hopefully by now the cavalry has arrived at the other parking area and our main crime scene is being secured. I'm going to call for another deputy to come and stay at this scene."

"I hope so too," Maya said. "Once Juniper has some water and a break, I want to go back to the crime scene and do an evidence search with her. Maybe we'll get lucky."

After Maya got Juniper comfortable in her compartment, she grabbed crime scene tape and checked her phone to see if Lucas had called. Nothing. Maya walked back to the pull-off where Josh waited. Together they strung the yellow tape around a large area. She knew that when it came to a crime scene it was better to tape off more area than you might think you'd need. It was better to discover evidence within the crime scene rather than taping off a small area and realizing important evidence could be outside the crime scene. Defense lawyers could have a field day with that.

"By the time we get done stringing this up, Juniper should be rested, and we can do an evidence search in the area," Maya said.

A sheriff's patrol car pulled up and a young deputy stepped out of the patrol vehicle.

"Hey there, Deputy Wilson," Josh said, then nodded toward Maya. "Have you two met yet?"

"We haven't," Maya said, holding out her hand.

"Taylor Wilson, ma'am," the deputy said.

"Nice to meet you. I'm Officer Maya Thompson. You don't have to call me ma'am. Makes me feel old."

"Sure thing." Maya thought the deputy looked like a kid. Did that mean she was getting older? Or maybe Pops was hiring younger?

Josh spoke up. "We just need you to stay here and watch the scene. You know the protocol. No one in unless it's Miranda, our crime scene investigator, or one of us."

"Yes, sir."

"Thanks. Radio us if you need anything," Josh said.

He and Maya started back down the road to the Big Gulch parking area. She glanced at her watch. It wasn't even noon yet and they had multiple crime scenes. But... someone had killed Kendra. Was it random? Maybe someone asked for her help and then ambushed her? Or was it someone Kendra knew? She'd never mentioned that she had any boyfriends or even friends. In fact, as

Maya thought more about it, Kendra was always just focused on her.

"You look like your brain is going a million miles per hour," Josh said.

"It is." Maya glanced up the mountainside. Large fir trees were silhouetted against the baby-blue sky. The trees blocked some of the sun. A small stream gurgled in the distance. "You ever wonder how we can live somewhere so beautiful and yet have so much ugliness around us?"

Josh shrugged. "To be honest, I haven't thought about it. After being in Chicago, one murder here and there seems pretty laid-back, although this is a bad one."

"I guess it's all perspective," Maya said. "My mom's homicide was the first one in twenty years in this town. Kind of crazy. And I guess we've had our fair share with Nana and everything that happened last summer with Doug. But now Kendra too? I don't understand it. Who would do this to her and why?"

"I don't know," Josh said as they approached the trailhead parking area. "But we'll investigate this and figure it out."

"I know we will. Let's start by getting Juniper out and doing an evidence search. Then we can tape off the scene depending on whether or not we find anything."

"Sounds good to me," Josh said.

Juniper started barking in the vehicle. Maya knew that meant that she was also turning circles and dancing up and down with her front paws.

"Guess she's ready to work again," Maya said. "She did well on the track and didn't test me at all."

"Has she been testing you?" Josh asked.

"Let's just say I think we're out of the honeymoon

period. Zinger and I went through times like this too.
We teach these dogs to be independent and think on
their own. We want them to follow their nose and we
follow them for the most part, so it's not unusual for a
dog to test a handler. I just hope I'm up for it," Maya
said, thinking about her military K-9. Zinger had also
been a Malinois but was a brindle color. She had loved
working him, but he had lost his life to an IED. She had
never forgiven herself for that.

"You're a good handler, Maya. You got this."

"Thanks," Maya said, wishing she felt the same confidence. Juniper had been working well for the most
part—it was more at home that she was testing Maya
by jumping at windows and barking. Maybe Maya had
relaxed too much on the at-home dog rules. She'd have
to think about that, but having Juniper helped her feel
better. Juniper wasn't a service dog, though. She had a
job, and when a dog cost around $50,000, Maya had to
make sure she didn't ruin that asset.

Approaching the vehicle, she opened the door and made
Juniper wait to come out. When Juniper settled, Maya
stepped back and allowed the fur missile to launch. Juniper flew out, landed gracefully and then started jumping up and down.

"Sit," Maya said.

Juniper sat, but her tail kept going back and forth,
scattering rocks from the gravel. Maya smiled. She did
love her dog.

She waited for Josh to grab more tape and evidence
markers and then the trio started together back toward
the crime scene. Maya's stomach churned, and for a
moment she thought she might throw up, but she willed
it back down.

She'd seen death. Smelled death and flouted death herself. Maya had learned to compartmentalize except when the nightmares came, and the flashbacks. But seeing a person she personally knew become a victim of such a brutal crime brought up different emotions. Ones she hadn't been expecting.

"You look a little pale," Josh said. "You need water?"

"No, I'm fine. Just upset," Maya said. She'd started sharing how she felt with Josh. It was something that Dr. Meyers wanted her to work on. Before the group sessions, Maya had tried unsuccessfully to stuff her feelings inside and tell everyone that she was fine. That only increased her drinking. Now that she was tackling being sober, she realized she had to feel again and she didn't like it, but she trusted Josh to share with him. "I mean, it's not like Kendra and I were great friends, but now I know that the next time I go to our group she won't be there, and this is the image of her I'll have in my mind."

"I understand," Josh said. "It's not easy."

"Makes me want a drink so I can quit feeling."

"I understand that too. We both know, though, that alcohol doesn't make you quit feeling. It just hides it to come out another day. This is a nasty scene. I don't like it either, but it comes with our jobs."

"I know," Maya said. "I hope Juniper can find something on our evidence search."

"I do too," Josh said, as they approached the sound of flies buzzing again. This time Maya knew what was around the bend.

Chapter Eleven

Maya stopped Juniper and checked her equipment to put off seeing the murder scene again. She even checked her phone again in case Lucas had called. Nothing. She took a deep sigh and started directing Juniper, telling her to "seek."

Juniper put her nose to the ground and started sucking in air. Maya took a large loop around the crime scene to start. Juniper hadn't alerted on any evidence during their track, but Maya was hoping that maybe the suspect made a mistake and had tried to hide or dropped something that would help them solve the case.

Josh was staying out of the way. He had his hand resting on his firearm just in case the suspect came back, since the person had been hanging around when they had first arrived. Maya directed Juniper toward different areas where a suspect might try to dispose of evidence, like bushes and rocky areas. Juniper followed Maya's instructions and happily bounded around stopping to sniff branches or even small holes in the dirt. But her body language didn't change, and after she checked an area, she continued on.

They'd just about done a full loop and come back around to where they'd started their track earlier when

Juniper hesitated near a large rock that was close to the trail. Maya was wondering if Juniper would pick up the track again as it was still fresh, but then Juniper paused and turned back in the direction she'd just come from.

Juniper continued the back-and-forth pattern. Maya sucked in her breath, trying to stay neutral and just let the dog work, but she knew she'd caught an odor and was working a scent cone. Juniper would go back and forth in the scent pool until she could pinpoint the odor exactly.

Suddenly, Juniper went behind the rock and then lay down.

"Is that an alert?" Josh asked.

"It is. I added to her training, and I've been working on her lying down for an evidence alert and sitting for a narcotics alert. Lets me know better what I'm dealing with."

"Pretty amazing," Josh said.

"Thanks. Let's see what she found."

Maya stepped around Juniper, who stared intently at some tall grass behind the rock. Her tail wagged. Maya was proud of her. Maybe Juniper wasn't testing her as much as she thought.

After pulling out some gloves, Maya put them on and then carefully moved the grass until she saw an object on the ground. It had a long blade, orange handle and was in a T shape. The blade was covered in blood. "I think I just found Sofia's tree borer and it's all bloody."

"Okay, once you get Juniper away, I'll mark it and we'll make sure it's inside the crime scene line."

Maya stepped back and threw Juniper her favorite ball with a large rope. She had been trying out different toys with Juniper. If a dog liked one toy over the other, then sometimes it would help bring up their drive more. Not that Juniper ever needed a ton of encouragement with her energy level, but rather her focus.

Juniper snatched the toy and started squeaking it, moving out of her down-stay alert and running around Maya. The dog tossed her ball and then pounced on it, repeating this several times before bringing it to Maya and shoving it against her leg. This meant Juniper wanted to play tug. Maya obliged by grabbing the rope and pulling on it. Juniper wagged her tail and got into the game, tugging with all her might.

Maya let go. "You're too strong for me, girly," she said.

Josh had put the marker down and was watching them with a grin. "You two always make my day better."

"Thanks," Maya said, attempting to get the toy back from Juniper. At first Juniper played a little bit of keep-away. Maya stayed firm in her request for the toy back, but she didn't escalate anything. There was no reason to fight with Juniper. This was all part of the testing process.

After a few seconds, Juniper relented, but she kept her golden eyes trained on the ball as Maya put it away in her BDU pants pocket. Juniper licked her chops and then let her tongue hang, panting in the warm day.

Maya unclipped the portable bowl from her duty belt and poured in some of the water that Josh had brought down, giving Juniper a quick drink. After splashing water everywhere, Juniper looked at Maya, telling her she was ready to go again.

Maya and Juniper continued checking the area but didn't find any new evidence. Maya hoped the tree borer would have a fingerprint or DNA. Something that they could use to identify who did this. Could Sofia be messing with them and be the suspect? Maya doubted it, but it wouldn't be the first time a suspect had done something like that. Some of them liked inserting themselves in the investigations.

"I have a text from Miranda. She's just about here. She started at the other scene and didn't find much, but she did do a cast on the tire tracks and took an oil sample just in case," Josh said.

"Great. I'll take Juniper back up and meet her at the parking lot. I can help her bring things down the trail after I put Juniper away to rest."

"I'll wait here then to keep the scene secure," Josh said.

Maya was grateful she didn't have to wait at the scene as she and Juniper headed back up the trail. Maybe tonight, after all this exercise, they would sleep well. She figured she'd have to call Todd and let him know she hadn't made it to Deer Valley Pass to check on more booby traps, though.

A thought did enter her mind: Would someone who tortured their victims want to set booby traps too?

Miranda was pulling into the parking lot as Maya and Juniper arrived at their vehicle. Maya had first met Miranda, the crime scene tech for the sheriff's lab, a couple of months ago. Miranda had helped process some evidence from the drug trafficking ring that helped Maya and Juniper find Pops after he'd been kidnapped. She thought Miranda was top-notch and they were lucky to have her up here. Originally Miranda worked crime scenes in Denver, but decided, much like Josh, that she wanted to leave the city life and live in the mountains. The Forest Service had a partnership with the sheriff's office to use their lab for some of the crimes.

Other times the evidence could be sent to the state lab or to the FBI at Quantico. It all depended on the crime.

"Hey there," Miranda said as she got out of her vehicle. She had her dark hair pulled back in a ponytail and looked ready to tackle the mountain environment with jeans, boots and a sheriff's department long-sleeve shirt.

"Good to see you," Maya said.

"I heard this one is a doozy."

"That's one way to put it," Maya said as she opened the door for Juniper to get into her compartment. This time the Malinois curled up on what remained of the blanket without even a hint at shredding it. She'd worked hard and was finally ready to rest.

Miranda pulled out some cases with equipment she'd need and things to gather evidence. Maya checked that Juniper's climate control was set properly and then came over to help Miranda carry things down to the scene.

"I did an evidence search with Juniper and she found a possible murder weapon, although who knows what the coroner will determine for the final cause of death. It's hard to tell from just looking at the deceased," Maya told Miranda. She wanted to fill her in, but also to prepare her for what she might see.

Miranda put down the case she was carrying and stared up at Maya. "I heard the deceased was a friend of yours. I'm really sorry. If you need anything, let me know."

"Thanks," Maya said, touched that Miranda would think of her. "I'll be okay, but I'll also be glad when the coroner gets here, and we can give Kendra some dignity."

"I agree," Miranda said. "I better get down there and see what we have. Hope the coroner gets here soon."

As if on cue, a white pickup with a camper top pulled into the parking area. The word *Coroner* was stenciled on the side of the truck. Doc Charles "Chuck" Clark stepped out of the vehicle. He played double-duty for the county as coroner and as the only general practice doctor in Pinecone Junction. Maya had always liked Doc Clark and was happy to see him. She just wished it were under better circumstances.

Doc ambled over to them. "Maya, good to see you. Sorry to hear about the investigation with your grandfather."

"Thanks, Doc," Maya said, realizing that if her grandfather were arrested, it would be awkward for Doc too. Especially since Doc and Pops were good friends and liked to get together with some other guys for poker night.

"I'm waiting on some search and rescue folks to come and help me carry the body back up to here. I think that's the easiest. One SAR person might even bring a horse and we can use it to pack the deceased out."

Maya stayed quiet. The deceased was a friend, and she still hadn't had time to process her death, much less how they might move Kendra's body.

"Let's all go down there so Miranda can start in on what she does, but I'll be on scene," Doc continued. Without waiting, he turned and started trudging toward the trail.

"You think he's up to this hike?" Miranda whispered.

"He's tough, kind of like Pops," Maya whispered back.

They all headed down and Maya helped carry some of Miranda's supplies. Josh was waiting for them when they arrived, and Miranda whispered to Maya again. "Heard you two are a thing."

"What? No. Where did you hear that?"

"It's scuttlebutt at the department," Miranda said with a wink. "And female hearts are breaking in Pinecone Junction." She gave a laugh and then headed toward Josh.

Maya shook her head. Nothing like department gossip and small-town gossip all in one. *I guess we do spend a lot of time together. Would I mind if those rumors were true?*

As she approached them, Josh was explaining about the tree borer they found and the shoeprints on the track.

"Let me see the borer first. I'll photograph and then bag it," Miranda said.

Josh pointed toward a marker, and they all headed over that direction. Miranda photographed the tree borer and then put on gloves, picking it up carefully.

"I think there's a fingerprint I can get off of this," she said. "Let's bag it and I'll hopefully be able to get to this right away when I get back to the lab."

Maya was hopeful that there could be a fingerprint, as that would be quicker to get a possible ID versus something like DNA, which could take months.

More voices could be heard as search and rescue volunteers arrived. Miranda was in full work mode and Maya stood back. She was at a point now where she was just an extra person at the scene that could help. Josh had been taking pictures, but when he saw Maya, he came over to her.

"I think this is going to be a long day," he said.

"Yeah, I think so too. I may go back up to the parking lot at some point since I have cell service there and let Todd know what's going on and why I didn't look for booby traps today."

"Sounds good," Josh said, resting a hand for a second on Maya's shoulder.

Maya fought the urge to lean into him and let him take her mind off the murder of her friend, but if the rumors were already running rampant, she didn't need to add fuel to the fire.

Chapter Twelve

Maya was up early the next morning after a bad night's sleep. She was exhausted, after tossing and turning all night long with visions of Kendra's murder mixing with memories from Afghanistan. She'd also checked her phone several times throughout the night hoping that Lucas would message her. Realistically, Maya knew that he wouldn't do that, but she couldn't stop hoping he would receive quick results.

She headed out the door and drove to the sheriff's station, draining her last sip of coffee as she parked. Juniper started to whine and give small yips in the back.

"I know, girly. You want to work. Let me go in and check on some things and then we can get out on patrol. Maybe we can even get up to Deer Valley Pass today and see what we can find up there as far as booby traps."

Juniper barked in response and pushed her head against the door that opened between her compartment and the front of the vehicle. All Maya could see was a golden eyeball staring her down.

"I'll be right back, I promise," Maya said, getting out of her patrol vehicle and hoping she wasn't lying to her dog.

She headed inside and found Pops sitting at his desk.

She was glad he was still allowed to work. If he went on leave, he would be at home by himself with nothing to do. She didn't think that would work out well.

"Hey there, Pops."

"Maya, good to see you."

"Good to see you too. Any news on your investigation? Has the sheriff's committee met yet?"

Pops shook his head. "Nothing more than what I already told you. I promise I'll keep you posted."

"Okay," Maya said, leaning up against the doorjamb.

"I'm sorry to hear about your friend," Pops said. "I don't think I've ever had anyone miss an interview because they were…uh…"

"Murdered?" Maya filled in.

Pops shrugged and said, "Yeah."

"We'll work hard to figure out who did that to her. I'm going to say hi to Josh and check with Miranda on the evidence before I head out on patrol."

"Sounds good. Stay safe."

"Always," Maya said with a smile. "You stay safe too."

"Always," Pops said back.

Maya headed down the hall toward Josh's office. She found him sitting at his desk behind a mound of paperwork.

Maya knocked on the door. "Hey there," she said, thinking she should have brought coffee for him. He looked as tired as she felt.

"Hey," Josh said, his face brightening. "Come on in."

She stepped into his office, which for the most part was pretty bare. Other than the desk, there was a beige filing cabinet. On the filing cabinet though was a picture of Maya, Juniper and Josh out on a hike. She'd forgotten that he took a selfie of them.

Josh followed her gaze. "I like that picture," he said.

"Me too. That was a fun day."

"It was. Do you want a copy?"

"I'd love one," Maya said.

"You heading out on patrol?"

"I am. I thought I'd stop in and see if Miranda had any results from the crime scene," Maya said.

"Just a couple things. She did a cast of the shoeprint we found on the track. It's a match to the boots Kendra was wearing. Miranda bagged the gauze in case we might need a scent article for Juniper. We also haven't been able to find Kendra's vehicle or cell phone. I was able to get a warrant so that the phone company could try pinging her phone and see if we can locate it. Who knows, that might lead us to more evidence."

"That all sounds good. If you can find the phone location or the vehicle location, let me know. Juniper could do another evidence search or she might be able to locate the vehicle with the scent article from the scene. She might pick up a track if someone dumped those items and then took off," Maya said, and then she went quiet for a moment as her mind processed that they were talking about evidence in not just any murder case, but a murder of one of Maya's friends. Josh didn't say anything. He always seemed to know when to speak up and when to let Maya sit with her thoughts. "I was thinking about Kendra and the worst part of our jobs—death notifications."

Josh nodded. "I was thinking about that too. Do you know if she had any family around here? Anyone we should talk to?"

"All I know about her is that she said her dad was in prison because he killed her mother. She never said anything about any siblings or other family, but that doesn't mean there isn't someone."

"I'll look into it more."

"Thank you," Maya said, feeling relieved.

"If I find anyone, do you want to go with me to tell them?"

She hated doing a death notification. Being the person who told someone that their loved one would never walk through the front door again was one of the most difficult things she'd ever done, but Kendra had been a friend. Maybe not the closest friend in the world, but a friend nonetheless. "Yes, I'd like to do that."

"Okay, I'll let you know if I find anything," Josh said.

Maya stood up to leave and Josh stood too. They stared at each other for a moment, and she wondered how many awkward moments they would continue to have like this before one of them admitted that they liked the other. It felt like being in high school all over again. She was getting ready to say something when there was a knock at the door, and someone cleared their throat.

"Hope I'm not interrupting anything," Miranda said. She gave Maya a wink.

"No," Josh said. "Come on in. Maya was just getting ready to head out on patrol for the day."

"Then this is good timing. I have a result from the fingerprint on the tree borer."

"Already?" Maya asked, impressed at the quick hit.

"It's because the person it belongs to was already in AFIS so that made it easier. I think you both will be interested in looking over this file," Miranda said, handing a folder over to Josh.

Maya knew that this was luck on their side. Even

though the Automated Fingerprint Identification System
was a national database, it didn't mean you would get a
hit this quickly. To say the system had a ton of fingerprints on file was an understatement. Josh flipped open
the folder and started reading. His expression changed
to a look of surprise.

"An ex-cop and wanted felon?" Josh said.

"What?" Maya asked.

Miranda nodded. "Yep. The fingerprint matches a
guy by the name of Eric Torres. He was a cop up in
Montana, but his fingerprints ended up in AFIS because
he's wanted for multiple felonies including murder of
two cops and a judge. All in Montana."

"What's he doing here?" Maya asked.

"No idea," Miranda said. "That's your jobs to figure
out, but I hope you find him. I don't think he's someone
we want running around loose in the forests."

"I'll put out a BOLO for him," Josh said, meaning
a *be on the lookout*. "I'll make sure our deputies know
to watch for him and call for backup if they spot him."

"I'll keep an eye out on my patrols too," Maya said.
"Is there a picture?"

Josh flipped the file around and Maya peered at the
attached photo. Butterflies started in her stomach and
she swallowed hard. Dark hair and eyes—a stare like
a snake ready to strike.

"I know him," Maya whispered.

"What?" Josh said. "How?"

"I'm pretty certain he was the one at the house the
night my mother died."

"Are you sure?" Miranda asked.

"No, I guess not. I was just a little kid, but I've been
having dreams and memories coming back. I swear it's

him. Does that look like the man that we saw on the trail in Fort Collins?"

"I honestly don't remember that guy," Josh said. "Sorry, but I'll call the department in Montana that has the warrant out for him. They may want to come down here and be a part of this investigation. I'll run it by your grandfather first, of course."

"I'll let Todd know too," Maya said. "And maybe when I'm out on patrol, I'll spot him."

"Just be careful," Josh said.

"I will. I promise."

Josh's expression told Maya that he didn't quite believe her. Not that she blamed him. She knew she could be impulsive at times, but at least she had Juniper. Juniper was better than any backup officer, in Maya's opinion. Although since Josh was often her backup officer, she thought she'd keep that opinion to herself.

"I wonder if Kendra knew him somehow," Maya said.

"I'll start looking into Kendra's background," Josh replied. "Not only for the death notification, but also to see if I can find any ties to her and this Torres guy or if this was a random wrong place, wrong time kind of thing."

"I think she had an apartment near Fort Collins," Maya said. "Maybe we can get a search warrant too and see what we can find there."

"Good idea," Josh said. "I'll work on that too."

"Sounds like a busy day," Miranda said. "Call me if you need anything else. I'll keep processing the other evidence from the crime scene and see what I find."

"Thanks," Josh said.

"Yeah, thank you," Maya said.

"No problem."

Miranda headed out the door and Maya found herself staring at Josh again. She decided to end the awkward moment and head out herself, but before she could say goodbye, her phone rang.

Her caller ID read Lucas.

Chapter Thirteen

"It's Lucas from the CBI. Maybe he has some results from the DNA he submitted to CODIS." Maya hit the answer button on her phone along with the speaker button so Josh could listen in. "Hey there, Lucas. What's up?"

Josh put the folder about Eric Torres on his desk. Maya sat in the chair on the other side of his desk.

"Hey, Tree Cop, I'm so glad I caught you. I was worried you'd be out of cell phone range for the day playing in the forest or something," Lucas said.

"One of these days, I'll let Juniper bite you for calling me a tree cop. Lucky for you, I'm still in town, so you have good timing. I'm in Josh's office right now and have you on speakerphone."

"Oh, cool. Hey there, Josh. Are you both sitting down?"

Maya worked hard to keep her patience. Lucas would only sound this excited if he had news about the DNA. "We are both sitting down and I'm guessing you got a hit in CODIS."

"I did. I can't believe how lucky we were and how fast that came back. I have a name for you and get this, he's an ex-cop from Montana."

Maya sucked in her breath.

No way. Could it be?

She glanced at Josh, who also had a puzzled expression on his face. "Ex-cop? Does he have a record? Wanted for murder?"

"He is."

Maya shook her head. No way could it be Eric Torres. "I don't suppose his name is Eric Torres?"

"How did you know that? Good grief, Maya. You're always one step ahead."

She didn't know what to say at first. How could the DNA from her mother's and Nana's crime scenes connect to Eric Torres?

Hearing only silence, Lucas said, "Are you still there?"

"I am," Maya finally said. "It's just that…"

Josh, sensing her shock, said, "Lucas, we had a murder yesterday in the national forest and got a fingerprint hit off of what could be the murder weapon. That fingerprint matches an ex-cop from Montana named Eric Torres."

Lucas paused for a second too and then said, "Well, I guess he's here in Colorado then. Catch him and it looks like we can tie him to two more murders. Keep me posted. If this ties in with your family cold cases, then I'll be coming up to your area to help investigate."

"Thanks, Lucas," Maya said, finding her voice again.

"You're welcome, and keep me posted on this new investigation. I'll email you both the DNA report."

"Thanks. I'll keep in touch." She ended the call and flopped back in her chair, suddenly exhausted. "I was not expecting this. I thought I'd be happy when I received DNA results, but all this has done is gone from bad to worse. Who is Eric Torres and why is he in Colorado killing more people? Kendra, of all people?"

"I don't know, but I don't like it," Josh said. "Maybe

you and Juniper should come stay with me until we figure this out. I have a guest bedroom."

"No, I'm good. Your house is really nice. You've worked hard redoing it. Juniper could undo all your work in a short time unless she's crated, and I don't think she'd be very happy to live in a crate."

Plus, I haven't lived with anyone in years and I need my own space. Not to mention, I'm not sure I trust myself to stay only friends if I'm living with you. I don't know how to handle a relationship right now.

"I have a yard."

"Not one set up for a Maligator. You have a nice lawn and landscaping. She'd ruin it in a heartbeat," Maya said. "I was going to head out on patrol, but now I'm wondering if we should head to Kendra's apartment and see what we can find there. Maybe Lucas should join us too. I think the drive time would be about the same. You want to call and see if you can get a search warrant and I'll send Lucas a text?"

"Yeah, let me do that now." Josh got on the phone and contacted a local judge. Maya only halfway listened in as she thought about Eric Torres while she texted Lucas. Who was this guy? The only connection she could think of was that her mother ran away to Montana when she was a teenager. Maya knew her mother had been arrested. Maybe Eric Torres was somehow connected that way.

"I was able to get one," Josh said, hanging up. "I'll call Fort Collins PD and let them know we'll be there in case they need to get involved."

"Okay," Maya said. "Juniper isn't going to be happy if she doesn't get to work, but I want to see if we can figure out any connection between Kendra and Eric

Torres. If there's not one, then maybe he's a serial killer and picks random people. Maybe my mother and Nana were random victims."

Josh sat back and put his hands behind his head, interlacing his fingers. "But a serial killer who just happens to kill two people related to each other twenty-four years apart? I think there's more to this. I'm going to stop by Miranda's office on the way out and have her come with us. That way she can process the apartment and log any evidence we find. Let's get going."

"Agreed," Maya said, standing up. "Lucas is going to meet us at the apartment." Her mind was racing, but there were only questions, no answers.

About an hour later, they pulled into Kendra's apartment complex parking lot. They all drove separately in case Maya was called to something else in the national forest. Juniper was in the back circling and whining, letting Maya know that she didn't like being stuck in the vehicle. Often when out on patrol, Maya would let Juniper out in safe places to burn off some energy. Today, that wasn't going to work since they were in Fort Collins with traffic and everything that came with being in a city environment. Maya knew she better plan on doing something with Juniper later or she'd pay for it by Juniper chewing and ripping something up. Maybe they could go for a run this evening.

Maya opened the door between the cab and Juniper's compartment. Juniper stuck her head through and gave her a few slurps on the face. Maya scratched her behind the ears.

"Sorry, girly. We'll do something fun this afternoon. I promise."

She waited for Juniper to pull her head back through into her compartment and then she shut the door. She made sure the air-conditioning was on in Juniper's area because being down in Fort Collins at a lower elevation meant hotter temperatures.

As Maya stepped out of her vehicle, Josh stood in the shade talking on his phone. He motioned for her to come over and join him. As Maya approached, Josh switched his phone to speaker. "Detective Harper, I just wanted to stop you for a moment."

Maya stepped in closer to him so she could hear.

Josh continued, "I'm being joined by U.S. Forest Service Officer Maya Thompson. She's helping with this investigation since we found one of Torres's victims on national forest land."

"Hello, Officer Thompson."

"Hello," Maya said.

"As I was saying," Detective Harper continued, "I received the results from CODIS this morning. I have it flagged to alert me for anything to do with Eric Torres. I've been trying to locate him for a while now and bring him back to Montana where he's wanted for many crimes, including murder. Then you called and left your voice mail. At least we have an idea of where he might be."

"Sounds like we all want him," Josh said. "Are you interested in joining the investigation here in Colorado? You can always extradite him back to Montana."

"I'd love to come to Colorado and help you find him. I know him better than anyone. In fact, we started out our careers together. Torres is cunning and, being an ex-cop, he knows how the system works and how to elude you. He's dangerous and would think nothing of shooting another officer or killing another person. He's even gone after witnesses. How about a multi-jurisdictional task force? My partner can come too."

"That sounds good. I ran it by the sheriff and he gave his okay for doing something along those lines," Josh said. "Just know that if Torres is arrested here first, we'll keep him until he can have a trial."

"We can figure out those details when and if we catch him. Like I said, he's not going to be easy to find."

Maya spoke up. "I'll run it by my patrol captain too since Torres just committed a crime on national forest land, but I'm sure there won't be an issue cooperating."

"Okay. That sounds good. We'll leave tonight."

"Let us know when you arrive," Josh said.

"Okay. We'll be there ASAP."

The phone went dead.

"I'm glad for the help," Josh said.

"Agreed. And it sounds like she knows Torres personally so that's good too."

"I'll call your grandfather and update him about the detectives coming and then get in touch with the building superintendent. He has a key for us to get into Kendra's apartment."

"I'll call Todd in a little bit," Maya said. "And hopefully there's some answers inside."

Eric Torres stepped back into the shadows of the apartment building. At least in this area it was easier to blend in and look like another renter who was taking out the trash or doing whatever it was normal people did.

He didn't know how the investigation was progressing. Was he even a suspect? Did they know who they were looking for or what he looked like? But the fact they were at Kendra's apartment meant he had to be careful. He knew what they would find, and it only complicated things.

Eric had parked his truck down at the neighboring business parking lot. The dang thing was leaking oil like crazy now, but he didn't have time to worry about fixing it. He just needed to stop somewhere and buy enough quarts of oil to get him back up to the Pine-cone Junction area.

Now that they'd decided to go into Kendra's apartment, it was only a matter of time before the investigation ramped up, and he needed to be ready. Eric opened the door of the truck. He'd parked under a tree not only for the shade during this warm September, but also because he was out of the line of sight of some security cameras he'd spotted.

Eric pulled out his Sig Sauer P320 and made sure his weapon was locked and loaded, along with extra 9 mm ammo in his extra magazines. Satisfied that everything was set, he placed the handgun on the seat next to him and fired up the old truck. It rattled to life.

He'd hoped this day wouldn't come, but he should have known better. He was ready for battle. No one would ever send Eric Torres to prison. He'd rather die first.

Chapter Fourteen

While Josh called Pops, Maya took a quick peek at Juniper. The Malinois was sitting up and staring out the window right back at Maya as if she was saying, *I can help.*

"Hang tight, girly," Maya said.

An unmarked black SUV pulled into the parking lot. Lucas. Maya was looking forward to seeing him, but wished it wasn't under these circumstances.

Lucas stepped out of the vehicle. He was short and stocky, about four inches shorter than Maya, but on the other hand, she was tall. His blond hair was still cut high and tight like when he was in the Marines and he wore a white button-up shirt, expensive-looking tie and slacks along with shoes that looked like they'd just been spit shined.

Maya gave Lucas a hug. "You look good. It's been too long since I've actually seen you."

"Same here, Tree Cop," he said with a grin.

"Better look out. Juniper is right over there and she'd love to bite you."

"You wouldn't do that to me, would you?"

"Maybe," Maya said. "Don't tempt me. Josh is just on the phone with Pops. We've had yet another twist in this case." She filled him in about the Montana detective as they headed over to Kendra's apartment, where Miranda was waiting. Maya introduced her to Lucas.

"What's holding up Josh? Anything to do with this apartment search?" Miranda asked.

"Yes and no, he just needs to call Pops. Although it does relate to this crime," Maya said, telling Miranda about the phone call from Detective Harper in Montana.

"Wow," Miranda said, when Maya was done. "It's always nice to have more help."

Maya shrugged. "It is, especially with such a small department, but I can tell this detective wants Torres first and I hope he doesn't get extradited before he stands trial here."

"Well, she can't have him until I have a crack at him," Lucas said. "Don't worry, we'll keep him here in Colorado. He can get transferred to Montana later."

Josh got off the phone and headed their direction. When he was in earshot, he said, "The sheriff wants to have a task force meeting as soon as the detectives arrive so we can create a plan to find Eric Torres. Hey there, Lucas."

"Good to see you," Lucas said.

The building superintendent came around the corner and handed Josh a key. Josh thanked him. "Let's see what we can find," he said.

He put on gloves and then opened the door. All four of them stepped inside and Maya gasped. She took in what was in front of her little by little. The far wall was covered in notes and photos.

All of Maya.

"What the…" she said.

Josh didn't say a word. Neither did Lucas. Both of them went over to the wall and began studying the pictures. Maya trudged forward, feeling the shock of seeing her image plastered up in someone else's apartment. But why? Already instead of more answers, there were only more questions.

Miranda set down her case behind Maya. "Holy moly…" she muttered. "We'll figure out what's going on, Maya."

Some of the pictures included Maya and Juniper out on walks, Maya and Josh together at dinner at the Black Bear Café and then Maya saw some of what appeared to be the latest photos if they were in order—of Maya and Juniper taken through her cabin window.

Josh followed Maya's gaze. "Maybe Juniper is barking at more than foxes," he said.

Stunned, she didn't know what to say. Why did she ever trust anyone? Kendra didn't want to be a friend or get a job—she was only trying to get close to Maya.

"Are you okay?" Josh asked.

"No."

He put his arm around her shoulders. "We'll get to the bottom of this and find out why Kendra was surveilling you."

Maya stood still, not sure how to react. She started to read one of the notes pinned up. It was a summary of their veterans' support group. Things Maya had shared that were personal. Not only did Kendra violate Maya, but now this would all be evidence and her personal thoughts and feelings would be out there for others to see. She clenched her fists, fighting the urge to put her fist through the drywall. Damaging a crime scene wouldn't go over well and she leaned a little bit into Josh.

Miranda cleared her throat. "I don't mean to interrupt, but if it's okay, I'm going to start processing this apartment starting with all these photos. Maya, I can't imagine how you feel right now. Are you okay with me doing that?"

"Yeah, that's fine," Maya said, trying to not show any emotion or vulnerability. "It's not that big of a deal. So, she was stalking me, but now she's dead, so I guess I don't have to worry about her. Let's just determine how she's connected to Torres and why she was following me."

"Okay, I'll get to work then," Miranda said. She carefully opened her kit and started taking out crime scene equipment and evidence markers.

"We'll start processing evidence and try to make sense of all of this," Lucas said. He put on gloves and went with Miranda to lend a hand processing the scene.

"Maya, can I talk to you outside?" Josh asked.

She nodded and followed him. They walked through the door and then Josh turned and stared at her. His dark eyes were intense, and Maya wanted to both lean into him for support and at the same time tell him she didn't need anything from him. She could take care of herself.

"Look," Josh started. "I know how you are. You're a strong person and you have fought more battles than I ever will."

"Just get to the point," Maya snapped. She felt bad after saying that, but she knew where Josh was going with this. He'd want her and Juniper to stay with him. She wasn't ready for that on so many different levels.

"Stay with me, Maya. Bring Juniper over and stay at my house so I know you're okay."

"And what if you get hurt because of that? What if something happens to you? I couldn't live with that,"

Maya said, crossing her arms. She was being stubborn, but she couldn't help it.

"I'm not worried about me."

"And I'm not worried about me. I can take care of myself. I don't need some macho guy coming in and taking care of me," Maya said.

"It's not like that. I'm not trying to be a macho guy or tell you you're incapable. I just worry that you're in danger and vulnerable on your own at the cabin."

"Well, I'm fine. If Kendra was the one watching me, then she's no longer a concern."

"Think about it, though," Josh said, stepping closer to Maya. "Maybe Kendra was gathering information for someone. Maybe even Torres. He's now linked to your grandmother's and mother's crimes, and you're the one who sent the DNA into the lab. You're the one investigating this on the side. He could be planning to come after you. Will you at least think about it?"

Maya stared away from Josh, trying not to be distracted by how close he was to her. How easy it would be to reach out and kiss him. She hated that she had these thoughts when she needed to focus and be professional. "I appreciate your offer, but it'll be better if I go to my cabin. I feel comfortable there and it's my home."

"I could come to your cabin. Sleep on the couch."

"I did a tour in Afghanistan where I bunked with other soldiers. I can still hear them screaming from their nightmares, smell the sweat in the air, not because it was hot, but because of the tension. We were always on high alert. There was always something going on with someone. I like being alone now. It suits me and I don't know that I could handle having someone else in my cabin even out on the couch."

Josh took a deep sigh as anger and frustration flashed across his face. Maya could tell he was struggling with his emotions too. She knew she had a way of doing that to others. She'd seen the same look from Pops. All the more reason to stay on her own.

Miranda appeared in the doorway. "Um, don't mean to get in the middle of this lovers' quarrel, but I need more fingerprint powder out in the vehicle."

Maya and Josh stepped away from each other, giving Miranda a chance to squeeze through.

"It's not a lovers' quarrel," Maya said to Miranda as she went by.

"You're in denial. Both of you," Miranda said over her shoulder. "Just admit it already."

"I agree," Lucas shouted from inside Kendra's apartment. "Admit it, Tree Cop, you're in love."

Maya stared off at the surrounding buildings, missing her forests. Lucas was right about her nickname. She was a tree cop and she liked it that way. She liked her solitude and having her own space out in the middle of nowhere without other people.

Josh rested his hands on his duty belt and studied the ground. Sweat trickled down Maya's back. Fort Collins was much warmer than the high country. She needed to escape and get back to where she was comfortable. The mountains always soothed her. City life only created more chaos and made her feel claustrophobic.

"I'm heading back up to go on patrol. There's nothing I can do here, and since the evidence in there deals with me, it's better I leave the scene anyway," Maya said. She heard Juniper giving short staccato barks meaning she wanted to get out and work. "Not to mention, Juniper needs to do something today before she goes insane.

Keep me posted on anything new. I'm heading up to Deer Valley Pass to see if I can find booby traps." She started to walk away.

"Maya," Josh said.

"Yeah?" She stopped and turned around. His face had a mix of emotions. Hurt, anger, frustration and concern. All because of her. What was she thinking even allowing herself to like him? She wasn't good for him. Juniper was the only one who understood her and accepted her for who she was.

"Be safe."

"I will be," she said, and then walked to her vehicle and left.

Maya was relieved to leave the city behind her and get out into the open space. Cattle grazed in fields that led to red cliffs. The sun was out, and the high mountain peaks sat in the distance, silhouetted against midday light.

Her heart pounded and she fought to slow her heart rate as she turned onto the road that would lead back toward Pinecone Junction and the national forest. She hated arguing with Josh, but she hated someone trying to take care of her even more. She didn't know why. It wasn't a bad thing to have someone care for you, but she wanted to be strong. Prove to everyone that she could take care of herself. That she wasn't weak after coming home from the war. Maya had learned though through her veterans' group that part of being strong was admitting when you were wrong and having the courage to change. Maya needed to have the courage to not push away those she loved. She should probably apologize to Josh later.

There were other complications too, though, when it came to giving in to her feelings for him. She would have to call her boss and tell him if she was in a relationship with another officer. He wouldn't be thrilled, but at least she and Josh were in different agencies. But it would mean they couldn't work cases together anymore because it would be a conflict of interest. One of them would have to excuse themselves and Maya wasn't certain Josh could even be her backup officer when she worked Juniper. Nothing about this relationship seemed easy and she wasn't ready to deal with the fallout. Not yet anyway.

She reached back and opened Juniper's door. Juniper stuck her head through and watched out the front window. Maya knew she liked it when she could see.

Her mind raced as she thought about what she'd seen in Kendra's apartment. Hopefully, Miranda, Lucas and Josh would be able to find something more. Something that might start giving them answers instead of just questions. She knew that was another reason she wanted to get away. Why would someone be after her?

The obvious reason was Maya reopening her mother's and grandmother's cold cases. There was someone who wanted to keep things the way they were—unsolved. She knew Josh had a point about staying alone at her cabin. She'd never admit it, but Maya really was vulnerable there.

She worked to quiet her mind as the road took her to a higher altitude. The trees became thicker and cast shadows across the road. The river was next to the road and ran slow and easy. Knowing that Kendra had been following her all this time, Maya kept an eye in her mirrors making sure that no vehicles were tailing her.

The roads were empty today, though, and there were no cars in sight.

A little while later, Maya took the turn to Deer Valley Pass. Her mind hadn't slowed down at all, but her breathing and heart rate were better. She parked in the area that led to the trailhead and stepped out of the vehicle.

Deer Valley Pass was a beautiful area. In the summertime, it was full of wildflowers. Most of the flowers had already gone to seed, but the aspen trees around the outskirts of the meadow were turning a perfect shade of gold. Nana used to love to bring Maya here as a kid to hike and camp. The area seemed like part of home for Maya. She took a deep breath. She had to admit that she was glad she had Juniper with her in case someone was following her. She still had to do her job even with Kendra's murder investigation.

Stretching, Maya could smell the vanilla-like odor of the pine trees. She decided to do some training just to keep Juniper sharp and get some energy out. She went to the back of the vehicle where she kept some training narcotics and put on gloves so she wouldn't get her scent on anything; she had to be careful that Juniper would never associate Maya's scent with the odor of the narcotics. She pulled out a piece of cloth scented with methamphetamine and put it in a small container so Juniper couldn't grab the cloth by accident.

Then she went and found a pile of rocks. She pulled up a few and placed the canister down underneath, making sure the rocks went back into place and were hidden from view. Juniper had a great nose, but if she could take the easy way out and use her eyes, she would.

Maya could hear Juniper yipping in the patrol vehicle. Juniper knew what was up and was excited to find something.

She went around to the other side of the vehicle and let Juniper out. A streak of brown fur flew by as Juniper landed on her feet and then shook, happy to be free of her area. She danced around Maya and at the same time gave some yips, expressing her displeasure at having to be locked up for the morning.

Maya waited for Juniper to settle down. She was holding Juniper's flat collar that was used for narcotics searches. Once the collar was on, Juniper would know what job Maya wanted her to do. Juniper, in her excitement, stood in front of Maya, jumping up and down, but never touched her. She knew better than to cross that line. Maya continued to wait for Juniper to calm down. She had the collar in her hands, and all of a sudden, Juniper sat and poked her head through the collar.

"Good girl," Maya said, loving on her dog. Her mind was finally forgetting everything that had happened this week. She was glad to have Juniper as a distraction.

Juniper was alert and listening. The tension vibrated up the leash.

"Go find it," Maya said, directing her dog toward a bush with her free hand while letting the leash out longer with her other hand.

Juniper leapt toward the bush and placed her nose down on the ground. For the most part, Maya let Juniper go, but every once in a while, she would ask Juniper to check up higher or lower. Air flow was funny, and the odor could go up high or even drop down low. So much of it depended on the environment conditions including wind, temperature and humidity.

Continuing to sniff, Juniper was a couple feet away

from the rocks where Maya had hidden the meth. All of a sudden, Juniper's head whipped around, and her body tensed. She headed in the direction of the rocks, pushing her nose into the rock pile. Then she sat, staring at the pile of rocks. Maya waited a moment, making sure Juniper committed to her alert. Then she threw Juniper's favorite toy in front of her.

Juniper took off, playing with the toy in her mouth and squeaking it in a staccato rhythm. She jumped around and tossed the ball out of her mouth and then pounced forward, grabbing it again. Maya smiled. Juniper could always take her mind off anything that was bothering her. She didn't know what she'd do without her dog.

Maya picked up the hide and put everything away. Juniper came over and pushed the ball against Maya's leg. She indulged the dog by grabbing the rope and playing tug with her. She asked Juniper to release, and for a moment, Maya thought Juniper might ignore her, but then the Mal let go of the toy. Maya spent a few minutes playing fetch with Juniper as a reward. That way the toy wasn't just being given away, it was being given back too.

Eventually, Maya took the toy away for a final time and put it in her BDU pocket. She got out a bowl and put some water in it. Juniper happily lapped it up.

Satisfied that Juniper had been able to burn off some energy, Maya put her back on leash and they started hiking the pass.

The events of the morning filtered back into her mind. She checked her phone to see if she had any messages, but she was out of range. That was probably for the best. Easier for her to concentrate on her job.

Usually, Maya let Juniper run out ahead of her, but with the threat of a possible booby trap, she kept Juniper close to her as she scanned the trail. In Afghanistan, she would have relied on her K-9, Zinger, to help her find the booby traps, but that was because they had explosives attached to them and Zinger was a bomb dog. Maya still found herself heartbroken over Zinger and her mistake as a handler. Maybe at some point she could discuss what had happened in the veterans' group. If she could ever feel safe talking to the group again. Kendra had created some distrust for Maya.

They wound up the trail when Maya noticed the sun glint off something near the next switchback. She stopped Juniper and put her on a down-stay so she could inspect the area closer without Juniper by her side.

Sure enough, as Maya crouched down to look from a different angle, she saw a wire that they could have easily stepped on. She spent the next few minutes tracing it to where the trap was, and then Maya carefully disarmed it. Juniper sat and stared at her, head down between her paws. Maya was glad she'd gotten some energy out before, or else Juniper might not be as happy to stay in place.

When Maya was satisfied that everything was safe, she released Juniper from her down-stay. Maya made notes for her report and gathered the evidence. If they'd stepped on the booby trap, it would have released a ball with very sharp sticks. Sharp enough to go into a body and cause damage. She took pictures, documented things and gathered the evidence in paper bags. The sticks were not from trees, but rather wooden stakes from the local hardware store that had been shaped until they had a sharp end. The hardware store's logo was still on the end of a few of them.

Once she cleared the area, Maya decided to have Juniper do an evidence search. Maybe they would find something that would help her find the person setting these traps. She took Juniper over to where she'd disengaged the trap and took off her leash. There was no one in the area and she felt like the area was clear of any danger from booby traps. Juniper would like working off-leash.

"Okay, girl, seek," Maya said, sending her dog out to search the area.

Juniper scampered around, working the area back and forth in the grid-like pattern that she was trained to do. Maya would only direct Juniper when she thought they had possibly missed an area such as bushes or around rotted out logs on the ground. If Juniper got too far ahead of Maya, she would turn and wait. Even though Maya felt like Juniper was testing her at times, they'd definitely still formed a bond. Juniper waiting for her only proved that.

Maya caught up to where Juniper waited. They'd come to a small area near a creek that had an old firepit. She put her hand over the pit. There was still some heat coming off it. She was about ready to make sure the fire was completely out when Juniper snapped to attention. She worked a scent cone back and forth until she narrowed the odor down to an old tree. Juniper sat at the tree and stared up in the branches.

Sitting was Juniper's alert for narcotics. Maya praised her as she put on gloves. Juniper didn't move, her body shaking with excitement, waiting for her toy. Maya went over to the tree and stood up on an old stump where she could see better. Up in the tree was a bag that had been secured around a branch. Maya untied the strings of the bag and found a pipe, some dab and wax—all potent marijuana products. While marijuana was legal in Colorado, it was still illegal on federal land, so Juniper was trained to find it.

"Good, girl," she said, giving Juniper her toy. As Juniper played, Maya took pictures and documented everything. It was hard to tell if the drugs connected with the booby traps. No matter what, Maya would start patrolling this area more often. She would also see if Miranda could get fingerprints off the bag, pipe and containers with the marijuana dab and wax.

She made sure the campfire was out and then spent another hour hiking with Juniper and looking for any other traps, but didn't find anything. She'd go to the hardware store before she headed home and see if they had a record of anyone buying stakes like these.

"Come on," Maya said to Juniper. "Let's head back to town."

Leaving the mountains and heading back to reality made Maya think about Josh. Guilt washed over her at how she'd left things with him and what she'd said. He was only trying to be her friend and despite all the reasons Maya had to push him away, she just couldn't. She had to go and make things right with him. That's what being strong was all about.

Chapter Fifteen

After finishing her patrol, Maya figured she'd drive into town and stop by the hardware store and see if they could remember anyone buying a large amount of wooden stakes. Maybe they'd even have records and receipts too. That could help a lot. Maya would also give Todd a call and update him.

She wanted to stop into the sheriff's office too and see what they found at Kendra's apartment, but for now, she was putting that off. She both wanted to see Josh and avoid him. She knew she needed to make things right, but she didn't really know how.

All these years of being in the military and now law enforcement, Maya had worked with lots of guys. But after one serious relationship in the military, she had decided she would never mix work and relationships. Ever.

And then she met Josh.

Damn it, why did life have to be complicated? Of course, Maya reminded herself, she had no way of knowing if Josh really felt the same or not. After all, he'd offered her his guest bedroom, nothing more.

She pulled up in front of the local hardware store and got out of her vehicle. Juniper was happily napping in the back curled up in a little pooch ball. Maya was glad she'd been able to get some energy out but had no illusions that it would be a quiet night. Nothing was ever quiet when it came to a Malinois.

She headed into the store. A bell jingled as she opened the front glass door and stepped inside. The front cash register was near the entrance and Maya could smell wood and paint. The floors were wooden, and her boots clomped on them as she walked in.

"Hello?" Maya said.

"Be right there," a man's voice shouted back.

She waited, thinking that only in the small town of Pinecone Junction would a cash register be left unattended. Even in a small town, though, she was a little bit concerned. Thieves lived everywhere. As Maya took in her surroundings, she did notice some security cameras around the store. At least they had those.

She hadn't spent much time in the hardware store. Maya tended to not worry about cabin projects, but maybe she should get more serious about updating things or even just varnishing the wood to seal it for the winter.

Maya headed down the aisle with paints and varnishes. She had just picked up a sealant that might work for her cabin and was calculating how much it would cost to do the whole thing when a man came around the corner. He had thin graying hair that stuck out on top of his head, wire-rimmed glasses and a friendly smile.

"I'm sorry about that," he said. "How can I help you?"

"No problem," Maya said, setting the varnish back on the shelf.

"Do you have a log home? That's an excellent sealant that you had there."

"No—well, I mean yes. I do have a cabin, but I'm actually here on official business."

"Oh," the man said, adjusting his glasses. "What can I help you with?"

"First, my apologies, I should have introduced myself. I'm Officer Thompson, with the Forest Service," Maya said, holding out her hand.

"Daryl Brenton."

They shook hands and Maya said, "Nice to meet you. Are you new to town?"

"I am. My family and I moved up here a couple months ago and I bought the store."

"I'm sorry I haven't stopped in sooner to meet you," she said. "Can I ask you a couple questions?"

"Sure. I'm guessing it's not about cabin stain, is it?"

"No," Maya said. She pulled out her phone and brought up a picture of the spike end of the booby trap. She enlarged the picture and showed Daryl the photo. "Do you sell stakes like these?"

"We sure do," Daryl said. "Here, I'll show you."

Maya followed him back out to the front and down the rows until they got to an area with different types of flags and stakes for projects.

"Here," Daryl said, pointing at the wooden stakes just like what she'd found in the booby trap. Only these hadn't been sharpened as much.

"Looks like the same stake," Maya said. "Have you had anyone come in and buy a bunch recently? Maybe with some wire too?"

"I can't think of anyone, but I can go through our sales receipts. My wife works in the mornings and sometimes our son, Ethan, works during the weekend. I can look into it for you."

"That would be great. I really appreciate it," Maya said, handing Daryl her card. "If you find something like a name with the receipts, here's my number."

"Sure. Can I ask what this is pertaining to?"

"Just something we're investigating right now. I appreciate your help," Maya said.

"Of course. You need anything else? I'd be happy to help you load up some of that varnish."

"No, I'm good," Maya said. "But I probably should stain the cabin at some point. I'm sure I'll be back in. It was nice to meet you."

"Likewise," Daryl said. "Have a good rest of your day."

Maya nodded and headed back to her patrol vehicle and drove to the sheriff's office. Juniper had flopped over on her side and was still blissfully snoring, so Maya let her be and walked back to Josh's office. She found him typing on his computer; yet another stack of paperwork was in front of him.

"Hey there," Maya said.

Josh looked up and smiled, but she thought it looked forced. "Hey back," he said. "Come on in, let me finish typing this sentence."

Maya sat down and waited for Josh to finish. When he did, she said, "Lots of paperwork, huh?"

"Yeah, I'm trying to find a stopping point for today. You know how it is with being the deputy sheriff."

"Well, actually I don't," Maya said, trying to tease him a bit, but he didn't laugh. "Did Lucas go back to Denver?"

"No, he's actually around here somewhere. I found him an empty room about the size of a closet to work in. He's getting a warrant to try pinging Kendra's cell phone and see if we can locate it. Maybe then we can find her vehicle too."

Maya rubbed her forehead, feeling a headache coming on. "What all did you find in her apartment?"

Josh sighed and said, "That's some of my paperwork. She was definitely obsessed with you. Pictures, notes, maps marking where you patrolled most frequently and a log she kept with your schedule."

"Holy shit," Maya said, flopping back in the chair. "Any indication why?"

"No, nothing obvious. Is there any chance your paths would have crossed in the military?"

"Not that I know of, but I'll think about it more tonight," she said. "Did you find any next of kin?"

"Still working on that. From what I've found, it looks like her dad did murder her mother. She was telling the truth about that. No relatives stepped forward to take her in, so she was in the system and in and out of foster care. Arrested a couple times, but then got her act together and joined the military. Seems like she had a decent career there."

Maya didn't know what to say. Once again, she only had questions, no answers. "No obvious connection to Eric Torres?"

"As a teenager she was in foster care in the same town he worked as a cop. Her records are sealed because at the time she was a juvenile and it appears maybe the judge even threw out some of the charges or else she might not have been able to enlist in the military. If I can get a court order to open up the records, maybe we can see if Eric arrested her, but other than that, all I can say is they're from the same town. But you and I both know there are very few coincidences. He had to have known her. I bet he arrested her at some point."

Maya stared up at the ceiling and then back at Josh. He was keeping a poker face. No emotion. She hated it when he did that. It made it hard to know what he thought. *Now would be a good time for me to apologize. But what do I say?*

"Okay, that's at least a start," Maya said, thinking that maybe it would be better to buy Josh dinner and apologize then. "You want to grab some dinner at the Black Bear Café? It's burrito night. Our favorite."

"No, thanks for the offer, but I'm buried here. I have so much to get done."

"Okay," Maya said. She clasped her hands together and was about ready to say something along the lines of an apology when she sensed someone behind her. Lucas.

"Uh, sorry to interrupt," he said, "but I was able to locate the last ping on a cell phone tower from Kendra's phone. It's not far from where her body was found. I thought I'd go see if I could find it. Anyone want to go with?"

"Yeah," Maya said. "Juniper is resting and I bet by the time we get back to the area, she'll be ready to go again. If we bring the scent article from the crime scene, she might be able to help us locate the phone. If the evidence is fresh enough, she may also be able to find other items too."

"Sounds good to me," Lucas said. "Josh, you want to go since this is really your jurisdiction?"

"Yes, anything to get away from this pile of paperwork. Let's do it," Josh said, standing up.

He walked past Maya and she placed a hand on his arm, stopping him for a moment. She waited for Lucas to walk down the hall and out of earshot, then said, "I'm sorry, Josh. I didn't mean to hurt you when you offered to help me. I appreciate you doing that."

Josh shrugged. "It's okay, I understand wanting your own space, but I really care about you. A lot."

Maya took a deep breath. She had to start being honest with him, even if it was difficult. "I care about you too. I just don't know if I'm ready to stay with someone or have you stay overnight with me. I'm sorry about that."

"It's okay. Just promise me you'll be careful. You always talk about losing me, but I don't know what I'd do if I lost you, Maya."

"I'll be careful and I'll ask for help. I promise."

Maya followed Josh and Lucas to a trailhead parking area where Kendra's phone had last pinged. This trail was farther down the road from Big Gulch and many people used it to get back to some good fishing spots both along a creek and at a reservoir. The problem with finding the phone was that the ping happened on a cell phone tower. That meant the phone had been in range of that tower, which left a lot of open space where it could be. There were meadows all around the area.

Juniper had slept the entire drive, but when the vehicle turned off, she jumped to her feet and started spinning in circles, yipping in excitement.

"Geez," Maya said. "You go from comatose to a hundred miles an hour. Calm down, girl. You're going to get to work again."

Juniper shook and grunted. Maya went around to her compartment, glad Juniper's tracking gear was still on, and got her out. The pair went over to where Josh and Lucas were looking at a map. Josh was also holding the plastic bag that Miranda had placed the gauze in from the shoeprint. Maya hoped there was enough scent, but the good part of this search was that the temperature was dropping and humidity would slightly rise, which would start to bring scent out more for Juniper. Anytime the ground was warmer than the air, a scent trail became stronger.

"I have no idea where to start," Lucas said.

"Let's start on the path with Juniper," Maya said. "I'll let her work on the long leash and see what she can find. I don't want to let her off leash since we're near the road." If Juniper caught a good track or scent for evidence, she'd have tunnel vision and not worry about crossing the road with an oncoming vehicle.

Josh and Lucas agreed to Maya's plan and she took Juniper over to the start of the path, which wound its way to the reservoir. Josh opened up the bag with the scent article and let Juniper take a good sniff.

"Let's find it, girl. Seek."

Juniper immediately put her nose on the ground and Maya let the leash out. She watched her dog for the telltale signs that she was in odor. Josh and Lucas stayed back, Josh still in position to be her backup officer while Lucas made sure he didn't get in the way of Juniper working. He had often worked with Maya and Zinger in Afghanistan, so he understood the protocol.

At first, Juniper went off the trail, but then stopped, whipped around and came back to the path. Her tail went straight up and her body tensed. Then she took off down the middle of the footpath.

"I never get tired of seeing the dogs work," Lucas said.

Maya smiled. She never tired of it either.

Juniper went down the path straight toward the reservoir, and as they approached the shoreline, she suddenly veered off to some bushes. She went back and forth, working a scent cone, and then off to the side of the bushes, she lay down and stared at the ground.

"Good girl," Maya said. She wanted to reward Juniper, but she didn't know yet if there was anything in the bushes. "Release. Come."

Juniper stood up and came back and sat by Maya's side. Lucas put on gloves and started carefully inspecting the area where Juniper had indicated. A smile spread across his face.

"It's a cell phone," he said, taking some pictures and making notes before he removed it. "Hopefully it's Kendra's."

"I hope so too," Maya said. "I'm going to cast Juniper out again and make sure there's not anything else around this area."

"I'll back you up," Josh said. Maya thought he seemed quiet, but she was exhausted after this long day; Josh was probably really tired too.

She had Juniper sniff the scent article again and then started casting her back out. Almost immediately, Juniper's tail went straight up and her nose went to the ground, following the scent trail. Juniper headed back toward the reservoir shoreline.

As her front paws hit the water, Maya pulled her up. She didn't want Juniper heading into the reservoir, not only because she didn't want to smell wet dog all night, but also because she didn't know what Juniper might be smelling in the water. There could be something out in the middle of the reservoir and the odor could be coming back to them.

Josh and Lucas came up beside Maya. "I don't know

what to tell you," she said. "She tracked to this shore-line."

The sun started to dip below the mountains, casting an orange hue across the water. The change in color highlighted something just below the water's surface. Maya squinted, peering harder.

"Is that…"

"I think it is," Lucas said.

Josh nodded in agreement. "That's definitely a ve-hicle."

"Kendra had a blue Jeep," Maya said.

"Looks blue to me," Josh said. "I'll call Miranda and a towing company. I'll see if I can get some lights out here too. We have a long night ahead of us."

Chapter Sixteen

Early the next morning, Maya and Juniper headed to town. Once again, she was short on sleep, because she hadn't made it home until midnight. They hadn't found any more evidence around the reservoir but had managed to pull the Jeep out of the water. The plates were still on the vehicle, so it was easy to verify that it belonged to Kendra.

Miranda would be spending today processing the entire car. Maya was hoping they'd find something more that would answer some questions about why Kendra was spying on her and who had killed her. But first, they were meeting with the Montana detective Abigail Harper, and she couldn't wait to learn more about Eric Torres. Hopefully, something beyond the information that they already had.

Maya had left Todd, her patrol captain, a voice mail and filled him in as best as she could on both the task force and the booby traps. She knew he was out on some investigations, so she'd probably hear back from him later.

Maya swung into the local coffee shop and picked up some drinks for her, Josh, Pops, Lucas and Miranda. She didn't know if the detectives drank coffee, but in her mind, was there anyone who worked in law enforcement and didn't drink coffee? She added a few extra orders.

As she sat down in her patrol vehicle, Juniper was whining in the back. Maya waited for her to settle down for a moment and then let her stick her head through the door between the compartment and the cab. Juniper watched out the front window as they turned onto the street and pulled into the sheriff's parking lot.

Juniper grunted and pulled her head back through to her own side and plopped down on her haunches, giving Maya a look that said she was not happy because she knew she was being left in the vehicle again. Maya reached back and scratched Juniper behind her ears.

"I promise I'll get you some time out in the woods soon, girl. I know you're tired of this meeting stuff. Maybe if Josh isn't too mad at me, he'd even be willing to decoy for us and let you take a bite."

Juniper gave her a quick lick on the hand and Maya hoped that meant she was forgiven. If she wasn't forgiven, then there was a good chance Juniper would sneak something into her dog run and get payback. Maya still had a pair of chewed-up boots to take to the shoe repair shop. That had been her fault, though. She'd left them too close to Juniper's run and they had become casualties of Juniper's sharp teeth.

Carefully getting out of the vehicle, Maya carried the coffee holder across the parking lot. As she was approaching the door, she heard a female voice say, "Let me get the door for you."

Glancing back over her shoulder, Maya saw a smaller woman dressed in black slacks, a cream-colored blouse and a black jacket. She had her badge on her belt and gun holstered on her hip. Her dark hair was cut in a bob with some waves. Her makeup brought out her eyes, which reminded Maya of the color of some of the glacial lakes in the high country. The woman carried herself with an air of confidence and like someone who would get what they wanted.

"Detective Harper?" Maya asked.

"Please, just call me Abigail."

"Okay," Maya said as Abigail opened the door for her. "Thanks." She went inside, still balancing the coffees precariously.

"Here, let me help," Abigail said, taking a few of the coffees from Maya.

"Thanks again. I'm Maya…"

"Officer Thompson—yes, I know," Abigail said.

"I guess the Forest Service uniform gave me away," Maya said. She liked how direct Abigail was. With her help, this might be the chance they were looking for to get some good information on Eric Torres. Maya wanted to know if Abigail could connect Eric with Nana and her mother as well as how he might know Kendra. Hopefully she had some answers.

"My partner, Blake Conner, is parking our car. He'll be in in a minute. Where should we meet you?"

"Go through those doors," Maya said, nodding in the direction behind the front desk. "There's a meeting room down that way. We'll be there. And if you want those coffees, they're yours."

"Good, we had a long drive and I need caffeine. I'm sure Blake does too. See you in a minute," Abigail said.

Maya headed on down to the meeting room. Abigail Harper might be exactly who they needed. Maya could already tell she was sharp and didn't mess around. Her kind of person.

When she got to the meeting room, Josh was the only person in there. He was reading through some more reports.

"Hey there," Maya said. "Brought you some coffee."

Josh looked up and flashed his grin, which brought out Maya's favorite dimple and made her heart beat a little faster. She felt better seeing him look happier this morning.

"Thanks," he said, taking one from her.

She set the rest on the table. "You're welcome. You look better rested."

"I am. Even though we were out late, I slept really well."

"That's good," Maya said.

They stared at each other for a moment in awkward silence until someone behind Maya cleared their throat. Miranda. "You two making up?" she asked.

Maya laughed and shook her head. Miranda was to the point too. "I guess," she finally answered.

"Good."

"There's a coffee for you," Maya said, as Pops, Lucas and Abigail came into the room. A man followed Abigail. He was maybe a few years older than Abigail, but younger than Pops. He had the look of someone who'd been in law enforcement their entire life. He nodded at Maya but didn't greet her or acknowledge her more than that. His demeanor seemed cold and cut-off. She didn't know what to make of him but figured it didn't really matter as long as they all worked together.

Everyone took a seat around the table and Pops started the meeting.

"Let's just get to the point," he said. "We believe due to evidence that Eric Torres is in our area. We know he's dangerous and we'd like to work together. Maybe one of you can fill us in as to why you feel you both needed to come for one man. What don't we know about Eric Torres?"

Abigail jumped right in by saying, "First, thanks for having us come and allowing us to join in looking for Torres. There's a lot more to him than what's in the files."

Maya noticed that Blake's face tightened. Maybe he didn't like having to work with a female partner. She had experienced some of that too in her military time. There were guys that thought women shouldn't be there or be promoted, but the fact that Blake didn't talk was interesting to Maya because that could also mean he didn't mind Abigail taking charge. It was hard to read him. If they were going to work with these two, she wanted to know more about the dynamic in their relationship. It could affect the investigation and Maya needed to find Eric Torres. She wanted answers.

"Eric Torres is not your typical criminal or just a cop gone bad," Abigail continued. "He's cunning, he's ruthless and he's smart. He's eluded arrest for a long time and he's not going to be brought in very easily."

"Maybe you can give us more background on him," Pops said. "The more we know, the better. Did you two ever work together in your department?"

"We did. In fact, we went to the academy together. I liked him when I first met him, but that's the thing with Torres. People like and trust him. He's very charismatic and that's allowed him to manipulate others over the

years. We worked patrol together for a few years and I
started to notice problems even then."

"Like what?" Pops asked.

"He took bribes, for one. Usually from people he
pulled over. Simple things at first like being paid off
to look the other way on a speeding ticket or a DUI.
Then, he started working for some judges who took
bribes. They would get paid off by defense attorneys
and in turn, Torres would lie on the stand and help the
defense win. He would suddenly 'forget' certain details
or deliberately leave out some details when he wrote up
reports. Things that could legitimately get cases thrown
out. We believe the judges and attorneys gave him a cut.
I saw him intimidate witnesses a couple times and he
would arrest young women on drug and prostitution
charges, seduce them and convince them that if they
had sex with him, he'd let them off. I know it happened
many times. Never mind the fact that he was married."

Maya gripped her coffee cup almost to the point of
crushing it. Arrests on drug and prostitution charges.
Her mother had been arrested for those things and she
had run away to the same town in Montana. Maya knew
one question was possibly answered. She'd have to see
if she could find some old arrest records, but she bet
that her mother had been arrested by Eric Torres and
who knows what else happened based on what Abigail
was saying.

"I agree he sounds like a total scumbag," Pops said,
"While he deserves to be arrested for all of that, it
doesn't make him a cold-blooded killer. The crime scene
we had here was horrific."

"I understand and I can only imagine how bad it
was," Abigail said. "I've seen his work. It seemed like

Torres moved into harder crimes and now I suspect him for several more murders in our area including key witnesses in cases."

Maya watched Pops. He was taking in everything Abigail was saying and mulling it over. Blake stared straight ahead at the wall. He hadn't said one word. Maya didn't know what to make of that and wondered why he wasn't adding in information as Abigail's partner.

"I see the connection to your area and his motivation," Pops finally said, "but why Colorado? Why is he here? Does it connect to any of your cases? And do you know the most recent victim, Kendra Martin?"

"I'll get to all that, I promise," Abigail said. "We actually believe he's a pawn in a bigger crime ring. Believe it or not, there's someone above him calling the shots and we want to find that person. They may or may not also be in law enforcement. We're not sure, but we believe that Eric has connections here in Colorado and he's back to finish the job he started. There was a young lady he arrested several times by the name of Zoey Thompson..." Abigail trailed off.

Maya stared at her and then at Pops. She released her grip on her cup so that she didn't crush it and send coffee everywhere and willed herself to remain calm.

"I know that's a personal connection for you too, Sheriff Thompson and Officer Thompson, and I'm sorry for your loss," Abigail said.

Maya could tell Pops was trying to stay calm too. He had more practice at a poker face since he got together with the guys and played poker once a week. That along with his many years in law enforcement.

"Thank you," Pops finally said. "My daughter's cold

case has remained unsolved. Recently we've also connected the case with my wife's death through DNA
which is why Officer Thompson and I have not been involved. That DNA also goes back to Eric Torres. That's
why CBI investigator Lucas Tucker is sitting in on this
meeting because he's in charge of those investigations.
But I am curious, any ideas on why he'd want to kill
both my daughter and my wife? The same gun was
used in both crimes—what are your thoughts on that?"

"Again, my condolences," Abigail said. "I know for
a fact that Torres arrested your daughter a couple times.
We believe he asked her to do favors for him, probably
illegal ones. We don't have proof, but we also believe
that your daughter took evidence with her when she left
Montana. That evidence could connect not only Torres
to many crimes, but others in the judicial system too.
Unfortunately, we've had some issues in our area. And
we also believe that this evidence could help lead us to
the person in charge of the crime ring up in our area, but
that Torres is this person's right-hand man, so to speak.
Did your daughter ever mention any evidence to you?"

Maya leaned forward, holding her breath. Did her
mother have something that Pops didn't tell her about?
Was he holding back on her?

"No, she never mentioned anything..." Pops said.
She saw the realization hit Pops the same time it did
her. "But she and I weren't close. Zoey often confided
in my wife, but not me. Karen told me some things,
but not everything, so I'm sorry. If there's evidence, I
don't know where it is or even what it might be. Zoey's
house burned down and there wasn't anything left, so
it could be gone."

"Or it could still be out there somewhere," Abigail said.

"What makes you say that?" Pops asked.

"Because Torres is here and he's cleaning up his messes. You see, he arrested Kendra Martin too back when she was in foster care. She was in and out of juvie and Torres put her there, but then all of a sudden, he said she had her act together and he wasn't arresting her anymore. She probably started working for him back then."

Maya couldn't stay quiet any longer. "But Kendra enlisted in the Air Force. Would he have kept in touch with her?"

"Definitely," Abigail said, turning to look at Maya. "Once you work for Torres, there's no getting out."

"Then what about the gun that was used to kill my grandmother and mother?" Maya asked.

"That's definitely typical of Torres. He probably stole the gun from evidence or bought it off the street and then figured out how to register it to your grandmother. It's all part of his manipulation, to make you wonder if there was any chance your grandmother killed her daughter."

"No, I never wondered that," Maya said, as her chest constricted. Pops glanced at her and she knew that she had to keep her cool. "But I know the other investigators did."

That had been another difficult part of losing her grandmother. Since Pops was married to Nana, he couldn't technically investigate, so some state investigators came in to help. They'd immediately ruled Nana's death a suicide and had suggested that since the same gun was used in the crimes, Nana might have actually killed her own daughter and then years later taken her own life, no longer able to live with the guilt. Maya had still been drinking heavily then. After the investigators had suggested that, she'd gone home and drank until she passed out. It was how she dealt with her anger, and she wasn't proud of it. When they originally reopened the cases, even Josh had suggested the connection. He had been the one to point out that they needed to somehow disprove that theory so investigators could look at new leads. Lucas had agreed, which was why he had approved testing the DNA.

So many memories washed over her, and Maya rubbed her temples, working to pull herself together.

"That's why we continued this investigation." Josh. Maya was relieved to hear him speak. He probably had sensed that she and Pops were starting to feel overwhelmed with how personal this had become.

"When Sheriff and Officer Thompson told me about the cases," Josh continued, "I was with them, I didn't think everything added up. I've been helping with the investigation since I'm not family and with recent DNA evidence, we can at least place Torres at the crime scenes."

"I would not be surprised that he killed them both and tried to confuse the investigators, but when we catch him, we can interrogate him and find out more."

"What makes you think he'd talk?" Josh asked.

Abigail shrugged. "He may not, but if we can get some sort of plea deal to get him to give us the name of the person in charge of this crime ring, then he might rat them out. Eric Torres is a snake. He'd kill his own mother if he needed to. He even worked at the station for years while committing these crimes. Had us all fooled."

"Did he come back to work after he killed my wife?" Pops asked.

"No. We had started to investigate him and internal affairs was getting ready to arrest him, but then he didn't show up for his shift. Didn't even clean out his locker. That was around the time your wife was murdered. He just disappeared and we couldn't find him. Until now."

Pops spoke up again. "I can see why you want this guy and why you were willing to come to Colorado. We will do our best to cooperate with you. I'm assigning Undersheriff Josh Colten as lead investigator for our department. Colten worked in Chicago on many murder investigations and has the most experience."

Maya took a deep breath and sat back in her chair. Abigail had certainly provided more information. Now they just needed to catch the man responsible, and Maya had a great way to find him: Juniper.

Juniper had already tracked Eric Torres once. She could do it again.

Chapter Seventeen

As thoughts swirled through Maya's head about how she could find a good scent for Juniper to track, her phone buzzed. It was Todd.

"Excuse me," she said, stepping out of the meeting room and answering her phone. "Hello, sir."

"Thompson, sorry I couldn't get back to you until now. I was out on some other investigations but got your messages. Fill me in."

Maya took a deep breath and recapped everything Abigail had said. She also updated Todd on the booby trap investigation, which in Maya's mind had taken a back seat to this one, but she knew she couldn't let her other work slide just because of the Torres case.

"Okay," Todd said, after remaining quiet for a moment. "Good work on the booby traps and finding the drugs. Maybe they're connected, maybe not. Keep following up with that lead from the hardware store. I'm also guessing it's someone local. Hopefully, the hardware store can find the receipts so we can figure out who bought those stakes and question them."

"I'll let you know as soon as I have more information, sir," Maya said, pacing up and down the hallway.

"Good. As for this other case, even though it happened on Forest Service land, I need to pull you off."

Maya stopped and gripped her phone until her fingers hurt. "Sir?"

"Look, Thompson. I know this is tough and it's difficult for me too. I don't know what I'd do in your shoes, but this is your family, and you can't be on this case. Why do you think your grandfather put Colten as lead investigator? He really can't have anything to do with this either. If I had an extra officer available, I'd send them down to help, but you know that we're short-staffed so let the sheriff's office and CBI investigator do their jobs."

Maya pinched the bridge of her nose. This wasn't happening. A few months ago, she probably would have punched something. Today, she worked on her breathing and staying grounded, but it wasn't easy. She knew she'd been walking a fine line with investigating on her own time. Todd had talked about this with her before. She needed to let Lucas do his job, but it wasn't easy. "I understand, sir, and you're right."

"You want to nail this guy?"

"Yes."

"Then don't get involved more than you have. You and I both know a defense lawyer would get this case thrown out, and that's the last thing you want. You have to think ahead about this going to court. I know that's hard and it's not what you want to hear. You can still help with anything that doesn't have to do with the main investigation. And if you see that son of a bitch while you're out on patrol, arrest him. But then call in Colten or the CBI to take over and step away. Got it?"

"I got it, sir," Maya said. She knew he was right and that only made things more difficult.

"Good. Keep me posted on these booby traps, and Thompson…"

"Yeah?"

"Stay out of trouble. There's only so many times I can smooth things over with the higher-ups. You're a great officer and K-9 handler. I need you."

"Yes, sir," Maya said, saying goodbye and hanging up. She knew that he was talking about a few months ago when she'd used Juniper to apprehend some of the drug traffickers that had kidnapped Pops. She and Juniper weren't certified yet, but Juniper's help had led to taking down a big drug operation with a Russian mobster, which helped to defuse Todd's bosses.

Maya walked out the back door to get some fresh air and calm down. The sun was up high and already felt intense. She hoped for some afternoon clouds to roll in. She walked over to the edge of the back patio and stared at the mountain peaks, which were bare of snow except for maybe a few places that didn't get sun.

Todd was right. She had to behave herself, but he did leave the door open for arresting Eric Torres if she found him. He didn't say she couldn't use Juniper to get that done. And now they were certified. Juniper was her best way to find someone who wanted to disappear.

Eric parked his truck in a picnic area that connected to a trail that ran along the edge of town and ended just past the sheriff's office. There were plenty of trees to provide cover and not much foot traffic. He could hike down to the sheriff's office and not worry about being spotted.

Another complication had just arrived and now he

needed to get to Maya sooner rather than later. He wasn't happy that his plans had been disrupted, but he should have known better. Abigail Harper wouldn't stop until he was behind bars.

He would do everything he could to make sure she didn't accomplish that goal—even if it meant killing her. If he could grab Maya first, though, she might have the answers he needed, but then what would he do with her after he got them?

First, he needed to see if Abigail really was here. He'd started out his career with her and they had worked together for a while. Abigail was ambitious, he had to give her that. But he was better, and they both knew it. Especially now that Abigail hadn't been able to capture Eric. He was usually able to stay one step ahead.

But if the different departments teamed up, then that would make things harder for him. Luckily, he knew the mountains and how to survive, live off the grid and avoid capture. Having millions of acres to disappear in was an advantage.

Eric arrived at the area behind the sheriff's office. He had to be careful he wasn't spotted on security cameras, but he needed to see who was there and if he was right that Abigail was in town. Eric snuck around the next corner of the building, which led to a back patio and lunch area. He'd scoped out the building at night when there were less people around.

As he came around the corner, he sucked in his breath and stepped back behind a tree. Maya was there. By herself. She was the spitting image of Zoey. He couldn't believe how much they looked alike.

Eric chanced another peek. She was pacing back and forth and looked like she was ready to punch something. He remembered the first time he'd had to arrest her mother, Zoey—she was feisty too and hadn't made it easy for him.

Maybe this was his chance. Maybe he could distract her and get her now. The dog was out in the patrol vehicle, so that made things easier, but Eric wasn't prepared. He didn't have anything to subdue her, and he didn't know if he could handle a fight. She was strong and tough. He knew that much from watching her.

As he thought through his options the door opened again and the deputy that couldn't stop looking at Maya came out. Eric had missed his opportunity. He continued along the trail and checked out the parking lot. Sure enough, there was a detective's vehicle with Montana plates.

Abigail was getting too close. Eric had to act tonight. It was now or never.

Chapter Eighteen

Maya heard the door open. She took a deep breath and turned around. Josh.

"You okay?" he asked.

"Yes and no," Maya said. "I mean I'm glad we're finding out more about Eric Torres and his background. How he thinks and works and things like that, but I just talked with my boss and he's pulling me off the investigation because of the family ties."

"I'm sorry, Maya. I know how hard that is, but it's not a surprise. Your grandfather just let me know that he's stepping out of this too. I'll be in charge for the sheriff's office. We need this Torres guy to go to prison and not go free. If you want justice for your mother and grandmother, this is the best way."

"I know," Maya said. "It still sucks. Although Todd did say that if I happened to see Torres when I was out on patrol, to arrest him. And then call you."

"Todd should know better than to give you a loophole like that," Josh said with a laugh. Then his face became more serious. "We'll get him. I promise you that. And I'll make sure it's an airtight case and you and Pops will get the closure you need. Just promise me that you will be careful, and you won't do anything without backup."

Maya desperately wanted to go over to Josh and hug him, but she restrained herself. If someone saw them, that would only add to the rumors Miranda had been talking about.

"Thank you," she said. "That means a lot to me… and I promise I'll be careful."

She and Josh locked eyes for a moment, and as Maya's chest tightened, she cleared her throat and said, "I guess if I'm not on this case, I better go back out on patrol. I need to figure out who's setting those booby traps and it is hunting season. I should probably help check some tags."

"Okay," Josh said, holding the door for Maya.

She went back inside, and as she passed Josh, his frame seemed to fill the door, forcing her to step a little bit closer. She could smell his cologne and wanted nothing more than to have him wrap his arms around her and tell her again that everything would be okay. They would catch this killer and her mother and Nana would finally have justice. Instead, Maya continued down the hall, Josh following behind her.

As they approached the meeting room, Abigail stepped out. "Where's a good place to grab lunch?" she asked.

"There's only one place in Pinecone Junction—the Black Bear Café. But luckily it's good," Maya said.

"You two want to join me?" Abigail said. "Blake has some personal business he needs to attend to and Lucas said he's going to the crime lab to see if Miranda needs help with processing the vehicle, so I thought I'd grab lunch and then come back here to keep working."

"Sure," Maya said, turning toward Josh. "You want to come?"

"I wish I could, but I'm meeting up with Pops to fill him in on some other things. You two have fun."

"Okay," Maya said. She told Abigail she'd meet at the café because she needed to get Juniper out. After letting her play for a few minutes, she put her back in the vehicle. Juniper's pointy ears drooped slightly, and she appeared put out and pouty.

"I promise we'll go to the mountains today and do something other than have you sit in the car. You did get to have some fun last night," Maya said to her.

She felt a little guilty because she knew that after lunch Juniper would still be stuck in the vehicle. Maya needed to stop in at the hardware store and see if Daryl had found any receipts, and after that, help their local parks and wildlife officer check hunting tags. Then she would have to take Juniper and do something. Some training would be good. Maybe they'd even head back home and go for a run.

Home.

A thought started to form in her head.

Her cabin was the one crime scene that hadn't been processed. She knew now that someone had been watching her, and that was Kendra. According to Abigail, there was a good chance Kendra had been working for Torres, probably gathering intel on Maya. If Torres thought that she knew something about the evidence her mother supposedly stole, then he might have been surveilling her cabin too.

Maya thought about the cigarette smoke she'd smelled. Why had she ever doubted her instincts…and Juniper's instincts? There was a good chance there were more cigarette butts out there somewhere that Juniper could help her find and possibly some other evidence that could help them locate Torres.

Maybe Maya could do a "training" session with Juniper to work on evidence searches and older tracks. It was a long shot, but it could kill two birds with one stone—give Juniper something to do so she didn't tear apart everything at the cabin and find some more evidence.

Maya drove down to the Black Bear Café and parked in front. Juniper huffed and sighed in the back and turned around, so she was facing away from her. Maya smiled and said again, "I promise we'll do something fun this afternoon. You'll enjoy it."

She headed into the café, stopping long enough to do her ritual of patting the wooden black bear statue out front on the nose. There was a lunch rush going. There wasn't much to do in Pinecone Junction, so the locals often grabbed lunch together. Ranchers would gather and discuss things like hay and beef prices. Wives would get together and discuss how the kids were doing and gossip. Maya used to come with Nana for lunches like that. She'd enjoyed it, but after coming home from Afghanistan and with Nana being gone, she felt more like an outsider now.

She wound her way through the other lunch patrons over to where Abigail sat in a corner. It was the table closest to the bar. Part of her wanted to move tables. She'd love nothing more right now than to go to the bar and have a few beers. Make all these feelings go away. She didn't like having raw emotions pop up, but discussing the cases this morning had brought up deep feelings. Maya always worked to be stoic and tough, but the reality was, she was as vulnerable as the next person. It didn't matter what uniform she wore or what type of gun she had on her duty belt.

Abigail studied the menu. "What do you recommend?"

Maya picked the chair that faced away from the bar. "Everything here is good. I'm a burger and fries kind of person, but Josh loves the meat loaf."

"Meat loaf?" Abigail made a disgusted face and then laughed. "Maybe my mom just didn't know how to make meat loaf."

"No, you're not alone, I'm not a huge fan either."

The waitress came over and took their drink and food orders. Maya had her usual cheeseburger and fries while Abigail ordered a turkey sandwich. The server left and Maya suddenly felt awkward. She didn't know Abigail. What would they talk about? They couldn't really discuss the case in public and Maya wasn't on it anyway. Why had she agreed to come to lunch, especially when she had so much to get done?

Abigail broke the silence. "Heard your boss pulled you off the investigation because of the family ties."

"He did, but I understand," Maya said.

"Still, it must be frustrating."

Maya glanced over at the bar again. This conversation would be easier if she could order a beer. Maybe she'd better call her sponsor later too. The craving was hitting her hard today. "It is frustrating," she finally said.

"How old were you when your mom died?"

"I was four, almost five," Maya said.

"That's young. I'm sorry to hear that. You remember much about that night?"

Maya's memories were still fragmented, but she

could still feel the heat of the fire and the relief of Pops finding her and carrying her to safety. She could even taste the mac and cheese she'd been eating earlier that day. "I have some memories, but they're not great. The memories come in pieces, kind of like looking into a broken mirror. You can't quite see the whole picture, but I've been working on remembering more. The most vivid memory was when my mom told me to go hide."

"It's a good thing she did tell you that or you might not be here today."

"True," Maya said.

"So what made you want to become a cop and work K-9s? I mean, it's not a common profession for women. I should know."

"Pops and Nana adopted me after my mother's death. They were both grandparents and parents to me. I can't imagine how they felt losing their only daughter and then having to raise their granddaughter, but I loved them both and I always said I wanted to be just like Pops. I don't think he was happy at first that I wanted to be in law enforcement, but Nana always encouraged me to be what I wanted."

"You're lucky to have had them," Abigail said.

"I am. How about you? What took you down this career path?"

Abigail gazed out the window and then turned back to Maya. "I wanted to help people. I wanted to solve crimes and put the bad guys away, but I was naive. At the time I entered law enforcement, there weren't as many women as there are now and things were different. I wanted to quit several times because of the harassment, but I made it through the academy and started to prove myself, and now almost thirty years later, here I am trying to solve this last big case so I can retire."

"Women like you helped pave the path for my generation. Thank you."

"Oh, don't thank me. There's still a long way to go. The glass ceiling is still there for us."

"But you made detective," Maya said.

"True, but how many female chiefs of police do you see? Or sheriffs? Not many. Now it's your generation that's in charge of breaking through."

"I feel pretty fortunate," Maya said. "I served in the Marines, and I was given respect. I earned it, but everyone had to. As a Forest Service officer, things have been great too. I went through the training in Georgia at the federal law enforcement training center and was treated with respect there too. I never had any issues, so things have come a long way."

Their food arrived and Abigail waited to answer until after their server was gone. "Then you're lucky," she said. "I'm glad you've had a great experience. It wasn't the same for me and I've talked with other women in law enforcement. Some are lucky like you, but some still have issues in their departments."

"I'm sorry to hear that," Maya said.

They started eating in an uncomfortable silence. Maya wanted to ask more about Abigail's time at the academy but refrained. She knew she was lucky. Even in the military, she never had any issues, but other women had and often things were covered up. Maya's PTSD didn't involve rape or other types of assault, and for that she was grateful.

They finished lunch making small talk and then each went their own direction. Maya was glad that someone like Abigail was the one investigating her mother's and Nana's deaths. It seemed like she understood how important this was, not only to catch a dangerous criminal, but also how personal it was to Maya and Pops.

Chapter Nineteen

Maya spent the rest of her day catching up on her duties for the Forest Service. She spent some time investigating the booby traps. Daryl told her that he hadn't found any receipts that would help her. No one had bought that many stakes in bulk. She had noticed Daryl's son, Ethan, hanging around, but the kid seemed shy and just shook his head when she asked if he had any information. He didn't show any signs of being high either, but that didn't mean he didn't like escaping to the woods to smoke. Maya made a mental note to see if Miranda had been able to get a fingerprint off the pipe or containers. Probably not with how busy they'd all been.

She called their local parks and wildlife officer and asked if he needed help checking hunting tags and making sure no one was poaching. She helped with that for a few hours and then, exhausted, she headed back to her cabin. She couldn't remember if Josh was coming over for dinner or not. Maya sent him a text and he responded that he had some more paperwork to finish up but could come around 20:00 if that worked for her. She figured that was good. It gave her time to see if Juniper found anything around her cabin and then shower before they ate.

"Okay," Maya said to Juniper, who continued to pout in the back. "I know you think we're done for the night, but we're going to work. I've promised you that all day and I'm keeping that promise."

Juniper lifted and tilted her head at the mention of the word *work*. Then she jumped to her feet and started a little jig with her front paws dancing up and down. Maya smiled, happy to see her dog looking joyful again.

She figured she'd take Juniper back to where they found the foxes a few days ago. She'd made a mistake assuming that's what Juniper was barking at. There was a good chance Kendra or even Eric was watching her that day and the foxes just distracted Juniper at that moment. If Maya had been thinking, she should have cast Juniper out to see if she could find a human scent once the foxes left. Even though the scent would now be a few days old, Maya thought she'd give it a try again.

She came back around to the door to Juniper's compartment, and Juniper started some high-pitched yips. Maya waited for her to settle down and then let Juniper out of the vehicle. Juniper spun in circles, but she finally settled down and Maya snapped the leash on the tracking harness.

She continued to ask Juniper to settle until she felt the dog was ready to focus. Then they went over to where they had run into the foxes. How close had Kendra been to take pictures? Maya closed her eyes and visualized the wall with all her pictures. It seemed like most of them had been taken outside of the large picture window where Juniper would lunge and bark.

Feeling that Juniper was paying attention, Maya took her over to outside the window and started casting Juniper out. She would direct the dog in different directions, trying to read her body language and see if she was in odor.

"Go find 'em. Seek," Maya said.

Juniper, happy to be working, put her nose to the ground, but she continued to wander, which meant she hadn't found a good odor to track. Maya worked her way toward a stand of pine trees that could be a spot where Kendra would have hidden. Seeing her from inside the cabin would have been impossible. It would be hard to be much closer than that as Maya had cleared trees out to have defensible space around her cabin in case of a fire.

Juniper kept her nose to the ground and a few times brought it up to air scent. Maya had encouraged Juniper to do both. Some trainers wanted the dogs to track with their noses on the ground and not air scent. This meant the dog would follow the exact footsteps of the person they were after. The problem with that was the suspect could come back around and ambush a dog and handler, so Maya had worked with Juniper to put her nose up in the air too. That way if someone was hiding, they had a better chance of finding them. Juniper had been a superstar at figuring that out. Especially if it meant she could take a bite at the end of the track.

They continued their way back through the woods surrounding Maya's cabin, getting further away. All of a sudden Juniper paused. She whipped around and her tail poked straight up. Maya's heart rate picked up. She tried to remain calm so her dog wouldn't cue off her, but she really hoped they could find something. She knew that if they found evidence, she'd have to call Josh, Lucas and Miranda, but for now, it made Maya feel like she was still helping with the investigation and she wanted some sort of clue that would help them find Eric Torres and put him away for life.

Juniper put her nose back on the ground, making snuffling noises. Maya was ready to go. She knew once Juniper had the scent, she would shoot off like the fur missile she was. Sure enough, a few seconds later, Juniper headed east toward the road. Maya let the leash out, jogging to keep up with her. Juniper stayed on the track, keeping her nose to the ground, although she'd stop and air scent every now and then.

The thought occurred to Maya that she needed to be careful as Torres could be in the area. They suspected he was still in Colorado and wouldn't leave until he had what he needed which was probably the evidence Maya's mother had stashed. She was doing this track with no backup officer, and while Juniper would happily apprehend someone, Maya had to keep in mind that Torres was armed and dangerous.

Maya continued following Juniper, realizing they were headed toward the road. The track might end where Torres parked his vehicle, but that information could be helpful. She and Josh could set up surveillance for that area and see if Torres showed up. They might be able to catch him that way. Maya worked to keep her excitement about a possible trap under control. She couldn't interfere with Juniper's work.

They wound around and headed in the direction of a slow vehicle pull-off area. It would be a great place to park and hike to Maya's cabin. Juniper paused for a moment and started working a scent cone back and forth. Maya gave her more leash so she didn't pull her off the scent. Juniper went over to a tree and then went up on her hind legs, nose up in the air sniffing. She stayed up for a moment. Then she came off her hind legs and lay down, staring straight up.

"Good girl, Juniper. Way to find it," Maya said. She went and inspected the tree. There weren't too many branches at the bottom, but as she moved around, trying to figure out what Juniper had found, she saw the sun glint off something caught on the branch. It looked like a bracelet.

Maya continued to praise Juniper and pulled her favorite ball and rope toy out of her pocket. She threw the toy to Juniper, who joyfully latched on and ran around in a circle, squeaking it.

"You're going to kill that squeaker," Maya said. "Good thing I have some extra toys back at home."

She managed to get the toy away from Juniper, then sent Lucas a text and arranged for him to come right away since she couldn't collect the evidence herself and risk it being inadmissible in court. While they waited, she leaned in and carefully moved some tree branches so she could take a closer peek at the bracelet.

Maya gasped. She knew this bracelet and the good luck horseshoe charm that still hung off it.

It had belonged to her mother.

She leaned back against a tree and closed her eyes. Her breathing came in shallow gasps as she thought about the last time she'd seen this bracelet. She'd forgotten about it until now. The memory seemed so long ago, but Maya's mother had worn the bracelet the night she'd died. Maya leaned over, breathless as the memory flooded back in.

She remembered her mother answering the door when the loud knocks had started. The man who had reminded Maya of a snake had come back after Zoey kicked him out. He'd pounded on the door again, demanding that Zoey open it up. She took Maya by the shoulders and told her to go hide, the bracelet dangling right by Maya's face.

When Maya ran to the closet, her best hiding place, she remembered the man yelling at her mother. She hadn't recalled exactly what he said, but it had been threatening.

Maya squeezed her eyes shut trying desperately to remember what he looked like. Was it Eric Torres? *Can I trust this memory? Or am I wanting this to be what I remember?*

She worked to control her breathing. Juniper, sensing that something didn't seem right with her handler, came over and shoved her nose towards Maya's face.

"You're a good girl," Maya said, reaching out and stroking the dog on her head. She struggled to stand back up straight, trying to compose herself, but the memory brought with it smells of the smoke and fire. The sound of a gunshot. *That bastard shot her in cold blood. He's going to pay for this if it's the last thing I do.*

Not only had he killed her mother, but he'd been callous enough to steal this too. Had he given it to Kendra as a gift? Sweat dripped down Maya's face. A piece of her mother that would now have to be logged into evidence, but someday, when the bastard was behind bars, she would get it back.

Juniper continued to nudge her, and she sat down on the ground, petting the dog. She climbed into Maya's lap and tried to lick her face. Maya ended up with dog slobber all over her.

"Thanks a lot," she said with a laugh, wiping the slobber off. Juniper thumped her tail in response. Maya let the weight of Juniper calm her down and help get her breathing back under control.

A vehicle pulled into her drive. It was probably Lucas. Juniper hopped off Maya's lap and they went to greet him.

"So you found some evidence?" he asked.

"I did. I was just doing a training session and Juniper alerted. It's this way," Maya said.

"A training session, huh? Glad to see you haven't changed." Lucas chuckled and followed them back to the tree. They waited while he took pictures and logged the location of the bracelet.

"That bracelet was my mother's," Maya said as Lucas bagged it.

Lucas paused what he was doing. He stared at Maya with a bit of surprise. "Really? How do you think it got here?"

"I have no idea. I'm still in shock. I haven't seen it since the night my mother died."

"Yet another piece of the puzzle that doesn't make sense. I'll take it to Miranda and see if she can find any prints or other evidence on it," Lucas said. "Did you finish your 'training' track?"

"No."

"Well, I'm here now. I'll back you up. It'll be like old times and you can see if Juniper finds anything else."

"Works for me," Maya said.

She started casting Juniper out again and they picked up the track. Juniper continued to head in the direction of the pull-off and, as Maya suspected, that's where the track ended. She and Lucas inspected the area and found an oil leak. She wondered if Torres knew how bad his vehicle was dripping. It might give them the upper hand if they had to pursue him in a vehicle chase. Seeping that much oil, the truck might break down, especially if they were going up a mountain pass.

While Lucas took pictures of the area and the oil spots, she praised Juniper, who finally looked happy after working. She was proud of her dog. Because of Juniper, they had another piece of evidence tying Torres to her mother's death, and now Maya knew where he parked. She was one step closer to nailing Torres and putting him in prison where he deserved to rot.

As Lucas took some more pictures, Juniper started to growl.

"What's up with her?" Lucas asked.

"I don't know." Maya always trusted her dog. It was the number one commandment for dog handlers. She followed Juniper's gaze. An old truck was coming down the road. It was a two-toned beige Ford, probably an early '90s model.

The truck was slowing down.

She thought the driver was going to pull off and park, but then the driver shifted and the truck picked up speed. As it went by, creating a breeze that blew Maya's hair back off her face, she realized the driver was a male with dark hair. She snapped a quick picture of the license plate. Was there any chance that had been Torres? Even if she wanted to pursue the vehicle and pull it over, by the time she got back to her patrol vehicle, this truck would be long gone.

But Maya was definitely going to run the plate.

Eric downshifted as he passed his favorite place to park. The last thing he'd expected to see at the pull-off was Maya, her dog and another guy—he thought he was another investigator, but he didn't know for sure. Damn it, she'd probably used her dog to track to where he normally parked to hike in and do his surveillance. Now that spot was off limits.

And she'd taken a picture of his license plate.

They were Colorado plates—stolen at a rest stop on his way here—so that they wouldn't stick out. His Montana plates rested under the seat of his truck. He wondered how long before Maya ran the numbers and the plates showed up in the system as stolen. He hadn't worried about it because the rest stop was way up north in Wyoming and Eric figured that bought him some time.

Now that Maya had a picture of the plates, he would have to get rid of these. Maybe even get rid of the truck. Dump it somewhere where it wouldn't be found. The bottom of a reservoir always seemed to work. The thing was about done anyway. He was a little sad as he'd bought it new back in 1992 when he'd started out on the force. Back when he thought what he was doing was a noble cause. That being a police officer was the best job ever.

When had he changed? When had he become the monster he was now?

He stared at the butt of his handgun sticking out from the vehicle gun holster. He could go back right now. Maya might still be there with her dog and that other guy, but maybe he could take them by surprise. He could grab her.

Eric stepped on the brakes and whipped the old truck around in a U-turn. If he did this right, he could ambush her and grab her before the dog could do anything. Or so he told himself. This really wasn't a good plan.

He came around a curve in the road back to where he'd last seen Maya.

She was gone. He'd missed his chance.

Eric was tired of waiting and decided that he had to move now. Tonight.

He had to get to Maya as soon as possible. She'd seen him and would probably call it in.

Her fate was sealed.

Chapter Twenty

Once Lucas had left for the lab and Maya was back on her porch, she pulled out her phone and called Josh. He didn't answer, so she left a voice mail asking him to call. She needed to talk. Maya wasn't one for long voice mails—short and sweet worked for her. Juniper finished drinking and put her head on Maya's lap. Maya stroked the dog on her head and down her back.

"Thank you for finding that bracelet," she said to her. "You're such a good girl."

Juniper responded with a tail wag. Maya forced herself to get up and stared at the phone, willing Josh to call. She decided to send him a quick text too, just in case he wasn't in a good spot to answer the phone.

I know where Eric Torres is parking when he watches the cabin and I found more evidence. Lucas already collected it. Give me a call. I'll fill you in more.

Maya hit send. There was a part of her that even wanted him to stay with her for the night, knowing that she'd been under surveillance. But she was a Marine, for God's sake, and she really didn't need some guy taking care of her. She realized, though, that after she'd pushed Josh away when he asked her to stay with him, he'd been even more distant. She missed him and his friendship. She missed having someone to talk to. Even Marines needed friends.

She and Juniper went inside. Maya opened some windows to help cool off the cabin. At least when the sun set, the night would cool off. She didn't have air-conditioning because at this altitude the house cooled off every night and stayed cool until the afternoon. Juniper willingly went to her crate and went inside, curling up. They were both tired. It had been a long day.

Maya peered in her fridge and freezer. There was one frozen pizza left. If Josh didn't call soon, that would be dinner. She hoped though that he would call and come over.

The bracelet had triggered more memories and Maya was certain Eric had been at their house that fateful night her mother died. DNA only confirmed it. She could be a witness against him with what she remembered. He had threatened her mom—probably because of the evidence Zoey had. Where would that evidence have gone? Was there any chance it would be at Pops's house? Could that be why Nana was killed?

Maya let Juniper out of her crate and gave her the command to go lie on her bed. She hoped that Juniper would get better about this so that she had more options with her when she was home at night. The dog seemed tired enough that she listened to Maya and curled back up. Maya lay back on her couch and closed her eyes, trying to relax. She needed a break from everything.

She'd started to doze off when all of a sudden Juniper leapt off her bed, growling and barking. Maya sat straight up. "Juniper! Come!"

If Eric Torres was outside, they needed to be careful. She didn't want Juniper to be a target.

Maya rolled off the couch, grabbing her phone and staying low to the ground. Juniper came over near her and Maya crawled near the big picture window, but off to the side. She gripped Juniper's collar, not letting the dog get away from her. Juniper was not happy about being held down, but Maya didn't care. It took all her strength to keep her under control.

She carefully peeked her head up and peered out the window. Now that she knew the most likely place for Torres to watch her, she wanted to see if she could spot him. She had her phone still in her hand. She would rather have had her gun. Her shotgun sat by the front door. Maya was thinking about crawling to it and grabbing it when the first bullet pierced the glass.

She shoved Juniper underneath her body as glass shards sprayed around them. Maya pulled her back into the corner away from the window and the glass. More shots were fired in a staccato rhythm. Most likely a semiautomatic rifle. Probably a long gun like an AR-15. Maya clung to Juniper, who fought her, wanting to go out and do what she was trained to do—bite the person shooting at them.

"Pfui," Maya said, giving the command for Juniper to stop and hoping she would listen. Her arms strained as she continued to hold Juniper back.

More bullets were fired and, along with glass spraying everywhere, they hit Maya's kitchen cabinets. Dishes shattered and crashed to the ground. The bullets shredded the wood and pierced the cabin walls. Maya decided the shooter probably had a larger caliber weapon like a 300 Blackout.

No matter what kind of gun it was, she was tired of sitting and hiding while her cabin was being destroyed. Based on the shooting pattern, the shooter didn't truly know where she was, or they were deliberately missing to scare her outside where they could grab and/or kill her. Maya would not let them accomplish their goal.

Still clinging to Juniper, she waited out the gunfire. Eventually they'd run out of bullets. The question was, how many magazines did they have with them? She continued to wait, praying that a bullet wouldn't come through where she was sitting.

The noise was deafening, and Maya's ears were ringing. She wanted to cover them, but then she'd have to let go of Juniper. As she curled into a tight ball, she thought about that night in the closet where she huddled much the same way. The thing was, she wasn't that scared little girl anymore and when she had her opportunity, she was going to make Torres pay for this. The truck passing her, the dark-haired man, that had to have been him. He'd probably come back when he saw her.

Silence.

He had probably gone through his first magazine. Assuming Torres knew what he was doing, Maya would only have a few seconds to get out of her spot and to a better location where she could fight back. He probably had loaded magazines and would be doing a tactical reload and then another round of bullets would be coming her way again.

Maya stayed low and pulled on Juniper's collar. Much to her relief, Juniper willingly came with her. They managed to make it to the bedroom before the next barrage of bullets came. Luckily, the shooter seemed intent to focus on Maya's main living area. He'd probably been watching her nap on the couch and realized this was his opportunity. Based on the pattern she saw, he was aiming up and down, hoping to hit her.

Maya and Juniper sat near her bedstand. She needed to alert dispatch and get more deputies up here. She was all for fighting back, but she was outgunned and had to be smart about how she retaliated. Her long gun was locked in her patrol vehicle. She had her personal Glock in her bedside drawer, which was better than nothing, but the range on a handgun was short compared to a rifle. Maya would have to be within about thirty meters to get off a good shot. Closer would be even better. At least she had some sort of weapon.

Maya had to prepare for battle. She found her extra magazine and shoved that in her shorts pocket. Too bad she didn't have her duty belt to carry the extra magazines, but her pocket would have to do. She'd taken off her shoes while relaxing on the couch. There was no way she was going outside without something on her feet. Maya managed to find some tennis shoes and put them on. She also had an extra leash near the bed. She put that on Juniper so that she didn't have to cling to her collar.

She tried calling 9-1-1, but as the dispatcher answered, another round of bullets came through her bedroom window. Maya couldn't hear anything over the sound of the gunfire.

Frustrated, she hung up and texted 9-1-1 with her address and plea for extra officers, then hit send. Juniper lay next to her, waiting for a command, confused that she hadn't put a stop to this by now by biting the person shooting at them. Maya tried to count the bullets, but there was no way to do that. Maybe she could sneak out the back door, but she didn't know the shooter's location. She had an idea of where they might be standing, but the shooter had the upper hand. For now.

Silence.

Were they out of bullets already? What were the chances that the shooter only brought two magazines? If Eric Torres was the culprit, Maya figured he would have brought more. Unless he thought he could scare her out of the house. He didn't know who he was dealing with or the fact that this was really nothing new for her. She'd been through moments like this in Afghanistan. She knew how to focus and find that zone where you quit worrying if you were going to die. Instead, you let the training that was hammered into you kick in. You survived by waiting for the right moment to fight back.

Maya guessed he wanted her out of the cabin. If she could stay hunkered down long enough, then the cavalry would arrive and it would give her a chance to fire back at him and even deploy Juniper at the right moment.

Stubborn. Maya was definitely stubborn, and this was a situation where it was in her best interest. She was content staying under cover until the right time, even if Torres was out of ammo.

More silence.

Maya was beginning to wonder if Eric had even given up when she heard the crash of a bottle breaking. She scooted over slightly so she could see out of her bedroom door.

Son of a bitch. The asshole had thrown a Molotov cocktail into her cabin.

Chapter Twenty-One

The smell of gasoline permeated the cabin and the Molotov cocktail quickly lit up. Flames spread along the path of the gas and then spread to Maya's rug. Her log cabin was far from fireproof, and would be up in flames in minutes. She didn't have much time to react.

The barrage of bullets stopped, and Maya knew that Torres was outside waiting for her. She could get out the back door. Was that what he was counting on?

Maya found some scarves she had stashed away in a container under the bed, waiting for wintertime. She wrapped one around her face and then did her best to cover Juniper's nose with the other.

Wood popped as the flames spread and smoke poured into the bedroom. She and Juniper had to get outside. Maya took the bandanna back off Juniper. She didn't want anything on Juniper's face impeding her from doing her job. But that meant they needed to get out. Now.

Maya and Juniper crept over to the back door. Juniper seemed to understand that they needed to stay low as she followed Maya's lead, crawling on her belly. The back door out of her bedroom was solid wood with no windows. There was no way she could see. The window over her bed was the best bet, but Maya could feel the heat from the fire as it gained traction.

They'd have to take their chances.

Maya took a deep breath and left the leash on Juniper, grabbing it with her left hand so she could shoot right-handed. It wasn't the ideal situation, but better than nothing. She inhaled again, sucking smoke into her lungs, forcing her to cough.

They had to go now.

She flung open the door, staying down low. Juniper crawled next to her until they were on the porch, then sprang forward and rushed down the back stairs, pulling the leash out of Maya's hand. She followed the direction her dog went and scanned the area for the suspect and Juniper. Where did Juniper go?

Maya sprinted down to the stream where she could take cover behind some large trees. Even though the creek was barely running right now, it seemed the safest place to be because of the fire, but the worst place to be if someone was pursuing you. Maya continued to scan the area to see if she could see anyone and withheld gunfire. You didn't shoot and waste ammo until you had a target. Plus, she had texted dispatch so there could be officers responding. She didn't want to hurt another officer or Juniper with friendly fire.

Where was Juniper?

Maya had to get away from the house and back onto a ridge away from her cabin where she had a better vantage point. At least she knew the area. That gave her a small advantage.

Where was her dog? Normally she wouldn't have been holding a gun and the leash and would have had a stronger grip on Juniper. Maya had to trust that Juniper would take care of herself. Getting to the ridge would help her see the shooter and her dog. As hard as it was to leave Juniper, Maya continued down the bank of the streambed.

She would stop every now and then and duck behind a tree for cover, while she checked and cleared the area, gun out ready to fire at anything that moved. In the distance Maya could hear sirens echoing off the mountains as they came along the road. She checked her cell phone to see if she could get a call into dispatch.

No signal. The only reason Maya ever had any signal at her cabin was because she used Wi-Fi for calling or the good old-fashioned landline. Both her router and the landline phone were currently either being burned or had been destroyed by bullets.

Maya peered around her area, looking for her dog, hoping to see brown fur running through the trees. She didn't want to whistle and give away her location, but she had to try to find Juniper. She let out the shrill noise and waited.

No Juniper.

Maya fought the panic rising in her. She couldn't lose Juniper. She'd never forgive herself.

Smoke filled the air and Maya glanced at her cabin. Her chest constricted with anger and fury as she saw flames destroying her home. Her cabin. The cabin Nana had left to her and that held so many special memories.

Maya couldn't think about it all right now. For now, she had to keep moving and stay safe. There was a man out there trying to kill her.

The Molotov cocktail was obviously used to flush her out. Or was it? Maybe it was a diversion to escape. Maybe Torres thought Maya was dead and of no use to him. Whatever the reason, Maya still wanted to make it to the ridge where she had a better vantage point. For all she knew, Juniper had Torres by now and was waiting for Maya to come help her.

Get to the ridge and find your dog.

Maya trekked a little farther and took cover behind a rock. She peered up over the boulder and looked for signs of anyone in the area. Scanning around, she couldn't see any movement, but that didn't mean that Torres wasn't still there. And who knew if he was on his own? This could still be a trap.

Red and blue lights flashed through the trees as several sheriff's vehicles pulled up. Maya saw Josh, Pops and another deputy park on the outskirts of her driveway, staging a safe distance away. They were being careful.

Good.

Her message had reached dispatch. She had to let them know she was okay.

She pulled her phone out and texted another message to 9-1-1. She held her phone up, hoping to find enough signal to send a text. If it went through, it would go to dispatch, and they could relay to Pops and Josh that Maya was okay and would be making her way to them and that she didn't know if the suspect was still in the area. She sent her message and then started heading toward Pops and Josh.

They put their fingers up to their earbuds that connected with their radio. Maya hoped that meant they were getting the message she'd sent dispatch. Josh started looking around and was the first to spot her. He said something to Pops and pointed in her direction. Maya headed toward them as fast as she could.

Pops ran forward, hugging her. "Maya, thank God you're okay," he said.

Maya returned his hug and said, "I'm okay because Juniper warned me, but she's missing. She took off."

"Shit, we'll find her," Pops said.

Maya gave a shrill whistle again and peered around, straining to see anything moving in the woods. She was about ready to whistle again, when she spotted movement off in the woods from the direction she suspected Torres had run.

Is it...?

Maya held her breath, and sure enough, Juniper shot out of the woods straight toward her, looking pleased with herself.

Juniper proudly took her place by Maya's side. Josh came over and joined them. Maya could see they were all, including Juniper, still scanning the area for a suspect waiting to ambush them. Her home was almost completely up in flames and she was glad she'd cleared out the trees last year for the defensible space. While it was meant to keep a forest fire from destroying her home, she hoped it would help firefighters keep the fire from spreading to the forest and creating a bigger issue. At least Juniper was okay.

"I'm glad she came back," Pops said, putting a hand on Maya's shoulder and giving it a squeeze. "Everyone is okay and that's what matters."

"But Pops, the cabin that Nana left for me is gone. I feel like I've completely lost her," Maya said.

"No." Pops shook his head. "She'd only care that you're okay. She'd say the cabin could be rebuilt."

"Have you seen any signs of the suspect?" Josh asked. "The firefighters have staged a mile down the road. We need to clear the area before they can do anything."

"No," Maya said, shaking her head. "And Juniper hasn't reacted. I think the person is gone. I came out my back door and along the creek and back up to the ridge. I didn't see anyone, but I haven't cleared the other side of the house that leads to the road."

"Wilson," Josh shouted to the other deputy. Maya recognized the young deputy from the day Kendra died. "We need to clear the east side of the woods so the firefighters can get in to do their jobs."

"Yes, sir," Wilson said.

"Be careful," Maya said to them both. "I believe the suspect had a long gun."

Josh and Deputy Wilson pulled their guns from their holsters and headed toward the east side of what used to be Maya's cabin. She watched them use trees to help conceal them as they walked deeper into the woods.

Pops hugged her again. "I thought I'd lost you too," he said. "You know how to give an old man a heart attack. It reminded me of the night I heard the call about your mother's house up in flames."

"This has to be Torres," Maya said, hugging Pops back. Juniper stuck her nose in between them wanting attention. Maya stepped back and loved on her dog. "If you hadn't warned me, I could be dead. She barked and lunged toward the window. I was able to get down and pull her out of the way before the shooting started."

"I'm just so glad you're okay." Maya thought she saw some tears in the corners of Pops's eyes.

They stood together and watched as Josh and Deputy Wilson came back from clearing the east side, radioing the firefighters that they hadn't found anything.

The firefighters drove down the road, parked and went to work, but Maya knew it was too late. Her cabin was gone. Her home was demolished.

Part of her wanted to cry, but the other part of her was pissed off beyond belief. Anger coursed through her veins. She wasn't just going to find and arrest Eric Torres. She was going to destroy him and make him pay for everything he'd taken from her.

Chapter Twenty-Two

A few hours later, Maya and Juniper stood in the same spot. Her cabin was gone except for the stone fireplace which somehow looked awkward and out of place without the house around it. The firefighters had been able to contain the fire. Maya had heard Josh and Pops directing several deputies to tell the neighbors to be on alert to evacuate. Around this area, neighbors were a good distance away and behind some of the ridges. Some of them might not even know what was going on until it was too late.

A headache threatened to come on and she finally moved over to Pops's sheriff's vehicle and leaned against it. Juniper came with her and plopped down on the ground. Maya rooted around in Pops's patrol car until she found a water bottle and a cup. She poured some of the water into the cup and Juniper lapped it up, drinking a couple rounds.

Maya took a swig out of the water bottle and then put it back in the vehicle. She closed the door and leaned back, staring away from her cabin. She couldn't look anymore. It was too painful. Instead, she started focusing on plotting. She wanted revenge. She wasn't going down without a fight.

A vehicle pulled up and Miranda hopped out. "I'm so sorry, Maya. I'll do everything I can do to find evidence so that we can figure out who did this."

"I'm pretty certain it was Eric Torres."

"Probably," Miranda said. "But you never know. He could be working with someone."

"True," Maya said. "It sounds like this crime ring is bigger than we realized."

Miranda tried to give Maya a reassuring smile. "Well, I guess I better go get to work. From the sounds of it, I have lots of brass to process."

"That's for sure," Maya said. "Let me know if you need help. I have some contacts in other counties from working the national forests in their areas. They might be willing to lend a hand."

"I appreciate it, but I think I have it handled. If not, you'll be the first to know. I may have to talk to your grandfather about hiring another CSI tech if crimes keep happening around here at this rate," Miranda said, picking up her case with all her supplies. "I'll let you know if I find something you don't know about."

"Thanks," Maya said.

Miranda headed off toward the smoldering cabin. She would probably start to process the scene from the outside in and only once the firefighters told her it was safe. Pops and Josh were walking in Maya's direction. Pops placed a hand on her shoulder and squeezed.

"It'll be okay, Maya," he said. "The main thing is that you're okay."

Josh studied her, and Maya had to look away. She had a feeling he knew what she was thinking about: finding Torres and getting revenge. He would definitely try to talk her out of it, but Maya didn't want to hear it right now. Her temper was as hot as the fire that had just blazed through the cabin, only her fire was still burning.

"I know, Pops," Maya finally said. "I just feel like I lost my life down there though. The only good thing is I had just picked up my uniforms from the dry cleaners and they're still in my patrol vehicle, so at least I don't have to ask my boss for more. But I lost everything else. At least Lucas has the evidence that Juniper and I found today."

"What did you find?" Josh asked. "I'm sorry I missed your call."

Maya hesitated. It seemed like Josh was missing a lot of her calls lately. What was he up to? Of course, why did she care so much and what did it matter right now?

"I did a track with Juniper," Maya said. She saw the looks both Pops and Josh gave her and knew they weren't happy she had gone on her own. "I realized we'd never treated my cabin like a crime scene and yet we know for sure Kendra was here watching me and probably Eric Torres too. I thought I'd do a track and see what I could find."

Josh put his hands on his duty belt. It was the cop equivalent of crossing your arms, only cops didn't do that because they needed their hands free to protect themselves. Josh was definitely not pleased with her. She didn't care. She could take care of herself.

Maya took a deep breath and continued. "Juniper alerted on a tree, and I found a bracelet. It was silver with a lucky horseshoe charm. I called Lucas and he came out and gathered it for evidence, so I didn't process it. I remember that bracelet, though. It belonged to Mom. I remember it and it triggered another memory from that night."

"Your grandmother and I gave her that bracelet," Pops said. He stared off in the distance. "She wasn't wearing it when she died."

"But she was," Maya said. "I remember it because I was always fascinated with it. She'd let me try it on sometimes and tell me when I was older, she'd get me a bracelet just like this one. I remember seeing it dangle by my face the night she died when she grabbed my shoulders and told me to go hide. Torres must have taken it off her. I remember him there that night too."

"You do?" Pops asked.

"I do." Maya glanced at Josh, who now had his poker face on. It was the neutral face he used when he listened to people tell him both sides of the story. Somehow this only irritated Maya further. After she found Eric Torres, she had to figure out her relationship with Josh. Friends? Or were they more? She was tired of trying to guess. "The memory came back when I found the bracelet. He came to our house that night demanding something. I went and hid in the closet, so I don't know what he wanted, but based on what Abigail told us, I bet he was looking for the evidence Mom hid. When she refused to give it to him, he killed her."

"Why would he take the bracelet and then lose it at a crime scene twenty-four years later?" Josh asked, finally speaking up.

"I don't know," Maya said. "But I know what I remember."

They all stood in silence staring at the ground. Juniper gave a grunt and a sigh and then stood, shaking off the dirt from lying on the ground.

"I'm going to head into town," Maya said. "I can't stand being here any longer and seeing everything I owned destroyed. I need to get some clothes, toiletries and dog food for Juniper. I'll stay the night at my office. There's a pretty comfortable couch, and Juniper's dog bed is there. Plus, I need somewhere quiet to write up my witness statement. I just need to get out of here."

"You still have clothes at the house," Pops said. "I know some of it is from a while ago, maybe even high school, but you could see if anything fits. And you're welcome to crash at the house until you figure out what you want to do. You're always welcome, you know that."

"Thanks, Pops. I'll see if any of those clothes still fit. And thanks for the offer to stay with you. I just want to be on my own right now. Process everything, you know?"

"I understand," Pops said.

Maya knew he did too. They were a lot alike.

Josh stood quietly and Maya hesitated. She knew he wanted her to stay with him, but she didn't need protection. She had to admit, there was a part of her that wanted to be with him, but somehow, she wasn't ready for that even if it didn't mean anything more than a friendship where she stayed in the guest bedroom. It would start rumors she wasn't ready for, and she was so used to being on her own.

They stood there awkwardly, and Pops stared back and forth between them.

Before he could say anything, Maya said, "Okay then. I'll be in touch."

She started toward her patrol vehicle. Luckily, she had left the keys in the car when she ran the track because she hadn't wanted to risk losing them in the woods. She'd forgotten to go back and get them. Juniper seemed a little bit more herself as she kept in sync with Maya.

"Maya. Wait."

She hesitated. It was Josh. She turned around. "What?"

"I just… I just wanted you to know again that you can stay with me anytime. I'm not trying to be some macho guy protecting you, but if Eric Torres is after you, it's worse if you're on your own. Safety in numbers."

"I know, Josh. Look, I really appreciate your offer, but I just need to be alone. Think things through."

"Yeah, okay."

There was something she needed to ask. Juniper sat by her side and gave a big sigh. "I'll call you and check in. Let you know everything is okay. I promise. Will I be able to reach you? You've been kind of hard to get ahold of lately."

"I'll be around, and I'll answer if you call," Josh said, stepping closer. He tucked a loose piece of hair behind Maya's ear and let his hand linger there for a minute. "I'm sorry I haven't been available. I should have let you know what was going on."

"Are you doing okay? I mean, I know you're a lot further along with your recovery but with everything going on it's been tough for me. I'm sure you have days like that too. You need anything?"

"No, but I have gone to extra meetings," Josh said, getting that faraway look in his eyes again. "I don't know why, but I've been having horrible cravings for drugs and alcohol. I went to the bar and even ordered a beer. Sat there and stared at it until I got up and left. I knew if I even took one sip, all these years of sobriety would be gone. And all I could think about was you."

"Me?" Maya asked. Her heart rate quickened.

"You. I didn't want to disappoint you. So, I left and

talked with my sponsor. So anyway, that's where I've been. Your grandfather knows. He's supporting me through this, but remember when I told you sobriety could be beautiful?"

"I do," she said. "You made it sound pretty perfect."

"Yeah, well, it's also difficult. It's a constant battle."

"I hear you on that one," Maya said. "I thought maybe it was because I'm only a few months in."

"I think there's ups and downs like that, but I went to several meetings and I'm better. For now. So anyway, that's why I've been hard to get ahold of. I just wanted you to know."

"Thank you," Maya said, reaching out and placing her hand on his shoulder. "Thanks for being honest. I promise I'll check in with you."

"Please do and you know where I live."

"Okay. I'll call you later."

Maya turned to leave, feeling bad that she'd been mad at Josh for blowing her off. She needed to stop jumping to conclusions, something she and Dr. Meyers had discussed at times.

She loaded Juniper up in her compartment and shut the door. Juniper curled up in her shredded blankets. Maya was glad to see her resting. They were both tired and the adrenaline was wearing off. She just wanted to find some comfy clothes and dinner, and crash on her couch at the office.

Miranda came up behind her. "Hey there, before you go, I wanted to let you know I found more cigarettes. The kind Eric Torres smokes. I also found a piece of a shirt that was snagged on a branch."

Miranda opened a paper bag and Maya peered in. Another idea formed. One that no one would be happy about, but especially not Pops and Josh. "Would it be possible to have you cut a small piece of that shirt and put it in a plastic bag for me?"

Miranda narrowed her eyes. "Do I want to know what you're going to do with it?"

"Probably not," Maya said.

"Okay, then. I didn't do this."

Miranda set down the bag and pulled a pair of scissors out of her case. She snipped off a small piece and then put it in a plastic evidence bag and handed it to Maya. "Hopefully, I didn't just screw this whole case up by giving you that."

"If anyone asks, I won't tell them where I got it," Maya said. "It'll be our secret."

Chapter Twenty-Three

The next morning Maya woke up early. It was still dark
outside. She had a kink in her neck from sleeping on
the couch in her office. Juniper had her dog bed and,
much to Maya's relief, had stayed on it all night. Her
usual overnight crate had melted in the fire and leaving
a Malinois loose was never a good idea. In fact, when
Maya had first brought Juniper home, she had destroyed
the cabin one night when Juniper had escaped her crate.
That had also been Maya's fault for drinking heavily
when she first had Juniper.

She sat up and stretched. She'd talked with Josh last
night, and Miranda hadn't found anything unexpected.
The fire, of course, along with all the water doused on
it, damaged much of the evidence at the cabin. Lucas
had also called and apologized about not being able to
help. He had been in the process of logging the bracelet
into evidence and couldn't leave it until all the paperwork was done. Maya had told him not to worry about
it. They had plenty of responding officers. The more she
thought about it, the more she decided that the bracelet
had been planted for her to find.

Eric Torres was playing games and Maya was done.
She had the perfect weapon to find him—Juniper.

As if she knew Maya was thinking about her, Juniper sat up and wagged her tail. Then she stood and stretched, doing a downward dog and curling up her back while yawning. She sat down on her bed and stared intently at Maya.

"Don't get too used to this," Maya said. "When I get a chance, I'll get another crate, but thank you for being a good girl."

Juniper thumped her tail on the ground.

Maya stood up and walked over to her desk where the piece of fabric Miranda had cut for her sat in the plastic bag to preserve the scent. The bag could even help intensify the scent for Juniper.

There were two ways of tracking—one was the "hottest" scent of the last person on the scene. That was what Maya and Juniper most often did because suspects didn't usually leave scent articles behind, which was the other way Juniper was trained to find a specific person. Scent articles were more commonly used in search and rescue. Juniper was trained to do both.

Maya now had Eric Torres's scent from the piece of clothing Miranda gave her. She could take Juniper to the area around her cabin and have her track him. Hopefully, they would get further than a parking spot showing an oil leak. The scent article gave Maya some hope for that.

She quickly dressed—relieved that she'd found jeans, a T-shirt and a sweatshirt that still fit at Pops's place—made some coffee and let Juniper out. The morning sun was starting to peek over the trees. The air was cool and crisp. It wouldn't be that long before snow was flying.

And Maya had no home.

She could probably rent a room at the local hotel for

a while. There was always Pops too, but she didn't know how long they could live together. Maybe a camper? Or if she was lucky, there might be a house for rent in town. There was also Josh's place. She shoved that thought aside and focused on her number one priority—finding Eric Torres.

Juniper came back over to Maya and jumped up on her. Maya firmly told her "Off" and then rubbed all over her. Pops was right—at least they were okay. Things could be a lot worse.

As they were getting ready to go back inside the office, a white minivan with a stick figure family on the back window pulled up and parked in front of the Forest Service visitor's center. Juniper growled a little bit, but Maya told her to relax. Juniper sat down and peered up at her.

The driver of the car got out and Maya took a deep breath. It was her mother's friend, Denise Douglas.

"Denise?" Maya said. "Is everything okay? You're up here early."

Denise shut the car door and looked up and down the street. "I haven't been back up here since I left for college. Yeah, I'm fine. I told my husband I had an early yoga class and that he needed to make sure our daughter got off to school on time this morning. Do you have a minute? I don't have much time before I have to head back."

"Sure," Maya said. "Come on into my office. I'll get us some coffee. You okay with dogs?"

"I am, although your dog is a little scary."

"I'll keep her on leash. Come on in."

Maya opened the door for Denise, and they stepped inside her office. Maya got a chair for Denise, poured her some coffee and put Juniper on a down-stay next to her. Denise gripped the mug. Her hands shook.

"You know, you look just like her," she said. "Your mother. I thought I was seeing a ghost when you showed up at my door. I panicked. I'm sorry. I know you were looking for information and I know that you probably don't have many leads to help with that. I thought all of that was in the past and then there you were standing there, and I was terrified."

Maya took a sip of coffee. "Based on pictures and what people say, I know I look a lot like my mother. I'm sorry for just showing up at your house and surprising you like that. I should have called first."

Denise shook her head. "It's okay. You really do look like her. She was so beautiful, but part of my reaction is that you brought the past with you and that scares me to death. I always felt lucky that no one came after me. Zoey was killed because of what she knew. She protected me by not telling me much, but I knew more than I let on. I'll answer your questions this morning, but if you call me to testify, I won't do it."

"I promise you won't be called to testify," Maya said. "I understand why you're so afraid."

"It's funny, my husband doesn't know about my past. He thinks I'm the perfect housewife. My kids think I'm boring and don't understand anything they're going through, and my parents have never talked about what I did. And yet, I can remember it all like it was yesterday."

"Maybe you can start at the beginning when you and my mom ran away."

Denise took a deep breath. "Sure. Zoey and I didn't have many friends. We were kind of the outcasts, but Zoey was always adventurous. My parents thought she was a bad influence, but I didn't care. When she suggested we run away together, I thought it would be fun. Little did I know about the nightmare it would start.

"We always wanted to see Montana. Don't ask me why. Looking back, there were probably better places to go explore, but we loved the outdoors and wanted to see Yellowstone National Park. I was naïve and followed Zoey anywhere she wanted. So up to Montana we went, and we settled in a midsized town a few hours away from the park. Things quickly changed when we ran out of cash. I wanted to go home then, but Zoey refused. She said we could figure out how to make money. I went and got a job at a fast-food place, but Zoey thought she could make better money doing other things. I don't know when she began selling herself, but she was making good money. I joined her, but it was awful the way we were treated and how I felt about myself. We sometimes smoked some dope, but then Zoey began trying harder stuff—that's when she started getting arrested.

"But the justice system up there was crooked. Zoey was arrested and when she got out of jail, she came home and told me about things that were going on. Things she shouldn't have seen, including a murder. She'd been approached by a cop to do some dirty work. I begged her to just leave then, go back home, but she said she was going to do what they asked, record conversations, take pictures and gather any evidence she could to link this cop to the crimes. I don't think she knew at the time that it was more than one cop that was dirty. In fact, based on what she told me, there were judges and lawyers involved too. I think Zoey thought if she could get evidence to take to the state or even the FBI,

she would make your grandfather proud. She didn't
know it would cost her life. I didn't know that either."

Maya leaned forward. She normally wouldn't tell a
potential witness much about an investigation, but this
might be the only chance she had with Denise. "Do
you remember names? We've linked a cop named Eric
Torres to the crime scenes. I believe he killed not only
my mother, but also my grandmother. I also think he
came after me last night and burned down my cabin."

"What?" Denise said. "That's terrible. I'm so sorry.
I didn't know about your grandmother. She was always
so good to me. And your cabin? That's terrible too. Eric
Torres... I do remember him, but not as a bad cop. He
actually took care of us in a way. He was the one cop
who tried to help us. In fact, when I wanted to go home,
he bought me the bus ticket and told me to stay safe, go
to school and not come back. If it hadn't been for him,
I don't know where I'd be right now."

Maya didn't know what to make of that information.
That was opposite of everything she'd heard about Eric.
But if he was a good manipulator, then maybe there
was another side to him that Denise didn't know about.
Maya needed more information. "What about my mom?
Did he help her too? Or did he take advantage of her?"

"He helped her out, but..." Denise set down her mug
and clasped her hands together. "I had your mom convinced to come with me and thought Eric would even
buy her a bus ticket, but then she found out she was
pregnant with you. She said she could never go home
and tell her parents. They would freak. She said she
would figure out how to get clean. Eric would help
her, she knew it, and she would raise you on her own.
I told her that was crazy, that her parents loved her and

they would help, but she refused to come with me. I always wonder what things would be like if she had just agreed to go.

"Eric was also trying to convince her to leave. He told her it would be safer for her. I don't think he knew about the evidence at that point, but I think he suspected it. Zoey met me at the bus stop and made me promise to never talk about anything I saw and forget that she even existed. She said that was the only way she could protect me. I feel so guilty about leaving her. I should have told your grandparents where she was, but I was happy just to get home and see my parents again. I went to college that fall and 'forgot' everything like Zoey told me to. I never saw Zoey again, but she sent me a letter at one point with a picture of you as a newborn. I could tell motherhood had changed her in a good way, but I never wrote back. Maybe if I had…"

"It's okay," Maya said. "You obviously cared about my mom and you're here now helping me. I appreciate the information. Do you remember the names of any cops that were crooked?"

"I remember two. They were horrible. Blake and someone else… I can't totally remember. Kind of an Irish sounding last name. They were related. Like cousins or something."

"Blake Conner?"

"Yes. That was it. He was an awful person. He and the other guy even tried to take advantage of Zoey once, but she fought back. Blake said she would get what was coming to her. He's the one I remember the most. I was so scared and that's when Eric offered to help me and I got out of there. Your mom was so much tougher, but I don't know if that was a good thing."

Maya sat back in her chair. Blake Conner had tried to assault her mom and he was here now. She had to find out more about him. Maybe he and Eric were working together. That could explain why he was here helping Abigail. He probably had an ulterior motive to finding Eric. "Did you know an officer by the name of Abigail Harper?"

"No, that name isn't familiar."

Maya reached over and put her hand on Denise's. "Thank you so much for this information. It really helps. Is there anything else that I should know? Any other cops that my mom may have threatened by gathering the evidence she did?"

"I can't think of any right now, but I can call you if I do think of something."

"That would be great," Maya said, standing and grabbing one of her cards from her desk. "Here's all my contact information. I do have one last question if you don't mind."

"No, I don't mind, although I do need to get going soon."

"Do you have any idea who my father is? Did my mom know?"

"No, hon, I'm sorry. To be honest, once Zoey was doing the harder drugs, I think she was with quite a few guys. I'm not certain she even knew, but I do know that she would be proud of you and what you've accomplished with your career. I think she secretly wanted to follow in your grandfather's footsteps, but she never wanted to admit that. I better be going now."

"Okay. Thank you so much," Maya said.

"You're welcome. I hope you can find your mother's killer."

After Denise left, Maya went back into her office and took out a notepad, writing down everything she'd been told. She tried to stay unemotional, but all she could think about was her mother and all the ways she'd tried to do the right things. Life hadn't been fair to her mom, although Zoey had certainly made her own choices.

Maya glanced at the scent article sitting on her desk and then down at Juniper who had decided to take a morning nap. If what Denise said was true, then why was Eric's DNA at every scene? Why did Maya remember him at their house the night her mother was killed? Denise had said herself that Zoey protected her. Maybe she didn't know everything about Eric. If she could find him, then maybe she could get more answers. But the fact that Blake Conner could also be dirty made Maya wonder if she should tell Josh and Lucas to talk with him.

Juniper lifted her head and looked at Maya with her golden eyes. Something had to be done, and Juniper was her best bet to find Eric. She couldn't question Blake, but she could certainly do another training track.

She quickly texted Josh and Lucas that she would fill them in more later, but that Denise had come and talked with her this morning. They needed to look into Blake Conner's background and not trust him. He could be involved with Eric Torres.

Then she grabbed her purse and a backpack. The camping supply store opened early this time of year. It not only outfitted campers, but also sold ammo and other supplies for hunting.

Maya and Juniper got in her patrol vehicle and headed down the road to the store. They parked in front. Juniper's ears pointed straight up, and she made little whining noises.

"I'll be right back," Maya said to her.

She went in the store and bought supplies, including ammo, nonperishable food and a special backpack for water. Maya paid and headed back out to her vehicle, where she grabbed the Forest Service maps in the glove box and put them in the backpack along with a compass. You couldn't rely on cell phone service and GPS out in the woods. It was best to be prepared the old-fashioned way.

Once she had everything together, she drove out of town and arrived at what was left of her cabin. As she stepped out of the vehicle, a wave of sadness hit her and then anger. This had been her home. Her safe place. Her place to recover from the war and find some solitude. How dare Eric Torres do this to her? Or could it be Blake Conner?

Whoever it was, Maya would figure it out and they would pay.

She slipped on her bulletproof vest and tightened it down, grabbed her satellite phone, then put Juniper's collar for working narcotics in her backpack, along with the squeaky toy. She didn't know what she would be asking Juniper to do workwise, so she wanted all options available.

Maya put on her backpack, which felt bulky and awkward over the vest, but she didn't want to confront Torres without it. She grabbed her long gun from her patrol vehicle and slung it over her shoulder. Her Glock was already in the holster on her hip. She hadn't had this much gear on since Afghanistan.

Maya let Juniper out of the vehicle. Now fully awake,

Juniper bounded around, excited at the prospect of going to work, but Maya managed to wrestle her tracking harness on.

She settled Juniper down and took her down near the cabin, careful to avoid any of the debris from fire and all the glass shards from the shooting. Maya got her rifle in place where she could quickly access her firearms. This time she was prepared with both her Glock and rifle. Once she felt organized, she pulled the scent article out of her pocket.

She let Juniper sniff it and then told her, "Track. Go find 'em. Let's get the bad guy."

Maya cast Juniper out in different directions and Juniper put her nose to the ground, zigzagging back and forth, searching for the scent. Maya had to move around a bit before Juniper's body language changed and her tail went straight up.

Maya smiled.

The hunt was on.

Chapter Twenty-Four

Juniper shot forward and Maya gave some slack in the leash, following her. So much of the work with a dog felt like a dance, but Juniper always had the lead.

With all her gear on, Maya strained a little more to keep up. Juniper stayed on the trail that led to the ridge. There was a path that eventually went back onto Forest Service land and, if you stayed on it long enough, went to a campsite at a glacial lake. Maybe Torres was camping there?

That thought quickly went away when Juniper veered off the path. As Maya worked to stay on her feet and not get tangled in the vegetation and fallen tree branches, she noticed that the grass was stamped down where Juniper was tracking. So apparently Torres not only parked and watched her, but he hiked in. Maya didn't like that, but with her cabin gone, it didn't matter much anyway.

She started huffing and puffing as Juniper continued tracking. She stayed on the scent, never losing it. Her tail pointed straight up in the air, and as Maya watched her work, she knew that she was a sitting duck if they did come upon Torres. It was always best to run a track with a backup officer to help keep you safe. Josh would be furious with her right now.

At this moment, though, Maya didn't care.

Maybe she was being reckless, but underneath it all she wanted first dibs on Eric Torres. She needed to know why. Why did he take everyone from her? Why couldn't he just leave her alone now and turn himself in? Who else was involved? Could Blake really be a dirty cop? Maybe his cousin was the ringleader?

As a law enforcement officer, Maya knew some questions would never be answered. Sometimes you never knew why and there was no closure. Eric would probably lie to her too, but at least she would have a chance to interrogate him before he lawyered up and Abigail claimed him.

But first they had to catch him.

Juniper kept sniffing, never wavering from her path. Sometimes she would take some sharp turns. Maya worked to remember those turns in her mind so that she could find her way back out. Juniper had settled into a steady pace and Maya was able to find her rhythm with her.

They were heading toward a wilderness area. Wilderness areas were special designations within national forests. They were meant to be exactly what they sounded like—wild. People were only allowed in on foot to camp. Motor vehicles of any kind were prohibited, along with no mining or logging and other restrictions. And they would be a perfect place to escape.

Juniper's nose stayed close to the ground, and she kept up a solid pace. They headed into the trees, which were large and thick. Some of them had been decimated by pine beetle kill, but others seemed to be managing fine. The trees were close together, blocking some of the sun and casting dark shadows.

Maya pulled Juniper up for a minute and let her eyes adjust to the change in light. Juniper sat down and was panting, so Maya got them both some water. Not only would the water help Juniper with dehydration, but it would also keep her nose moist so she could scent better.

The bad thing about where they were was that it would be easy for someone to ambush Maya and Juniper. This was where a backup officer would have been a good idea. She thought about turning around and getting to an area where she could radio Josh and ask for his help, but she was already this far along.

"What do you think, girl? You up for this?"

Juniper wagged her tail in response. Maya pulled the bag with the scent article out of her pocket and let Juniper sniff it again just to keep her sharp on the odor.

"Track, girl. Let's go. Let's go find him."

Juniper immediately put her nose back down on the ground and found the scent trail quickly. They picked up their pace together. Maya was glad to be moving again as she had worked up a sweat on the first part of the track; now, being in the shade of the trees, she had cooled off and felt chilled.

They came to a small stream. Juniper hesitated there and then turned to her left, following the stream from the bank. People often thought dogs couldn't smell a track if a person ran through water. That was a myth. Dogs could smell just fine in water and Juniper proved that when she came up to an area that Torres must have used to cross the stream. Maya could see why. There were places to jump to that kept her feet from getting wet.

Juniper didn't care about her paws getting wet—she kept her nose down and trotted through the water with no hesitation. Maya didn't want to deal with wet boots and socks, so she took the path that she assumed Torres had also used.

They went back farther, and Maya swore she could smell smoke from a campfire. Juniper's body language changed from the easy rhythm of following a track to indicating that a person might be near. She paused and a low growl came up in her throat.

"Quiet," Maya said, not wanting the dog to sound off yet. She wanted the element of surprise. Juniper listened but stayed in front of her.

Maya peered around some of the trees blocking her view and saw a tent. There was a man outside of it who appeared to be cleaning up from breakfast over the campfire. He had dark hair, but without his hat on, she could see flecks of gray. He wore an old jacket and camouflage pants. Even though the man was older, maybe in his fifties, he was in good shape. He turned in their direction, and Maya pulled Juniper back with her into darker shadows. She held her breath. His eyes were exactly like she remembered—dark and snakelike, ready to strike. This man was definitely Eric Torres.

"You're a good girl." Maya rubbed Juniper's head, proud of her for finding Torres. Now she had to figure out the best way to arrest him with the least amount of conflict since she was on her own.

Maybe it's time to stop being stubborn and always on my own. I'm still at a point where I could radio Josh and ask for help. And if I arrest Torres, that could complicate prosecution in the case. It would be safer to have backup.

There was a thick stand of trees they'd come through when they had first approached the campsite. The trees would give them some concealment, so Maya and Juniper crept back that direction. They had to be careful that they didn't make any noise and tip Torres off. Maya pulled out her satellite phone and sent Josh a text with all the information about where she'd found Torres. She put the phone back in her pocket and decided she would wait until Josh arrived before approaching Torres.

"We'll just sit tight for now and wait for backup, okay, girly?" Maya said.

Juniper wagged her tail and gave a small whine. Maya hoped Torres hadn't heard them. When she peered back around the tree, he was gone.

Where is he?

Crap, maybe he did hear us.

Maya remained concealed behind the tree, Juniper in front of her to also keep her hidden. When she took another look around the tree trunk, Eric Torres stood about fifteen feet away and he had his gun drawn, but it wasn't pointed at them. Another person had arrived, and he and Eric were in a standoff.

Chapter Twenty-Five

Maya quickly pulled her gun out and unsnapped Juniper's leash.

"Stay," she whispered to her dog. She wanted Juniper to be free in case they needed to go after either or both guys. The whole situation had changed and Maya wasn't sure she could wait for Josh to arrive. She might have to intervene, but for now, she would wait and assess the situation.

At least she had Juniper in case she had to get involved. She and Juniper had worked on bite and redirect exercises to help take down two suspects by Juniper apprehending one, releasing the bite, and then under Maya's direction, biting the other suspect. Juniper did well with the exercise, but Maya didn't want to really test it out if she didn't have to.

"Harold," Torres said. "So nice to see you. I didn't think you cared anymore. Nice of you to find me."

Harold? Maya didn't know for sure who he was, but he had similar features to Blake. Could this be the cousin that Denise had told her about?

"Cut the crap," Harold said. "You know why I'm here. You're getting in the way, but you're not getting away with it. You can't save her. No one can."

Maya wondered if they were talking about her? Or maybe another witness? Could it be Abigail? Did she know more than she was letting on? Maya and Juniper remained hidden and kept watching.

"I will always protect her. I promised that. And I always keep my promises."

Torres's finger moved to the trigger.

With that change and Torres intent on shooting Harold, Maya couldn't wait. She and Juniper stepped out from behind the trees.

"I'm a Forest Service Law Enforcement officer. Both of you put your guns down or I'll send my dog."

Torres smiled. Maya was about ready to let Juniper go apprehend him when Harold pointed his gun at Maya and Juniper. "Get down *now*!" Torres yelled.

Maya dropped down, grabbing Juniper and pulling her down with her.

Torres fired off several shots in a row and then there was silence. Juniper was trained to automatically apprehend someone when shots were fired, so Maya clung to her harness, but Juniper got away from her, locking onto Torres as a target.

"Juniper! Off! Down!" Maya yelled, since Torres didn't have his gun aimed at them and had, technically, just saved her life. She hoped Juniper would listen. They had to run scenarios like this in training and for certification. It was a weak area for Juniper and the one part of certification they almost didn't pass, as Juniper loved taking a bite. Especially after a long track. Juniper listened and dropped to the ground, but stared at Torres.

Maya scrambled to her feet and kept her Glock out in front of her. Juniper trembled on her down-stay, waiting for the command to go apprehend him.

"Forest Service Law Enforcement! Drop your gun! Now!" she screamed.

Torres had his gun pulled into a low position, ready to fire again, but he didn't turn toward Maya.

"I said drop your gun or I'll send my dog."

Torres started to pivot toward Maya. She saw him scan the area where he had fired his gun. Just when she thought she would have to send Juniper or take a shot or both, he placed his gun on the ground and raised his hands. Maya strained to see Harold, but after he'd been shot, he had fallen back into some tall grass down a slight slope and was out of sight.

"Put your hands behind your head and get down on your knees."

Torres just smiled back at her. Maya didn't like his demeanor. It was off. Something wasn't right. He was different than what she expected. It was like he was enjoying this moment to a degree, but also completely on guard. *What does he have planned? I have to remember that Abigail said he's a good manipulator.*

"I said, put your hands behind your head and get down on your knees or I'll send the dog."

Juniper kept an intense stare in Torres's direction. She was looking for any reason to apprehend him. The silence stretched on, and Maya was about ready to send Juniper when Torres finally laced his hands behind his head and got down on his knees.

"Now, get down on the ground."

Torres shook his head and laughed but complied.

"Juniper, watch and guard," Maya said, as she slowly approached. Eric stayed in place, but she didn't trust him. He continued to let out little snickers. "What's so funny?"

"Go ahead and handcuff me. Then I'll tell you," Eric replied.

Maya didn't completely trust him, but his gun was out of his reach. She holstered her gun, now really wishing she had a backup officer. But this was her own doing so she would finish it. Hopefully Josh would arrive soon. Torres was making this too easy, though. Maya's gut feeling was that he was up to something, but she didn't know what. She pulled her handcuffs out of her back pocket and took his arms one at a time, snapping on the cuffs. Then she patted him down.

Juniper continued to stare at Torres, probably hoping he would do something wrong so she could go for a bite. Maya found a knife in one pocket and another ankle gun. She confiscated both items, grateful that Torres hadn't pulled the other gun on her. Then she rolled him over and helped him sit up.

"We have a lot to discuss," she said.

Torres's eyes darkened, but he kept a cool expression. "Do we?"

"Yes, we do."

"I don't suppose you'd like to thank me first?"

"For what?" Maya asked.

"For taking out a complete asshole cop and murderer."

Maya stared at Torres. He *had* saved her life. If Harold had been able to get a shot off, he would have hit her. In one respect she should thank him, but whenever Maya had killed someone in the line of duty, she always felt like a piece of her died too. Torres seemed so nonchalant about it all, like a cold-blooded killer and yet, he had saved her.

She should go and see if Harold was still alive. Torres

was in cuffs and Juniper could watch and guard, but Maya froze in place. Here was her chance to find out more, but she also needed to provide medical attention to Harold.

"Go on," Torres said. "See if that man has a pulse, but if he does, I'd recommend shooting him again and finishing him off."

Maya hesitated. This could still be a trap. He'd made the arrest too easy. He knew she was on her own because if anyone was with her, they would have stepped out to help her long ago.

"I promise I'll be good and stay here. Plus, your dog is itching to bite me, and I don't feel like having a Malinois hanging off my arm today. Been there, done that, don't want to do it again."

Maya didn't answer. Maybe if she stayed quiet Torres would keep talking. He was arrogant and manipulative.

"Guard, Juniper," she finally said.

She slowly backed away, keeping an eye on Torres and making sure he didn't try anything with her. Juniper licked her chops and her golden eyes stayed locked onto her suspect. Maya unholstered her gun and stepped down the incline toward the other suspect. Because of where he fell and the height of the grass, she couldn't see him.

"Forest Service Law Enforcement. Show me your hands," she said, trying to sound tough, but feeling like she was wavering. This whole situation had gone down in a weird way. "I said show me your hands."

There was no answer.

Maya crept forward, inching step by step. She kept her gun in a ready position in case the man popped up and fired at her.

"He's dead," Torres shouted at her. "You don't have to announce yourself to a dead person."

Maya ignored him. She had to keep her temper under control. He would have the upper hand if she got mad and he knew that. He'd probably keep doing what he could to goad her.

She stopped and cleared the area around her, making sure no one else had come with Harold, and then continued inching her way forward.

She heard a gasping and gurgling noise coming from straight ahead of her. She'd heard that noise before when she was in Afghanistan. Noises like that stayed with you and intruded on your sleep at night, causing nightmares. It was the sound of someone who'd been shot and was choking on their own blood.

Maya rushed toward the noise. Like Blake, Harold had short salt-and-pepper hair and a tanned face with lots of wrinkles. He'd obviously spent a lot of time outside. He was on the ground gasping for air; his gun had fallen out of his hand and off to the side. Seeing Maya, he struggled to reach his gun. She didn't know if he was worried about her killing him since she really wasn't in uniform or if he intended to hurt her, but she wasn't going to take any chances. She kicked the gun out of the way and holstered her weapon.

She had bent down to start first aid, when the man reached up and grabbed her by the hair, pulling her toward him. Adrenaline surged through her body, and with a mix of surprise, anger and fear, Maya took her elbow and slammed him in the face until he let go. If she had another pair of handcuffs, she would have put them on to keep her safe.

"Who are you?" she asked.

The man just shook his head and then took one more shallow breath, then went still. Maya, still not sure if she was safe, started CPR, but she saw as she did compressions that blood was coming out the bullet holes. She felt for a pulse, but there was none.

She stood back up and stepped back. There was nothing more she could do for him.

Dizziness swept over her. It didn't matter how many times you saw death or if the man was trying to kill her. It took a piece of you each time. She closed her eyes for a moment and could feel sand blowing against her face.

They'd been out on a patrol and Zinger had found several IEDs. She had been sitting with him in the shade by a Humvee. Her buddy Zach had come over and petted Zinger and given them some more water.

Zinger lapped some of her water, grateful for it. Zach was getting ready to say something when the first bullet hit him. It had come off a mountainside. Sniper.

Maya and Zinger moved fast, getting around to the other side of the vehicle and hopefully out of the sniper's view. Zach was still lying there. She put Zinger on a down-stay and crawling low, she managed to get back over near Zach. She grabbed him by the vest and pulled him in her direction. More shots came, pinging around them, but somehow Maya managed to not get hit.

She had radioed for help when she had heard the same wheezing and gasping noise. Zach hadn't lived for long either.

Maya opened her eyes, the memory flooding back in so strong and unexpectedly. She held up her hands and saw blood. Where the hell was she?

Stepping back, she could hear a voice in the distance. Maya pulled out her gun, sprinted back up the small hill and pointed her Glock at the sound of the person talking.

"Whoa. Easy there. I'm cuffed already. You don't have to shoot me. Is he dead? I hope so."

Maya started shaking. She had to control herself. She couldn't lose it like this every time she saw a dead body. Not in her line of work.

She fought to control her breathing and remind herself that she was in Colorado. She wasn't at war. At least not like the one in Afghanistan. That war had no rules. Here at home at least there were some rules, although suspects didn't like to follow policy and procedure. Maya's breathing calmed down and she stared down at the man one more time, then turned and walked back toward Eric.

Maybe out here with no one else around, she didn't have rules either.

Chapter Twenty-Six

Maya strode back over to where Eric was sitting. Sweat poured down her back and face after her flashback, as if her body were in Afghanistan too. She thought about the grounding and mindfulness Dr. Meyers had been working on with her. Then she decided, screw it. She wanted answers. Now. It didn't matter where her mind was.

Maya grabbed him by the arms, hoisting him to his feet with strength that surprised even her.

"Tell me what's going on now. Why did Harold Conner come after you?" she said, her face inches away from his. Juniper growled, feeling Maya's anger and frustration, but she stayed in place. Maya was to the point she didn't care if Juniper bit this man. He had caused her nothing but pain and hurt since he had come into her life.

"He probably followed you and was sent to kill both of us."

"Why?" Maya snapped.

"That answer will take longer than we have right now."

"Then you're going to answer some other questions. Now," Maya said. She didn't know where to start.

Why had he killed her mother and Nana?

What did he want? Just the evidence?

Why did he have to burn down her cabin?

She decided to start there. It was the most recent crime. "I bet you're pissed that you didn't kill me the other night when you shot up and burned down my cabin."

"I didn't shoot at you, and I didn't burn down your cabin."

"Yeah, right, and Juniper is the Easter Bunny."

"Seriously, Maya," Torres said.

"Don't call me Maya. I'm an officer and that's what you're going to address me as. Give me that respect at least since you took everything from me."

"What are you talking about?"

"My mother. My grandmother. My cabin. All for what? So you could find some supposed evidence and destroy it?"

Torres shook his head and stepped back a little bit to lean against a tree.

"Don't move again without my permission," Maya said.

"Or what? You'll shoot me?"

Maya stared him down. While shooting him was tempting at the moment, she knew she had to keep her temper in check and maintain the upper hand. Somehow she had to keep him talking. "No, I won't shoot you, but I'd rather get answers before I take you to jail."

"I will answer your questions as best as I can. They may not be the answers you're looking for, though."

"I'll take my chances. First question: why did you burn down my cabin?"

"I didn't."

"Bullshit. Stop lying to me. We have evidence putting you at the scene. Juniper tracked you here today from some of that evidence."

"Juniper, huh? Good name."

Juniper bumped Maya on the leg with her nose as if she was telling her to calm down too. Maya took a deep breath. She needed to stay calm and try to get answers. Eric Torres did not make that easy. "I'll ask nicely one more time: why did you burn down my cabin?"

"And I'll tell you one more time that I didn't. But I was there."

"No kidding. Tell me something I don't know."

"Okay, here's something you don't know. I was there because I've been keeping an eye on you."

"No," Maya said. "Actually, I do know that. Juniper and I found your parking spot where you'd leave your oil-leaking truck and hike in to watch me like some pervert. That was you the other day on the road passing me, wasn't it?"

Juniper let out a bark at hearing her name. Maya knew the dog had to be frustrated at sitting and guarding this whole time.

"It was," Torres said.

"Finally, an honest answer."

He shook his head. "Why don't you let me try to explain?"

"Please, I'm listening."

"Are you?" Torres asked. "Let's start with your cabin. I've been watching you because there's a dangerous criminal after you and it's not me. I knew you were in trouble. I wanted to make sure you were okay. I know this person and I knew it was a matter of time before they showed up and went after you either themselves or with their favorite hit men. Harold over there is one of this person's favorite go-to guys. This person wants the evidence your mother collected. They're crazy and probably decided that the evidence was at your cabin and burning it down would get rid of it. If you died in the process, then that was too bad."

"So let me get this straight. Your story is that someone else is after me—a criminal mastermind who has hired hit men. You, the person wanted for homicides, are protecting me and everyone seems to think I had some evidence. That's your answer?"

Torres shrugged. "Pretty much, yeah. Do you have the evidence?"

"What? No. I don't have any evidence and if I did, I wouldn't tell you."

"You think your grandfather does?"

"Leave Pops out of this. He doesn't have anything either. He would have told me if he did," Maya said, not totally believing her last statement. Pops was known to keep things to himself if he thought it would keep others safe. Juniper took a step toward Torres. Maya put a hand on her head, settling the dog back down.

"Well, your mother had it and it's probably around here somewhere."

"Or else you and your pyromaniac friend already burned it. Maybe my mother had it at her house and it's been gone that long."

"No, I think she had it stashed somewhere, but if you don't know where it is then that's not good."

"Why isn't that good?" Maya asked.

"Because you're going to be in danger until we can find that evidence."

"We? I don't think so."

"I saved your life."

"And for all I know that was a setup. You could have staged that to try to gain my trust."

"It wasn't a setup," Torres said. "And if it was, then it obviously didn't work. I can tell you don't trust me at all. Not that I blame you, but there's something you haven't considered."

"And what's that?" Maya asked.

"Think, Officer Thompson. What makes me difficult to catch? It's the fact I used to work in law enforcement. I know how the system works. I know how investigations work. Why would I leave so much evidence behind? Could it be that I was being framed?"

For the first time in the conversation, Maya realized he had a point. Once again, her questions were answered by more questions. And Denise had said that Eric was the one cop she trusted. Was there actually a chance he had been framed?

"If you're telling me the truth, then I have more questions. And I need honest answers," Maya said.

Chapter Twenty-Seven

"I'll give you answers. Know that when it comes to killing your mother and grandmother and trying to murder you, I didn't do it. I've been set up," Torres said. "This whole deal is a lot bigger than one person. There are so many people involved in Montana. You have no idea. I was also framed for murdering those cops and judge. You should get the file on that case and look into it more."

"You have my attention," Maya said. "Keep talking."

"In your mother's and grandmother's cases, think about the evidence. I bet you had something with my DNA and a fingerprint. The clothing you used to track. All of that was probably planted by someone who wants to make me look guilty. What else have you found?"

"Why should I tell you?" Maya asked.

"Because it's been planted. I don't know what you have or haven't found."

Juniper let out a whine and stared at Maya. She knew her dog was getting tired, having done a track and now guarding. Maya rubbed her head, reassuring her, and wanted to tell her they would get out of here soon, but she wanted more information while she had the chance.

"A piece of my mother's jewelry was also found. She was wearing it the night she died."

"Was it her bracelet?"

"Yes, how did you know? Did you plant it to mess with me?"

"No, I'm not messing with you. I swear. I knew because I arrested her. Several times for prostitution and possession of narcotics. She always had it on, and it was always the first thing she wanted back when she received her personal belongings."

Maya swallowed and fought back more emotions. "Well, it's logged into evidence now and I'll probably never get it back."

"I'm sorry," Torres said. "But I swear I didn't kill her. I've been framed for the other murders too. Look into them. Two cops and a judge. They were having a party, and someone gunned them down, but it wasn't me. Call up to Montana and ask to see the files. You'll see that I've been set up."

Torres came across as genuine. The usual signs of a suspect lying weren't there, but then she remembered the warning about Torres being a good manipulator. For all she knew he'd planted his own evidence just to toy with her like a cat with a mouse, or just left the evidence by accident, like most criminals. If what he was saying was true, Maya could follow up and look into the case like Torres said. She decided to change tactics and get away from the personal parts of these cases. "What about Kendra? Why did you kill her?"

"Kendra? I didn't kill her either. That was another setup."

"Was it? When we responded, we heard someone in the woods. A twig snapped and Juniper and I tracked you."

At the mention of her name, Juniper gave a low growl and locked eyes with Torres.

"I'd look away if I were you," Maya said. "When she locks eyes, that's not a good sign."

"I hope you can call her off."

Maya shrugged. "Maybe. Maybe not. You never know about these high drive working dogs."

"Look," Eric said. "I'll admit I was there and had a talk with Kendra. I needed to get information out of her. I was trying to convince her to help me."

"A talk? What's your definition of a talk? Does it include torture, by any chance?"

"In her case, it did. She'd promised to get me information and then changed her mind."

Surprise registered in Maya. She wasn't expecting Torres to be so candid about it. "Did you kill her by accident then? Maybe you went a bit overboard on the torture?"

"No, I didn't kill her. I just needed some information out of her. I suspected she'd been hired by someone to watch you and gather information. I needed to know what she knew and who she'd told it to. Like I said, there's more people involved than you realize. But Kendra was just a pawn and I wanted to know what she'd found out. I didn't think it would get her killed. I swear, that's the truth."

Maya didn't know what to think or say. Because of her conversation this morning with Denise, part of her believed him. She was getting ready to ask her next question when Juniper suddenly started growling.

Juniper turned and faced in the same direction that she and Maya had come from earlier. Her body tensed and while Maya couldn't see anyone coming, she trusted

Juniper. Maybe Josh was finally here or maybe Eric had another person he was working with that was trying to surprise them. She grabbed Torres by his arm, staying behind him, and marched him over to an area where he wouldn't be out in the open, then sat him down.

"Stay here. I'll be back to get you," she said to Torres. Then to Juniper she said, "Let's go see who's there."

They moved forward together, and Maya drew her gun. Juniper pointed her nose up in the air. The day was still and quiet with hardly any breeze, but the humidity was low, making the scent more difficult. Maya knew, though, that Juniper was used to this environment and could manage this.

A shadow moved in the trees to their left. Juniper air scented again and then started wagging her tail.

"It is Josh, isn't it, girly?" Maya asked, noticing the change in her dog.

Juniper's tail wagged harder as a figure stepped out from behind some trees.

Maya saw the dark blue sheriff's uniform and lowered her weapon, holstering it. Juniper jumped up and down and went over to Josh to get some pets.

"I'm glad you're here," Maya said. "There's so much I need to fill you in on."

"Apparently so," Josh said.

"I have him. I have Eric Torres handcuffed."

"What? Where?" Josh asked.

"Follow me. And Torres just shot another suspect."

"What?"

Maya waved, indicating that Josh should come with her. Juniper bounded up alongside her, but kept running back and forth between her and Josh.

"Yes, another guy showed up. I thought it was Blake

at first, but it's not. It's his cousin. This man and Eric were in a standoff and Eric shot him. The body is down the hill over there."

The trio approached the spot where she had left Torres, but he was missing. All that remained was Maya's hand-cuffs on the ground.

Eric ran through the woods, putting as much distance between him and Maya as possible. He knew she'd come after him with Juniper once she found her handcuffs left behind. He'd learned a long time ago to always carry a spare key with him. Handcuffs had universal keys.

He continued sprinting toward his truck, which was parked on an old logging road. If he could get there, he could get a head start and get away, but now that he'd talked to her, he could only hope that she might be-lieve him. Maybe he could connect with her again and wouldn't have to do anything rash to get her to consider what he had to say.

In so many ways, the day had been perfect, better than anything he could have planned. If he'd taken her, convincing her that he was innocent would have been so much more difficult. It was one of the reasons he'd held off with his plan. Now he had made contact and hopefully she would think about what he'd said. She certainly had a lot of questions.

Luckily, she wanted answers and that delayed her taking him in and booking him. If he'd gone to jail to-night, he'd probably be dead by morning. Hopefully, whoever was coming wasn't another hit man, but Eric now had faith that Maya could take care of herself.

She was tough and feisty. So much like her mother and yet so different too. What he didn't know was what had happened to her when she'd discovered the body of the man he'd shot. It was like she was in another world. There were pieces to her that he didn't understand, but maybe someday he could.

Torres got to his truck and hoped the old beast would start. He turned the key and the engine sputtered to life. He needed to check the oil—again.

"Hold together, baby," Eric said to the truck.

He started to bounce down the logging road and a sense of relief washed over him. Maybe he could get Maya to listen to him. Maybe she could even help him. She knew something about the evidence, of that he was certain. She just might not realize it yet, but Eric vowed to help her remember. If he did it right, he could even keep his promise to protect her and clear his name.

Chapter Twenty-Eight

"You've got to be kidding me," Maya said. "I shouldn't have left him, but I didn't know if it was you approaching or someone with Harold."

Juniper gave a low whine. Josh had his hands on his hips, staring at her. "Don't be too hard on yourself. You didn't know who was approaching and you thought you had Torres secure and could leave him. Does Juniper have enough energy left to go after him?"

"Yes, she can do it," Maya said. Juniper barked in response as if she understood.

"Okay, I'll back you up." Josh radioed dispatch and gave them the coordinates of where they were located. Once he was certain that someone was on their way, he said, "Let's go."

Maya knew that normally they would stay with a crime scene until a deputy showed up, but right now, catching Torres was top priority. Juniper was by her side and Maya reattached her leash. She patted Juniper's sides and spoke to her in a high-pitched voice, pepping her up to start another track. She normally didn't have to do that, but Josh was right, Juniper was tired, although Maya had faith that she had enough energy to still do this track. She took Juniper over to where Torres had dumped the handcuffs and told her to find him.

With her tail up in the air, Juniper put her nose down and started working. She headed off on a trail, and Maya saw some fresh boot prints, which she tried not to step on in case they were needed for evidence. Juniper settled back into a solid pace and Maya was proud of her dog. She'd come a long way working and had figured out how to better pace herself.

Maya heard Josh breathing hard behind her as they went up a hill and her own legs were starting to feel like jelly. They had covered a lot of terrain today. Who knew how far away they were from her cabin at this point? If this was how she felt, then Juniper would be the same. She couldn't ask much more of her.

Juniper kept her nose down, and every now and then, she would slow and put her nose up to start air scenting. Maya did her best to not interfere. Juniper picked up a trot again and wound her way to an old logging road. There she started to act like she'd lost the scent. She turned back and forth, sticking her nose up in the air and back down on the ground.

"Good girl," Maya said. She figured this was where Eric kept his vehicle and he'd probably taken off, and made a mental note to start working with Juniper on tracking scent once a person was in a vehicle. She could do it, but it wasn't something they usually trained for.

"She's lost the scent," Maya said to Josh.

"He definitely parked here," Josh said, pointing at the ground. "Here's another oil spot."

"Damn it. I can't believe I lost him," Maya said. "Maybe I should see if she can pick up the scent again even though he's in a vehicle."

"Maya, stop. Your dog is worn out. You're exhausted. I know you want this guy and you had him, but you need to stop and think about your dog."

"You're right," she said, taking a deep breath to try to calm her frustration. Josh was right. Juniper had worked hard for her today and couldn't be asked to do more. Juniper would always work for Maya, and she didn't want to take advantage of that.

"Let's go back to the crime scene and wait for the deputy to arrive. Then we can regroup. If Torres wants this evidence and he really thinks it's somewhere here in Pinecone Junction, then he won't be leaving," Josh said.

Maya nodded, knowing that he was leaving out the part that she was also still a target.

"When we find him, we can put together a tactical team," Josh continued. "This guy is smart. No one gets away from you."

"He probably had a handcuff key," Maya said. "I didn't even think about that, and I should have patted him down better. Who in law enforcement doesn't keep one on them?"

"Come on, let's head on back to where Torres was camping. Maybe there's something there that will help us figure out where he's staying."

"I'll get Juniper some water there too," Maya said. "I left my backpack with all my supplies there."

The three of them started trudging back. Luckily, the campsite wasn't too far from where Torres had parked his vehicle. When they arrived, Maya gave Juniper some water. She happily took a big drink and then went over to some shade to lie down. Maya was tired too.

"This is why you need a backup officer," Josh said.

"I know," Maya snapped. She started to pace. It

helped her think and avoided his stare. She knew he was right, and she'd acted impulsively.

"Did Torres shoot the other suspect before or after you texted me?"

"After. I know, you don't have to say it again, I should have had a backup officer."

"I won't say it again, but I was guessing that you were out on your own doing something like this."

"What made you think that?" Maya said, with a little bit of sarcasm.

"Hmmm…let me think, you were gone from your office this morning, not answering your phone and I found your patrol vehicle at your cabin. I figured you had decided to go out on your own."

"I guess you know me well," Maya muttered.

"I do. Your independence is something I love about you, but I wish you'd be more careful. Where's this suspect you're talking about?"

"Over there." Maya pointed. "Follow me."

Juniper stood back up and shook. She took her place by Maya's side and they all headed in the direction of the body. Harold was still and lifeless, and flies were already buzzing around the remains. Maya shook thinking about how he had grabbed her hair as he gasped for his last breath.

"What if this had been you?" Josh said. "I don't know what I'd do if I lost you."

"I'm sorry. I know I need to be careful. I would never want to hurt you," Maya said, starting to feel bad. Part of being friends or even something more was thinking about others. "I know it sounds crazy, but I think Torres saved my life."

"I'm grateful for that, although you don't need to

take risks and prove yourself," Josh said with a sigh. "I have radio signal out here, I'll call it in."

"Okay," Maya said. She couldn't get out of her head what Josh had said—he loved her independence. What exactly did that mean? She'd have to think about it more later. Right now she just needed to focus on the investigation. She couldn't deal with her feelings at the moment. "Not too much to investigate. I saw Torres shoot him."

"I'll make sure we get a search warrant for his tent too," Josh said.

"Good idea," Maya said. Even though they were on national forest land, they didn't need a defense attorney getting evidence thrown out because they didn't have a warrant.

"I also won't mention that you went out on your own to anyone," Josh said. "I wouldn't want your boss to think you disobeyed orders."

"I'm sure he just assumes that's what will happen by now," Maya said.

"What he doesn't know won't hurt him. As far as I'm concerned, you and Juniper took a long hike and happened to run into Eric Torres, who shot a man following you. That's pretty much what happened anyway."

"Thanks," Maya said, feeling relieved. It was bad enough that Torres had escaped. If her boss knew she'd intentionally tracked today, he would probably be upset. Justifiably too.

"I'm here for you," Josh said.

"Why are you so good to me?" Maya asked.

"Because…"

She waited for his answer, her chest constricting. What was she hoping he would say? Because he loved her?

"Because you're a good friend," he finally said. "You gave me a second chance when others didn't. You understand me and so I'll always be there for you too. That's what friends do."

Maya smiled but felt some disappointment. He saw her as a friend and she was grateful for that, but she admitted to herself, she really wouldn't mind something more than friendship with Josh.

Chapter Twenty-Nine

Juniper curled up in the shade while Maya and Josh continued to wait for a deputy to come stay at the scene. Miranda was out on another call. Doc Clark was also busy with his appointments with patients who were still breathing. The body couldn't be moved and the scene couldn't be processed and released until they could arrive. Because of the location, they were also going to have to wait for a sheriff's posse horse to come and pack the body out.

A wave of exhaustion swept over Maya as they waited. The day had become warmer, and she took off her vest and sweatshirt and settled in the shade next to Juniper. They sat together and Maya tried to comprehend everything that had happened.

Josh leaned against a nearby tree. "You want a ride to your vehicle when we head out? I'm parked closer."

"That would be great," Maya said. She let out a heavy sigh. She had to stop being so impulsive. Her mother had been the same way and that didn't turn out well for her.

"What are you thinking about?"

"My mom."

"What about her?" Josh asked.

"I keep thinking about how much alike we are. She was stubborn and independent too, only she went down a road that got her into a lot of trouble. Sometimes I think I'm headed down the same road. I'm even an addict like her." Maya leaned her head back against the tree trunk. She rubbed her neck with her hand. It still had a kink in it from sleeping at the office. Tonight, she'd get a hotel. It wasn't like she was broke. She could afford a room for a few nights.

"We all have our faults. It doesn't mean we can't change or go down a different path."

"Yeah, true. Why do you put up with me? Why are you still my friend? I think I'm a pain in the ass," she said.

"You *are* a pain in the ass," Josh said with a grin.

Maya laughed and said, "You didn't have to agree so fast. I think I'm just being pitiful."

"No, you're not. You've had a lot going on and in the middle of all of it, you're working on staying sober. You're amazing."

"You always say that, but I don't know."

"I remember the first time I met you. You stormed into the sheriff's office because your grandfather had turned down your application to be a deputy. You weren't working for the Forest Service yet. You and your grandfather stood face-to-face. I'd never seen anyone stand up to him before. I mean, everyone loves and respects him, but no one, and I mean no one, myself included, would ever get in his face. I loved how strong you were and that you weren't afraid to stand your ground. Of course, then he tore up your application and that was that. But that was the moment I knew you were different. In a good way."

Maya chuckled at the memory. "I was so angry at him. I couldn't believe he wouldn't hire me."

"I was bummed he didn't hire you either. I saw your application and knew you'd be a great asset to the department. But I think things worked out."

"They did," Maya said.

Someone called out in the distance. Juniper lifted her head up and jumped to her feet.

"Sounds like Deputy Wilson is here," Josh said.

A few seconds later the deputy came into view on the trail. He had gear with him to tape off the crime scene. Maya and Josh helped him out, and then Josh told him to stay there until Doc Clark and Miranda arrived. Wilson agreed, and Maya, Juniper and Josh started hiking out to Josh's vehicle.

They were out of sight of the crime scene when Josh said, "How's your neck feeling? I see you keep massaging it."

"I slept on the couch in my office last night. I don't really fit well on it, and I gave myself a kink. It'll be better tomorrow."

"Where are you staying tonight?"

"I was thinking the local hotel."

"You know, I have a guest bedroom. I haven't slept in the bed, but when my sister visited a while back, she didn't complain. And believe me, she would let me know," Josh said. "We can get a crate for Juniper, and she can sleep in the room with you."

"I don't know," Maya said. "You don't need to keep worrying about me. I'm fine."

"I'm offering this...as a friend," Josh said, coming to a halt.

Maya stopped too and turned around. Juniper grunted

and sat down as if she knew this conversation could take a while.

"I mean it," Josh said. "I'm not trying to be macho or worry about you, but I want to help you, and I like to spend time with you and Juniper."

"Josh, what are we doing? I don't know where this is going. Or if there even is a 'this.' I mean, you just want to be friends, right?"

"This doesn't have to go anywhere if you don't want it to." Josh took another step closer and was now close enough to reach out and touch her cheek. "But good grief, you drive me nuts. I want to be with you more than anything, Maya. I've been afraid to say that because I didn't know how you felt. I'm asking you to stay with me because I care about you. I've been trying to be patient and I've convinced myself that we can just be friends, but I don't know if I can do that."

Maya didn't know how to answer. He continued to stroke her cheek and her face warmed under his touch. Without thinking, she leaned in closer and then drew him to her.

The kiss started a little tentative. They paused for a moment and then kissed again, this time deeper and more passionately. Juniper whined and poked her nose on Maya's leg.

Maya pulled back and laughed at her dog. "I don't know how Juniper feels about this, but maybe a few nights at your place until I figure out where I'm going to live isn't a bad thing. I wouldn't mind a real bed."

Josh smiled and said, "It's about time you came to your senses."

"You may regret this when you see what it's like living with a Malinois. She doesn't get this tired every day."

"I'll take my chances," Josh said again, leaning in for another kiss.

This time Maya was ready and even though her heart was pounding, she returned the kiss. Her stomach was in knots, and she found herself not wanting to stop, but the sound of someone clearing their throat interrupted them. Josh and Maya stepped apart. She started to rub her necklace.

Miranda stood on the trail that Maya and Josh were blocking. "Hey there. This way to the crime scene?"

"Uh. Yeah," Josh answered. "Just down there about a quarter mile."

Maya didn't know what to say. Her face warmed up and was probably turning beet red.

"Deputy Wilson is waiting there," Josh said. He'd stepped back away from Maya and Miranda walked in between them.

When Miranda passed Maya, she turned toward her and gave a thumbs-up. "You go, girl," she whispered. "About time."

Maya shook her head.

Miranda just laughed and said, "We'll talk later. You can give me all the details."

"Okay," Maya said, hoping that she really wouldn't have to do that. Although if she was going to talk relationships with anyone, Miranda might be the one person she would confide in.

"See you all later," Miranda said, with a wave over her shoulder.

"So that's going to be all over the department," Josh muttered.

"When my patrol vehicle is parked in front of your house, that information will be all over town. It won't matter what room I stay in. I need to call my boss and let him know that I'll be staying with you."

"Think we should warn your grandfather?"

Maya shrugged and said, "He may know by the time we get back to the office."

"In that case, this won't hurt then," Josh said, giving Maya one more kiss. When they moved apart, he added, "I'm glad you're going to be staying with me. It'll be nice."

"Just until I figure out a place of my own while I get my cabin rebuilt."

"Okay, whatever you say," Josh said. "You don't have to be nervous."

"What makes you think I'm nervous?" she asked.

"You keep rubbing your necklace. It's your tell."

Maya dropped her hand, realizing she was doing exactly what Josh had just said. She added, "Just remember, when Juniper chews something up, you invited us."

Chapter Thirty

Maya went into the front lobby of the sheriff's station, tired from the day's events. Pops was standing there speaking with the front desk deputy. She headed his direction.

"Hey, Pops, you have a minute?" she asked.

"I do," he said. He finished his business with the deputy and then said, "Let's go to my office."

"Okay." Maya followed him, feeling like a teenager again. He'd caught her once in high school making out in a truck with one of the football players and that relationship had come to an end quickly. She didn't know what Pops said or did, but the boy would hardly ever look at her again. But she was an adult now and could make her own decisions. She'd never mentioned the guy she dated when she was in the military, although she'd talked about him with Nana. Did Nana tell Pops? It just seemed weird to tell your grandfather relationship stuff no matter what your age.

They went into Pops's office, and he shut the door. "Maya, what the hell were you thinking?"

"Pops, I think I'm in love with him, but I don't know for sure. I mean, how do you really know?"

"What? What are you talking about?"

Maya stopped and then said, "What were you talking about?"

"I was talking about going out on a 'hike.'" Pops raised his fingers and made air quotes. "But really going after Eric Torres on your own. I really hope the guy you're in love with isn't Eric Torres."

"What? No. Just forget what I said about being in love. I thought you were talking about something else. As for Torres, I had him, but he got away. Pops, I think there's more to this."

"Great. That means you're going to keep investigating," he said. "We both need to step out of this or we're going to give the DA a nightmare. Torres will walk if we keep messing with this case, not to mention it won't help the investigation into me either."

"I'm sorry. I wasn't thinking about that."

"That's the problem," Pops said, his face turning red. "You need to stop and think, Maya. You're an amazing officer and K-9 handler, but if you keep acting impulsively, then you'll get yourself in trouble. You'll end up under investigation, just like me. I don't want you to be just like me."

Maya sat down on the chair near Pops's desk. "I've always wanted to be like you, Pops."

"I know," he said, leaning back on his desk. "I'm so proud of you, but I don't know what I'd do if I lost you too. I don't think I could handle it, so keep yourself safe. Be smart and take an officer with you when you're tracking. Will you do that for me?"

"I will," she said. "I have a favor to ask, though. You may not like it."

Pops sighed. "What is it?"

"Torres told me that I should investigate some of

the murders he's wanted for, especially the one of two cops and a judge. I don't think I'd be able to get those files, but maybe you can, and we can look over them together."

"I don't know. We could just mention this to the Montana detectives. See what they know."

"I don't think we should. Based on some information I've received, I believe Blake Conner could also be involved with the murders," Maya said, filling Pops in on what Denise told her. "We need to be careful who we talk to in that department. Mom had evidence. She hid it somewhere. That's the one thing that everyone seems to agree on. Do you have any idea where it would be?"

"No, I don't. I should have been there for your mother, but I was angry at everything she'd put us through. Your nana talked with her more and knew more. That's probably what got her killed too. As far as where the evidence might be, I wouldn't even know where to begin looking."

"Maybe if we can find out more about these murders, it'll give us a clue. I wonder if Miranda has even had time to process the evidence from Kendra's crime scene," Maya said.

"I don't know if Miranda has or not. She's been very busy these past few days and processing all the evidence might take a while. It'll probably be quicker to get information from the files. I'll make the call to the Montana department, see what I can find out, but the files need to go to Josh since he's the lead, and probably to Lucas too. We need to stay out of this."

"Great. I'll head on down to the meeting room so we can fill everyone in and figure out the next steps to finding Torres. I mean, I won't be involved, but I'd like to listen in."

"I think we also need to keep the information from Denise between us and Lucas and Josh. The less people who know, the better. If we can keep the information quiet, then maybe Blake will slip up and we can have some stronger evidence against him. Right now all we have is a person who refuses to testify."

"That sounds good," Maya said. "We can fill in Josh and Lucas after the meeting about our plan."

Pops shook his head and said, "Okay, but you're not leaving this office until you tell me one more thing."

"What's that?"

"Who are you so in love with?"

"That? It was just the moment. I didn't mean to say anything. Really, it's nothing."

"Uh-huh," Pops said. "Well, I already heard through the grapevine. News travels fast."

"What?" Maya said. "Did Deputy Wilson radio it in or something? I think that's a record."

"Deputy Wilson saw you two and texted his girlfriend who works in dispatch. You know what? I'm with everyone else. It's about damn time. At least you and Josh are finally admitting your feelings for each other."

Maya wasn't used to being speechless. She finally said, "So you're not upset? I mean, Josh and I work with each other. I know that I have to be careful about that."

"No, I'm not upset. You two are good together. I'm happy for you. And you do work together, but you're not at the same agency. You'll want to talk to your boss and there'll be challenges, but if you're happy, then that's what's important."

"So, you won't be upset if you find out I'm staying

with Josh until I can figure out another place to live? Or until my cabin is rebuilt."

"Nope," Pops said, standing. A grin spread across his face. "But I'm going to warn Josh to be careful. He picked a tough one with you."

"Thanks a lot, Pops," Maya said, with a laugh.

Josh knocked on the door and peeked inside. "We're all set in the meeting room. Everything good here?"

Pops continued to chuckle as he walked out the door and patted Josh on the shoulder. "Good luck, son. Good luck." Then he headed down the hallway.

"What's that about?" Josh asked Maya.

She stood. "I told him I was staying with you. And by the way, your deputy and our dispatcher are gossips."

They all filed into the meeting room. Abigail and Blake came in as well. Blake had a scowl on his face. Maya wanted to start asking him questions, but she knew she couldn't. Maybe if they played things right, Blake wouldn't know he was also a suspect. They might be able to catch him in a lie or surveil him. He'd be more likely to make a mistake.

Blake caught her staring at him. Maya tried to look away but wasn't quick enough. "Your dog keeps barking at me," he said. "I go by the vehicle, and she goes nuts."

"Maybe stay farther away from the vehicle then," she said, annoyed but also trusting her dog. "If you get close, she has every right to bark."

"Whatever," Blake said. Abigail handed him a coffee, smiled at Maya, and shrugged as if to say *it's just the way he is*.

Maya tried to smile back, but it felt more like a grimace. Everything that had happened today, starting with the track and finding Eric Torres, seemed like a million years ago. How was it only afternoon?

Josh took a seat at the head of the table. Pops sat off to the side. Maya was surprised at first, but she knew he was serious about staying out of the way. He was only here to keep up to date about what was going on in his county. She needed to wrap her head around doing the same thing, but she had a hard time not taking action. There had to be something she could do. If only she could remember more about her childhood. Maybe she'd been with her mom when she stashed the evidence and didn't even realize it.

Maya didn't know of anything like a safety deposit box, but she could look into some of those options. If she found anything, she could turn it over to Josh and Lucas.

"So." Blake spoke up again. "Are we going to sit around here discussing how Officer Thompson screwed up or are we going to get back out there and find this asshole?"

Maya sat straight up and leaned forward. She was about ready to snap a reply, when Josh gave her a look and jumped in.

"While Eric Torres escaped from Officer Thompson, she was able to locate where he was hiding out. We did get the search warrant for his tent and our crime scene tech is going through it now. She's already messaged me with some information about some possible locations, but we all know he's smart and he's managed to stay one step ahead. I've also heard from our coroner, and he has an ID already for the victim. It's Harold Conner. Do you know him? Any relation to you?"

Maya stared at Blake, looking for a change in body

language. Maybe surprise? Did he know his cousin was dead?

"Shit," Blake said, sitting back in his chair and taking a sip of coffee. "Yeah, I know him. That's my cousin. He was on the department with me, but recently he became a deputy up in the county that surrounds our city area."

"Any idea why he'd be here? Why Eric Torres would have shot him?" Josh asked.

"No," Blake said, putting his elbows on the table and leaning forward. "He's my cousin, but I don't know the guy well. It's not like I'm his mother. Not my job to keep track of him."

As Blake continued to lean forward, the air-conditioning kicked on, pushing air toward Maya. She caught a whiff of Blake's aftershave. The smell triggered another memory.

She sat back in her chair thinking about a night about a week before her mother died when a man came over to their house.

Her mother had told her to go play in her room and stay there, but Maya didn't like to be stuck in her room when the adults were allowed to go anywhere they wanted. She'd snuck out and down the hallway. When she was certain that her mom hadn't seen her and was distracted, Maya slipped behind the couch and listened in. She hadn't understood the conversation at the time, but she had smelled the same aftershave.

It was strong, whatever it was.

The man was upsetting her mother, Maya could tell that much. They had argued and then the man had left.

Her mother had turned around and said, "I know you're there, Maya."

Maya was bummed that she'd been caught, but she knew there was no getting out of this.

"Come here," her mother said.

Maya obeyed. She didn't want a time-out.

"Did you understand anything that you heard?"

She shrugged. "Not really."

"We can't talk about this man being here, especially to Nana and Pops, okay?"

"Okay," Maya had said.

A slight headache hit as the memory ended. Maya picked up a piece of paper and jotted down the main points. She stared across at Blake. What did he look like twenty-four years ago? Was he at their house too? Based on what Denise had told her, Blake would be very interested in the missing evidence and her mother.

Blake stared back at Maya, his eyes both haunted and piercing.

She looked away. If only she could remember more. Dr. Meyers had told her fragmented memories were normal for the age she was when the traumatic event happened, but Maya desperately wanted to recall the events of that night. She was the one and only witness. Why couldn't she do better and get justice for her mother and Nana?

Another thought started going through Maya's mind. If Blake was at their house before the murder, then could Eric Torres be telling the truth? Had he been framed for the murders and only there to warn her mother? Maya would give anything to talk with Torres again. Dangerous or not.

"We'll regroup in the morning," Josh said. "I'll get all the information together from Miranda, Lucas and

Doc Clark and put together a report. Then we'll figure out how to find Eric Torres and end this."

Maya had a bad feeling that even if they found Eric Torres, the investigation might be far from over. She had to figure out if her mother's evidence was still out there and locate it.

Chapter Thirty-One

Eric parked his truck near another logging road and studied the map. He couldn't go back to his campsite, and it wasn't like he could stay at the local hotel. He'd probably sleep in his truck tonight or maybe find somewhere that provided shelter in the wilderness, like a cave. Wherever he slept, he was certain that with the events of this morning, his time was limited.

They would go through all of his things and try to figure out his next move. The problem was, Eric was out of next moves and money and everything else, but that had never stopped him in the past. It shouldn't stop him now.

The previous week, he'd stolen some cash from the cab of a Forest Service vehicle and had rationed it out, but what he had left was at the tent along with his food and other supplies. He couldn't go back now.

He had two things in the truck that could be of help—a granola bar and a burner phone.

The granola bar would be dinner. He'd be a little hungry, but it wasn't anything he hadn't done before. How many night shifts had he worked where he didn't even have time to eat dinner?

The burner phone was his one chance to maybe connect with Maya. He'd managed to figure out her phone number. But the big question was, had he established enough trust with her to get her to meet with him?

There was only one way to find out.

Maya followed Josh to his home. Juniper stirred in the back and then popped her head up.

"You feel rested, girly?" Maya asked her. Juniper stuck her head through the door into the cab. Maya scratched behind her ears and Juniper gave her a few licks on the face. "So, here's the deal. We might be staying here a few nights or maybe even longer. Who knows, but you have to be on your best behavior. Okay? No shredding the couch. No pulling branches off trees. No bed stuffing all over the floor. None of that, got it?"

Juniper gave a whine and stuck her head back inside her compartment.

"I know this is hard on you. I miss our cabin too. It's hard on both of us."

Josh stepped out of his vehicle and Maya did the same. She had a small duffel bag with her only belongings. Everything else had burned or been destroyed by the water the firemen used to put out the blaze. She'd need to go shopping in Fort Collins soon and at least buy some essentials. She didn't want to wear her high school clothes all the time. She should also probably get another teddy bear for Juniper. Although Juniper might just rip a new one up.

"You talking to Juniper?" Josh asked.

"I am. Better get used to it," Maya said. "We have some pretty good conversations."

He laughed and said, "Deputy Wilson had an extra dog crate. I had him drop it by before he headed up to watch the crime scene, which may have added to the speed of the gossip. Anyway, I may have never lived with a Malinois, but I have an idea of what it might be like so I asked him if we could borrow it."

"I'll see how she does," Maya said. "The crate may not be bad. I grabbed her bed from the office, but the stuffing is coming out from the holes she chewed. I need to duct tape it some more and probably buy her a new one."

"Stuffing coming out doesn't bother me," Josh said. "Let's get you two inside."

She went to Juniper's door and let her out. She hadn't been over to Josh's place in a while. Because Maya's cabin was set up for Juniper, they usually hung out at her place.

Maya awkwardly climbed the steps with Juniper by her side. *What am I thinking? Is staying here really a good idea? I'm here now, so I better figure it out. I can always stay at the hotel or my office again if this isn't working out.*

She and Juniper stepped inside. The house was about one hundred years old, and Josh had been redoing it on his own in his spare time. He'd started with the major things that older houses needed like updating the plumbing, but Maya hadn't seen it in a while.

He'd redone the floors and finished the sunroom that overlooked some mountain peaks to the west. The kitchen now had new appliances and Josh had painted the cabinets. There were sliding barn doors that were open, revealing the living room. He'd mounted a television on the wall but hadn't gotten around to getting furniture. There was a camping chair in the middle of

the living room with a TV tray next to it. Josh came up
behind her and followed her gaze.

"I have another camping chair, but you may want to
hang out in the sunroom. That furniture is much better. I'm going to get a love seat or couch with my next
paycheck. Sorry."

"No need to apologize," Maya said. "Camping chairs
make great furniture. I mean, they were my porch furniture at the cabin, and I had no plans on upgrading."

"I do admit, I'm looking forward to getting some
more furniture soon. I'd like to be comfortable watching the Chicago Bears."

Maya nodded, her bag still slung over her shoulder.
"The place looks great. I haven't seen it in a while.
You've done an amazing job."

"Thanks, I feel good about it. Gave me a feeling of
accomplishment along with keeping me out of trouble."

"You? Get into trouble? I thought that was just me,"
Maya said.

"True, I think you outdo me."

"Thanks," she said, with a laugh. Unfortunately, she
knew he was probably right.

"If you want, you can put your bag on the guest bed.
I have towels in there and the crate for Juniper. I'll go
out and grab her dog bed. We can put it in the sunroom
and maybe she'll like it there when she's out with you.
The backyard fencing is pretty solid. Deer were coming
in and eating the trees, so I made the fencing higher. I
think it'll work for Juniper, but that's your call. I have
some steaks and potatoes too. Thought I'd throw them
on the grill."

"That all sounds fantastic," Maya said, grateful that

they didn't need to leave again to get dinner. "Thanks for letting us crash here."

"Of course," Josh said, reaching out and touching Maya's cheek. "I'm glad you're here."

She smiled and Josh put his hand back down. Juniper stared up at them and whined. Maya swore the dog rolled her eyes. Juniper loved Josh, but Maya didn't know what she would think about living with him—especially if Juniper thought Josh was getting between her and Maya. This could get interesting.

She and Juniper made their way down the hall to the guest bedroom. Maya put her bag on the bed and took one of the towels. She needed to freshen up. She put Juniper in the crate and took a quick shower before changing into the only other clothes she had with her. After she pulled on a pair of jeans and a T-shirt, she let Juniper out.

Maya figured they could check out the yard and see if the fence would hold Juniper. For a while she probably wouldn't let her out unsupervised. Juniper was good at digging and finding ways to escape. She didn't want to call Todd and explain that Juniper had gone missing while she was staying with the local deputy sheriff. That would only bring on more complications.

They headed out of their room and found Josh out back cooking on the grill on the porch. Maya let Juniper out in the yard to explore and then stood near Josh so they could visit while she kept an eye on her dog.

"I just received an email in regards to the murder of the cops and judge," Josh said. "I haven't looked at the files attached yet. If you want to get on my phone and look at them, go for it. Just don't tell anyone I let you do that."

"More secrets to keep," Maya joked as she picked up his phone. Josh gave her his pass code and she opened the emails. Juniper was running around the yard, exploring and sniffing. She flushed a couple birds out of some bushes, but luckily didn't catch them.

"I was thinking about getting a bird feeder, but maybe with Juniper here, I'll wait," Josh said.

"Probably not a bad idea. And the black bears are still out right now anyway. They're getting closer to hibernating and would probably love to snack on bird food."

"Good point. I'm lucky to have a Forest Service employee here to help me with these things. See, you staying here is already working out," he said, as he checked the potatoes and then threw the steaks on the grill. The sizzling sound made Juniper pause and look their direction.

"Don't even think about stealing our dinner," Maya said to her. "Just keep exploring." To Josh she added, "I'm happy to help."

She scrolled through Josh's email until she found one from the Montana police department that Abigail and Blake worked for. Maya opened the attachments and started reading, but didn't find anything out of the ordinary. The report was pretty straightforward and went through what had happened based on witnesses' testimony when the judge and cops were murdered.

It listed the evidence collected and how fingerprints and DNA left at the scene matched Eric Torres. *Similar to our crimes here. Is that a coincidence?* Maya skimmed through more of the report, but it revealed very little.

"Is there anything that screams that Eric Torres is innocent?" Josh asked, flipping the steaks.

"No, not yet."

She continued reading and then she saw the name of the first officer on scene—Harold Conner—and signature of the detective—Blake Conner.

"I think I just found something."

Chapter Thirty-Two

Maya stared at the phone, rereading the report just to make sure she had the information correct. She thought about her memory of Blake coming to her mother's house a few nights before her murder. Could Blake be in charge of the crime ring? Did he convince his cousin to come after her and set up Eric?

"What is it?" Josh asked, putting the meat and potatoes on a plate.

"The lead detective on this case was Blake Conner. The first officer on scene was his cousin, the person Eric shot today. Along with the information from Denise, I had another memory at the meeting today. I know this sounds weird, but it happened when I smelled Blake's aftershave."

"Let's go inside and eat while you tell me about your memory."

"Okay," Maya said. Juniper was still running around the yard, now pouncing on grasshoppers.

"Leave her," Josh said. "She's good."

"I don't know. I don't think we should leave her unsupervised."

"She's enjoying the yard and we can see her from

the sunroom. Let's sit there and eat. We'll keep an eye on her."

Maya wondered if there was anything in the yard like a hose that Juniper might be inclined to chew up, but decided Josh was right. They could watch Juniper, and it was good for her to run around and relax.

They sat down and Maya told Josh about her memory. She was now certain Blake had been to see her mother before she died. "I think he was lying about not keeping in touch with his cousin too. He's acted suspiciously since he arrived here."

"We could talk to Abigail about him," Josh said. "See what she knows."

"I don't think we should trust anyone from that department," Maya said. "But I also don't think this will all be over even if we do catch Eric Torres. There's this evidence my mother supposedly had. It must be damning if everyone wants it. Maybe we need to focus on finding that."

"Any ideas where it might be?" Josh asked.

Maya shook her head. "I've been thinking about that all day, and I have no idea, but I think Nana must have known. That's probably why their deaths tie together."

"But then why would their deaths be so far apart? Why not kill both of them at the same time?"

"I don't know," Maya said.

"Back to Eric Torres. So maybe he's just a pawn too, but if we can catch him, maybe we can get him to tell us more."

"I agree. You have any ideas on how to find him?" Maya asked.

"None at all. I was trying to make it sound like we had some good leads today, but Miranda called me when we were heading home. They really didn't find anything that would tell us where Torres might be going or staying. That truck is our only lead, so I put out a BOLO on it, but as you know, it's not the big city up here. We'll have two deputies on duty tonight and there's a ton of places he can go hide."

"If we get any leads, we can use Juniper to track him," Maya said.

"I'll let you know if that happens. And hey, I don't have to call you now. I can just come wake you up."

Maya nudged him in the shoulder and said, "Just be careful. I don't wake up well."

"Are you going to shoot me or something?"

"Maybe." Maya laughed and went back to her dinner. *Maybe this whole deal with Josh will work out.* She cut another piece of her steak. "This is really good. So much better than frozen pizza. Thank you."

"You're welcome."

"I'll make you a deal. I'll buy the food, you cook it," she said.

"Deal," Josh said, "but my menu is limited. It's mostly beef."

"Works for me," Maya said. She hesitated and then said, "Have you been able to get to more AA meetings? You told me you were having a hard time. You want to talk about it? I mean, you always listen to me. It's time I return the favor."

Josh shrugged and Maya thought he might not want to discuss things. She understood that. She was about ready to say something when he spoke up.

"This Thanksgiving it will be three years since my partner died. I can't believe how fast time has gone. I also can't believe he's gone and I'm still here. It doesn't seem right. He had a wife and two little kids. I remember watching them struggle with Christmas that year. I tried to help, but I was already spiraling out of control myself."

"I understand," Maya said. "There were so many soldiers killed in Afghanistan who had families and children back home. I always wondered why I lived and they didn't."

"Survivor's guilt, I guess is what it's called," Josh said.

"Yeah, and it sucks."

"A couple weeks ago, I started thinking about how we were heading into the holidays again. They're not that far away. I was wondering how his family was doing. Now that I'm sober and taking care of myself, I thought maybe I should reach out to my partner's wife. See if she needed anything."

Maya nodded. "Did you call her?"

"I did…" Josh trailed off.

"Was she angry with you? Upset?"

"No, actually she was doing really well. The kids, both boys, are doing fantastic. One plays soccer, the other football. School had started and everything was good. Then she told me she remarried one of the guys on the Chicago PD. He's a nice guy, although he wouldn't have anything to do with me after my partner's funeral, but that's the way it goes. I told her congratulations and we left it at that, but when I hung up, I was so angry. I know that's stupid. I should be happy she's moving on with her life and that she's remarried and that the kids have a father, but all these emotions hit. And they hit hard. That's when I walked down to the Black Bear and ordered a beer. I almost called you, but I didn't want to bother you with my troubles. I managed to leave without taking a sip of anything, and I called my sponsor and your grandfather. Your grandfather told me to get to some meetings and get my head back on straight, so I did."

"I'm so sorry," Maya said, reaching over and resting her hand on his arm. "You can always call me. Always."

"Thanks," Josh said. He locked gazes with her.

They leaned over and hesitated. Maya's heart raced as she peered into Josh's eyes. Then they kissed, tentative at first, and then deeper. She put her hands on his chest and then up around his neck, pulling him closer. Josh tenderly cupped the back of her head, drawing her in tighter.

"I could get used to this," Josh said when they broke apart.

Maya stared down at the table and then back at him. "I could too…"

"But?" he prompted.

"You've been there for me in a way that no one else has," Maya said. "I'm so grateful for you, but I still don't know if I'm ready for a serious relationship."

"Why not?"

Maya wanted to come up with her usual lame excuses: She didn't have time. She liked her space and whatever else had come to mind over the years. But with Josh, she felt the need to be honest.

"I had a relationship when I was in the military. I thought he was the one, but it ended because I discovered he was a liar. He had a kid and wife and didn't tell me about it. Not only was I horrified that I was the other woman, but I could have been court-martialed. The military doesn't look very kindly on adultery. I broke it off when I found out. He said he was getting a divorce, but

I swore off relationships—especially with someone I was working with. They get too complicated. Luckily, no one found out and I was deployed, so it worked out. I'm lucky he didn't ruin my career."

"I'm sorry to hear that. You're talking about what it could have done to your career, but you're not mentioning how much it probably broke your heart."

"That too," Maya said, softly. "The only person who knew that part was Nana. I called her crying the night I found out. She talked me through it and said there was someone else for me. Someone special. She was sure of it. Then I met you. But I don't want to mess this up."

"Why would you mess this up?" Josh asked. "Look at the things I've done. If anyone is going to mess this up, it's me."

"I still feel broken. I have flashbacks and nightmares. I wake up screaming sometimes. I had to sleep with the television turned up loud after I returned home. I was stationed out of Bagram, and since that was mainly Air Force, there were jets taking off all hours of the night. You could hear explosives all night long too. I couldn't sleep when it was quiet. That's gotten a little better. Sometimes all I need is the radio. Juniper has learned to live with me, but I figured I was meant to be alone. When you're broken like me, no one wants you."

"You're not broken, and I want to be with you," Josh said. "Plus, I've heard I snore. Maybe that'll be enough noise for you."

She laughed. "Maybe, but let's just take it slow, okay? I'll stay in the guest bedroom and that way I won't keep you awake."

Josh leaned over and gave Maya another kiss. "Just know you can join me anytime you want."

Maya felt her face go red again. "Okay, thanks." She sat back and suddenly realized something. It was quiet. Too quiet. "Crap, we started talking and lost track of Juniper."

She jumped up out of her chair and Josh followed her to the backyard. There were no signs of Juniper. Maya willed herself not to panic. She whistled and hoped the dog would come bounding up to her, but there was still no Juniper.

"The yard goes around to the other side of the house," Josh said.

Maya followed him, hoping Juniper hadn't escaped. They turned the corner and stopped in their tracks.

"Oh no. I'm so sorry," Maya said.

Juniper peeked up at them out of a deep hole she'd dug near the back gate. Maya stepped forward to investigate. Juniper had just about managed to dig under the fence but must have decided she was tired and enjoyed lying in the cool dirt.

"I'll fill it back in and re-sod it. I'm so sorry."

"It's okay," Josh said. "I was thinking about planting a tree there anyway. I think it's a good spot."

"You want a tree near the gate?" Maya said, as she started giggling and then, not being able to hold it in anymore, erupted into laughter.

"Well, maybe there's a better spot we can get Juniper to dig," Josh said, as he started laughing too.

Juniper slunk out of the hole, coming over to Maya and leaning up against her. She rubbed on her dog and told her all was forgiven.

"I guess when we have serious talks, we should kennel her," Josh said. "I don't want to plant too many trees."

"I just hope your house survives us," Maya answered.

Josh's phone rang and he looked at the caller ID. "It's Miranda."

He answered it and walked off a little distance and then started pacing around the yard. A few minutes later, he hung up.

"Did she have some results?" Maya asked.

"Yeah. She did. Are you ready for this? She found more fingerprints on the tree borer. Along with Eric Torres, there were more prints that belonged to Harold Conner. Doc also agreed that the cause of death was stabbing and the tree borer was definitely the murder weapon."

"I'm beginning to wonder if Eric could be telling us some of the truth," Maya said. "I wish we could find him and bring him in for questioning."

"There's more," Josh said.

"What?"

"Miranda managed to collect some of the glass used for the Molotov cocktail. There was a partial print and it looks like it matches Blake Conner. Lucas went to pick him up for questioning, but he's gone. Abigail doesn't know where he is."

"Let's go look for him. Based on the giant hole in your yard, Juniper is ready to work again."

Chapter Thirty-Three

The next morning, Maya woke to the sound of Juniper whining. She rolled over and looked at the clock—0430 in the morning. Even though it was early, she had actually slept pretty well. The bed was comfortable, and she snuggled back under the covers. Maybe Juniper was just dreaming. She'd worked hard tracking last night.

She and Juniper had been tired after helping Josh and Lucas look for Blake. They'd only turned up dead ends and had decided to go home and regroup. Abigail had no idea where Blake might have gone and expressed surprise over his prints being on the Molotov cocktail.

Then she heard another whine. Nope, not dreaming.

Maya pushed back the covers and sat up. The room was pitch-dark, so she turned on a light. Juniper stared at Maya through the crate and wagged her tail, making a thumping sound. Maya was glad that they were in the guest bedroom since Josh might still be asleep.

"Give me just a second," Maya said, trying to find something to wear. She located her jeans and threw back on her T-shirt. Josh had lent her a sweatshirt too, and she pulled that on as well. The morning air was chilly.

Maya let Juniper out of her crate, and they headed to the backyard. This time she would supervise Juniper. No more holes or other damage. She grabbed her phone off the table to check her email while Juniper took care of business.

Juniper scampered around the yard, enjoying stretching her legs and getting some energy out. Maya realized she was technically off today, but she should probably follow up on some of the things on her to-do list, including the booby traps.

She enjoyed watching Juniper play and have fun. No matter where they stayed, Maya would have to get another dog run or something to let Juniper be outside. Maybe there was a spot near the yard for a large dog pen that didn't involve Josh having to redo landscaping.

Maya was enjoying the sunrise and watching Juniper sniff around when her phone buzzed. It was a text from an unknown number.

This is Eric Torres. I would like to speak with you on the phone, but it needs to be somewhere private where your boyfriend can't listen in.

Maya didn't know how to respond. Was this really Eric? Or was this Blake setting up a trap? Of course, if it was Eric, he might also be tricking her. But she could call him if it was on her terms. She typed back:

Give me five minutes. I have a spot I can go, and you can call me.

He responded, Where?

Not information I'm giving out but call me in exactly five minutes.

Maya's phone buzzed again. His response was two letters—OK.

She whistled to Juniper and the dog came running. Obviously, Eric Torres knew where she was staying since he'd mentioned Josh. Five minutes only gave her a certain radius to go, but she would have Juniper with her in case he was nearby. Juniper would warn her.

Juniper followed Maya back inside the house where she grabbed her holster, radio and Glock. She wouldn't be on the phone and be unarmed. Maya put on her work boots and snapped on Juniper's leash, then headed outside. She stopped at her patrol vehicle and grabbed some flex-cuffs. There wasn't a universal key to those and they would make it harder for Torres to escape. There was an aspen grove a little bit down the road. It also sat up on higher ground where she had a better vantage point and cell phone service.

Maya glanced at her watch. She had about thirty seconds to get there before he called. If he was punctual. She had a feeling he was. He came across that way. In an odd way, she felt like she knew Eric Torres. There was a strong pull, like he could answer questions about her mother no one else could. He had arrested Zoey several times and remembered the bracelet. Maybe she could get more information out of him even if it had nothing to do with the case.

Zoey Thompson was like a ghost for Maya. She remembered her mother in flashes and small memories, but in so many ways she didn't know her. Even now, as an adult, she craved information about her mother. Anything that would help Maya remember her better.

Maya and Juniper arrived up on the small ridge in the aspen trees as her phone rang. She answered but didn't say anything. She wanted to see if he was watching her right now. If he would give away anything.

At first there was only silence. Then Eric said, "I want to meet in person. There are things you need to know. I've stayed silent for all these years, but it's time to tell someone the truth. I feel like I can trust you."

"Why me?" Maya asked, thinking that while Eric might trust her, there was no way she trusted him. Juniper sat by her side but didn't react like anyone was coming near them.

"Did you look into the murders of the cops and the judge?"

"Maybe, but you didn't answer my question. Why me?" she asked again.

"What did you find?"

"I'm the one asking the questions," Maya said. She decided to try a different tactic. "How'd you get my number?"

"If you read the reports, you saw what I wanted you to see. Let's meet in person and I'll answer your questions."

Maya sighed. She had to play his game. Juniper was still quiet.

"I saw that Blake Conner signed off on the reports for the murders," she said. "His cousin was the guy in the woods. He was the responding officer. Is Blake a higher-up in this crime ring?"

There was silence. She checked to make sure her phone hadn't dropped the call.

Then Eric spoke again. "Blake Conner signed off on those reports?"

"Yes, isn't that what you wanted me to find?"

"We need to meet as soon as possible," Eric said. "You could be in danger."

"Why are you so concerned about me? Why do you care?"

"Because you're too close to all this and it puts you in danger," Eric said. "I also just want my freedom. I'm tired of being an old man on the run."

"Then meet me at the sheriff's station. Turn yourself in. I'll let the DA know you're cooperating and make sure you stay here in Colorado. I can help you."

"You can't help me, but I can make sure you stay alive and that's what's important to me. Meet me on the edge of town by the Pinecone Junction sign in five minutes. You can bring the dog, but don't tell your boyfriend. Leave him out of this. See you soon. You're already halfway there in those aspen trees."

The phone went dead.

Maya scanned around and strained to see anyone watching, but there were no signs of anyone there. He had to be close, though, and he was letting her know that. Juniper still was relaxed. If he was nearby, he was doing a good job of making sure she didn't catch his scent. Or he could be a good distance away but using a spotting scope.

Maya debated what to do. She should go wake Josh, tell him what happened and then let Eric Torres be arrested at the sign he was talking about. But Torres would see them coming and probably flee.

Knowing that Pops and Josh would be furious with her, Maya sent Josh a text.

I'm sorry. Torres contacted me. I'm going to meet up with him. He's willing to talk to me and give me more information. I think it's better if I go alone. He seems to trust me for some reason. I promise I'll check in

and try to let you know that I'm okay. Keep working
on finding Blake. You and Pops stay safe.

   Maya almost texted I love you, but at the last minute
she hit send without adding that. She could only imagine how much crap she'd hear from Josh and Pops. Probably well deserved, but she had to do this. The truth was
close. She could feel it. And Eric Torres was the key…
she just had to stay alive.

   She shut off her cell phone to make it harder for
someone to track her. She could always turn it back on,
but she didn't want Josh to panic and come after her.
At least not right now.

Chapter Thirty-Four

Maya and Juniper navigated back down the small ridge they were on and walked along the two-lane highway that went to Pinecone Junction. The sign Eric was talking about was about a mile down the road. It was wooden, made from pine beetle kill, and read *Welcome to Pinecone Junction. Elev. 8,523 feet.*

It was a good sign to conceal yourself behind and it was near a trailhead parking area. Would Eric be so bold as to park out in the open when he knew everyone was looking for him? Maya's stomach flip-flopped. She could be walking straight into a trap, but she had to have answers and so far, Eric Torres was the only person who even came close to giving her those.

As she approached the area, she saw a man standing near the sign. It was him. Juniper let out a low growl.

"It's okay, girl," Maya said. "If he tries anything, you can bite him. Otherwise, let's see what he can tell us."

Juniper stopped her growling, but tension vibrated up the leash as they stopped about ten feet away from Eric.

"I'm glad you came," he said. "Glad you're alone too. Well, except for Juniper."

"Quit wasting my time with chitchat. Are you going

to answer my questions or not? If not, then I'm out of here and I'll call the cavalry."

"You do that, and I'll be long gone. You'll never find me. But I don't want that. I'll give you answers. But you have to trust me. We need to go somewhere more secluded."

"What? So you can kill me?" Maya said.

"No, I'm not here to kill you."

"Just be a creepy stalker then?"

"Look," Eric said. "You can handcuff me if it makes you feel better. I promise I'm not here to hurt you. I know you're not going to stop until you get answers, and those answers will get you killed. Trust me. Please."

Maya stayed quiet, uncertain how to answer. She was usually good at verbal judo. She used it all the time in her job to get people to cooperate, but for once she was stumped. She finally pulled out the flex-cuffs and said, "Okay, I'll go with you, but you stay ahead of me, cuffed. Any wrong move and Juniper will bite you."

"Fair enough," Eric said, turning around so Maya could put the cuffs on. When she finished, he started up the trail. "I think I've scouted out a good spot for us to talk."

Maya and Juniper followed Eric as he kept a steady pace on the trail. He didn't speak or try anything, but she didn't let her guard down. She wondered if Josh had received her message by now. Would he forgive her for this? What about Pops? She'd have to work to get their trust back again too.

But if she could get answers and justice for her mother and Nana, then it would be worth it.

Eric took a split in the trail and headed back into a thick grove of trees at the top of a ridge. The trees gave way to an overlook of the road and trailhead where they'd just come from. Maya could see for miles. She was guessing that they were looking northwest at the Snowy Range in Wyoming. The trees, though, gave them good cover. It would be hard for anyone to spot them from the ground or even the sky if a helicopter were to fly over.

"Okay," Maya said. "I've played your game. Now I need you to cooperate."

"Let me start at the beginning," Eric said.

"No, I'm running this interrogation. Not you. Is Blake the head of the crime ring?"

"No, those reports must have been changed, although his cousin, the dirty bastard, was the responding officer at the scene of the murders."

"The reports were changed?"

"Yes," Eric said. "I think Blake is also being framed— at least for this case. Maybe his own cousin did it, but I'm guessing it's the ringleader who's behind this."

"And who's that?" Maya asked.

"Abigail Harper."

Maya stared at Eric, stunned. In some ways it felt like she'd been sucker punched. The evidence had pointed toward Blake and Harold, but nothing had been linked to Abigail. She had trusted Abigail, but maybe everyone involved in this case was manipulative. Maya had to hunt down the truth no matter the consequences. She needed to know more and get justice for her mother and Nana.

She decided to see what Eric told her. Hopefully evidence would either back his story or not, but either way, she needed more information. "Abigail? Seriously? What are you talking about?"

"Think about it, Maya," Eric said. "Abigail was really friendly with you. Knowing her, she asked you questions that seemed empathetic, but in reality, she was trying to see what you knew. She needs information from you and then she'll kill you too. She was the one shooting at you and burning down your cabin. She needed to scare you into action, and you took her bait. She knew you would try to find me."

"I can see your point, but I don't know how Abigail asking me questions would mean she's out to kill me. And evidence is pointing toward Blake burning down my cabin, so how do you explain that?" Maya asked.

"Because despite Abigail being an awful person, she reads people better than anyone I know. She knows you're proud of Juniper and that you work well with the dog and that you wouldn't be able to resist using her to find me. She left my clothing there not only to frame me, but to give you what you needed to track me. We may not be K-9 handlers, but we've worked with enough teams in our careers to have some idea of how dogs work. Blake was with her when your cabin was attacked. She probably made him start the fire and handle the evidence so nothing would lead back to her. I was at your cabin too, trying to figure out how to stop her. I was definitely outgunned. I think she saw me. I took off once I knew you were safe and realized she wasn't going to kill you then. She could have shot you when you came out of the cabin, but she didn't."

"How did she get all this evidence to plant? Like your clothes and your cigarettes?"

"Some clothing went missing out of my personal locker at the department, right before your grandmother died. Along with that, I'll admit that I'm not careful with my cigarettes and leave them in ashtrays in public areas. She could have collected them from any of those areas. After your grandmother's death, I knew I was being framed and went on the run."

"And what about the evidence linking back to Blake? You didn't answer that."

"I don't know. I didn't see him there, but Abigail could have set him up or I may just not have seen him."

Maya absorbed the information. What Eric was saying made sense. But Abigail had said similar things— that Eric was cunning and manipulative. One of them was lying, but Maya didn't know who. All she did know was that she wasn't safe, and neither were Josh or Pops.

Chapter Thirty-Five

Maya stared down Eric, debating everything he'd told her. Some of it seemed true, and it was convenient to find his clothing and cigarettes at the crime scenes. No officer would ever leave behind such obvious evidence. Maya had to be careful he didn't lull her into a false sense of security. He could be telling the truth or he could be setting her up. Maya was relieved to have Juniper on alert next to her to help keep her safe.

"You know, you look just like your mom," Eric said softly.

Maya had so many questions, but she wanted to know more about her mom. "How did you know her? I mean, I know you arrested her—I figured that much out—but it seems like you knew her better than just an arresting officer."

Eric shrugged. "I did arrest her, several times, for prostitution and possession of narcotics. She was heading down a bad road. I just wanted to help her, but then Abigail got to her first."

"What do you mean?" Maya asked. Juniper leaned into her leg, and she reached down and petted her, trying to help calm her nerves.

"I don't know how else to put this…she was a regular."

Maya nodded. They had a few of those in town. They were the people you arrested over and over to the point you knew them on a first-name basis.

"I was trying to help her by convincing her to go back home and finish school. Get herself straightened out and do something with her life. She was so smart, and she was throwing everything away."

"Why did you care so much about her?" Maya asked.

"There's just some people you feel like are meant to be in the system and will live their lives in and out of trouble, but she wasn't like that. Then Abigail arrested her and threatened to pin a murder charge on Zoey. It would have been easy to do as it was a guy who was a regular with the girls. I don't know who actually killed him. Zoey begged and pleaded. She knew she was in serious trouble. Abigail finally agreed to pin it on someone else, but only if Zoey started to help with doing favors. Zoey agreed, and from there on out I was in frequent contact with her since I was blackmailed into helping Abigail at that point."

"Funny," Maya said, "Abigail said you were the one taking all the bribes and doing all this stuff."

"Oh, I was involved. I won't ever say I was a good person—I have a lot of sins to pay for—but I drew the line at things like murder. Bribes were one thing. They helped pay for extra clothes for my kids or a night out with my wife. Murder, that was another thing."

"Glad you had some standards," Maya said, sarcastically. "What happened after my mother started working for Abigail?"

"I think she saw and did things she didn't want to.

Abigail is not a good person. Zoey knew that and realized if she ever wanted out, she needed leverage. I
think there were so many times she wanted to call your
grandparents and just go home, but she knew Abigail
would at the very least drag her back and maybe even
kill her. Then you came along. She loved you so much,
Maya. I've never seen someone so happy to be a mother.
She decided to get herself clean. She didn't want this
life for you, so she continued working on gathering
evidence. She took pictures, recorded conversations,
wrote down notes with names and kept collecting all
of this until she had evidence so airtight that she could
go to the FBI. If she'd done that, this would have all
been over, but because of the people she would have
implicated, Zoey knew she'd probably be in some sort
of witness protection. She'd never see her parents again
and would always be looking over her shoulder, so she
made a deal with Abigail."

"What kind of deal?" Maya asked.

"She told Abigail about the evidence but said it would
remain hidden forever if Abigail let her go home with
you. She just wanted to live in peace. Abigail agreed.
I personally never thought Abigail would let it go, but
for quite a while it seemed like she did. Then things
changed."

"What changed?"

Eric took a deep breath. "A state investigator and FBI
agent caught wind of what was going on in our neck
of the woods. They talked with people and eventually
Zoey's name came out. He called her and asked about
the evidence. Zoey denied knowing anything and Blake
drove down to make sure it would stay that way, but
then she changed her mind. I don't know why. Knowing

her, Blake threatening her would have made her mad and she might have decided to do something about it.

"Zoey might still be alive if she had stayed quiet. Word got back to Abigail, and I overheard her talking about needing to destroy the evidence. She decided she would go visit Zoey and remind her of their deal and get the evidence from her. I knew that meant Zoey was also in danger. And you. I drove to Colorado hoping to get to you and Zoey first, and I did, but she wouldn't believe me. I tried to get her to come with me, but she wouldn't. She didn't trust me, and I didn't blame her."

Maya nodded. That fit her memory from the night her mother died. "I remember you coming to our house that night."

"It was the last time I saw you—until recently."

"If Abigail killed her, why not just shoot her? Why stick her with heroin? It's not like the cause of death was an overdose."

Eric peered out over the ridge. Maya realized he was making sure no one was pulling up.

"That's Abigail for you," he said. "To say she's messed up is an understatement. It was probably her way of showing that in her eyes your mother was nothing more than a drug addict and whore. That she wasn't worth anything to Abigail."

Maya stood trying to stay stoic, but it was hard to imagine someone viewing her mother like that.

"I know it's hard to hear," Eric said, "and I'm sorry. But you wanted the truth and that's the truth."

"You could be making all of this up. You and Abigail tell similar stories about each other. You could be working together. Why should I believe you?"

Eric sighed. "Good question. I want out of this too.

I'm tired of being on the run, although I probably don't have a choice. Maybe I can be a witness and get a deal or something. I don't know. But there's so many people involved, from judges to police officers to lawyers in both the defense and the DA's office. It's crazy. Things are out of control up there. I understand if you don't believe me, but let me give you a little more insight into Abigail. Did she discuss being a female in law enforcement and the glass ceiling and all that stuff?"

Maya sucked in her breath. She didn't mean to give away her answer, but that lunch was one of the reasons she'd trusted Abigail. Even respected her. "She did," Maya finally answered.

"She's not totally lying. Being a female cop in our area when she started was horrible. She was one of two women in the police department at the time. The other one took her own life because things were so horrible. Abigail was raped by her FTO."

"What?" Maya asked. An FTO was a field training officer and someone who should help a young officer, not hurt them. Juniper sensed Maya was upset and shoved her nose into her palm. Maya reached down and petted her.

"Yeah, it was at a party and her FTO came onto her. She played along a little bit, but he took it too far. She tried to do the right thing and report it through the right channels, but she was laughed at and told to quit. She was told that this is why women shouldn't be cops. I have a feeling a similar thing happened to the other female officer, but Abigail was the type of person to wait to get her revenge. And that she did. She killed her FTO in a shootout. Said he got in the way and she nailed him by accident, but I have no doubt it was deliberate.

"By that point she'd started figuring out that it didn't pay to do things by the book. She had blackmail on half the department, including the chief, and she wasn't afraid to use it. Before long, Abigail was the cop people came to for help when they needed something. She's done everything from destroying evidence, to arranging hits, to taking bribes and who knows what else. She was also making good money from her side gigs. Your mother threatened to destroy all of that."

Eric took a deep breath. "Abigail is probably a millionaire by now. She loves the power and she's greedy, and with this evidence out there, she's threatened. When you reopened these cases, she probably thought you had found the evidence. I knew you were in trouble, and I came to help protect you. She knew I would be here and put out as many warrants on me as possible and put my info in the system. You ever wonder how you got a hit so fast in CODIS? That never happens, but Abigail made sure my DNA was there so it would be found. Then she could manipulate you. We need to find that evidence. It's the only way to put an end to this. You need to remember what your mother did with it."

Maya stared at him, so many raw emotions hitting her at once. She didn't know if she should believe a word. It was quite a story Eric had just spun, but if any of it was true, she wasn't the only one in danger—Pops and Josh were too. They were working directly with Abigail to find Blake. That would only push the people Maya cared about in Abigail's direction.

"Do you have any idea where it might be?" Eric asked.

"Why would I remember?" Maya finally said. "I was four years old when my mother was killed. I can barely remember her, much less where she might have hidden evidence."

"We can work together and find it. If we talk more, maybe we can come up with places to look for it."

"Why would I work with you?" Maya asked. "For all I know you're in on it, and even if you aren't, you need that evidence too. It's all that's standing between you and prison."

"True," Eric said. "But I also want Abigail and everyone else involved in these crimes over these years to go away for life. Our town is corrupt because of it."

"My mother is dead because of it," Maya snapped. "You ever think about that?"

"I have. Everything was taken from me too, including my family. My children. I want some of my life back. I want to see my children without them looking at me like I'm a criminal. I have a grandchild I've never seen. My wife divorced me years ago. I have nothing left."

"Except you're a criminal," Maya said. "Maybe that's what you deserve."

Eric shrugged. "Maybe. I've made mistakes, some serious ones. But people can change. I believe that. I want out of all of this. I want to change. I'm not a young man anymore and I'd like to see if I can salvage some sort of relationship with my kids. Let's work together and find this evidence."

Maya stepped away and peered over to the parking area below. There were still no vehicles. She never turned her back to Eric, still not trusting him. If everyone thought that she would know where her mother had hidden things, they were wrong. She had no idea who to trust. Maybe Eric, Abigail and Blake were all working together to find this evidence. This could be the plan they had come up with. Or Eric really could be on his own, but as soon as the evidence was found, he wouldn't need Maya anymore. He might just kill her.

She still had an advantage, though. A weapon that could help keep her safe and maybe keep the bull's-eye on her and off Pops and Josh. That weapon was Juniper. With Juniper by her side, she had backup. Maybe Maya could manipulate things too. What was the saying about keeping your enemies close?

"I'll help you and work with you to try to find this evidence, but if you try anything or do something I don't like, I'll arrest you and take you in. I won't help you get a deal with the prosecutor," Maya said.

"It's a deal," Eric said. "Let's get out of here. We need to keep moving. The longer we stay in one place, the better the odds that either Abigail or Blake will find us."

Chapter Thirty-Six

Maya contemplated everything Eric had told her. All of it seemed surreal, but many of his points fit the evidence and answered her questions. She had a choice—continue on with him or take him in. She had him in cuffs already. What was she waiting for? Maya had to admit she wanted more answers, and for now, she felt safe.

"Before we leave, I'm texting Josh," Maya said. "I'm going to warn him about Abigail and Blake. He can also verify some of your information. I don't want him or Pops getting hurt. I know I'll have a cell phone signal here, so you just need to have some patience."

Maya turned on her phone, while Eric leaned against a tree. Juniper moved so that she was between them, which made Maya feel better. She petted Juniper and praised her while she waited for her phone to turn on. When it did, it started chiming with messages coming in. They were all from Josh.

Most of them said, Where are you? Let me come help you.

Maya felt bad. Hopefully, Josh would forgive her after all this or else her stay at his place really would be short-lived. She typed a quick text trying to fill him in.

Don't trust Abigail either. I'm okay. Keep an eye on Pops and keep him safe. You need to be careful. There's more to this than we realized. Don't worry about me. I have Juniper. I'll be fine.

Maya hit send and then shut her phone back off. Not only did she want to make it more difficult to be tracked, but she didn't know how long she'd be out in the woods. She didn't have a cell phone charger with her and even if she did it wouldn't matter. There was nowhere to plug it in.

"Ready?" Eric asked.

"I am," Maya said.

The trio headed off, and she kept Eric in front of her. No way would she let him get behind her. But at the same time, he could be leading her to a trap. She kept her right hand on her Glock and her left hand on Juniper's leash. Juniper tugged and pulled on the leash in excitement. She was ready to work and do whatever Maya needed her to, which was reassuring. A four-legged backup officer was the best kind, in her opinion.

The trail went back into the woods and wound its way around. Maya thought that if you hiked it long enough, it might end up near her cabin. Maybe that's why Eric knew this trail.

"Where are we going?" she asked.

"I just want to get away from the road. I found a good place to camp last night, and I thought when we got there, we'd sit and chat. Maybe I can help you remember where your mom would have taken the evidence."

Maya shook her head. This guy didn't seem to be getting the point and he made this sound like they were meeting up at a coffee shop for a light conversation. "I told you, I don't remember anything. I was four years old. Do you remember things from when you were four?"

"Probably not. That was a long time ago."

"No kidding," Maya muttered.

"Heard that."

"Glad your hearing is still good," she said. "What makes you think the evidence wasn't burned up by now?"

"Because," Eric said, stopping to catch his breath. "Your mom said she hid it somewhere in the mountains. She told me that the night she died."

"She told you that? Why didn't you say so earlier?"

"She did. I had to know I could trust you before I told you more."

"You were worried about trusting me? And 'somewhere in the mountains' doesn't narrow it down," Maya said. "That gives us an area of millions of acres. I don't suppose she mentioned anything else?"

"No, she didn't." Eric turned around and started hiking again.

Maya realized he was headed back to an area where there were some caves. For all she knew that's where he had set up camp after losing his last camping spot. Sure enough, as they rounded the corner, she saw a large opening to a cave with a fire pit inside and some tree branches spread out. That might have been his bed.

"You sleep here last night?" she asked.

"I did. Wasn't the best night's sleep, but you and your crew sort of took my camping spot and gear."

"Yeah, well, that happens when you shoot people."

"It was in self-defense, you know that."

Maya couldn't argue with that. She'd smashed the guy in the face with her elbow when he tried to grab her.

"Sit down," Eric said, nodding toward a rock.

"What are you going to do? Hypnotize me to help me remember?"

"No," he said. "You know, you really remind me of Zoey. You are definitely her daughter. I mean that in a good way."

Maya didn't know what to say, so she took a seat on the rock. "You don't happen to have any water and a cup, do you? For Juniper?"

Eric surprised her by saying, "I do. Everything is over there in my backpack."

Maya stood and walked over to the bag. She found the water and was glad to see the bottles weren't open. It made her feel better that he wasn't trying to poison them or something. She should have brought her backpack with her supplies, but she didn't realize she'd be trekking back into the woods. She poured water in the bowl and offered it to Juniper, who happily drank it up.

"So," Maya said, "what's your plan? What's next?"

"I want to see if we can brainstorm where your mother may have taken this stuff."

"How much are we talking about?" Maya asked. "Boxes?"

"She had a duffel bag packed full of everything that she collected. A large one."

"Okay," Maya said. "She said the mountains. Did she give you any indication if it was around here?"

"No, but she loved to go camping. It was one of her favorite things to do."

"True." Maya allowed herself to smile at the memory coming back. "We'd just gone camping a few days before she died. We made s'mores. I loved them. Still one of my favorite things to have in the summer."

"See? You have memories from your younger years. Where did you go camping on that trip?"

"I don't remember," Maya said. She started rubbing her necklace. "We lived over on the other side of town, and she rented a house there. After it burned down, the people didn't rebuild it. You don't have to go far from there to access Forest Service land and lots of great camping areas."

"Are they high-traffic camping spots?"

"Yeah," Maya answered, still rubbing her necklace. "They are. The campgrounds often fill up in the summertime too and then less campers as we head into this time of year."

They sat in silence. Maya continued rubbing her necklace until she suddenly dropped her hand. Kendra had commented on her necklace. What if the key was literally the key?

"You look like you remember something," Eric said.

"This necklace. Nana gave it to me, but she said it was a special gift from my mom. I haven't taken it off since Nana gave it to me. Not even in Afghanistan. I always thought it was my good luck charm and kept me safe, but what if it's the key to something that's holding the evidence?"

"You have any ideas of what that might be?" he asked.

"I do," Maya said, standing. Juniper was right by her side. "Come on, let's go. I think I might know where this evidence is stashed, and it's not out in the wilderness."

Chapter Thirty-Seven

Maya made Eric walk in front of her and Juniper again. They had a good hike ahead of them, but they couldn't risk using either of their vehicles and being spotted.

"Mind telling me where we're going?" Eric asked. "And I don't suppose you want to take these flex-cuffs off?"

"To Nana and Pops's ranch, where I grew up, and no, you can leave those on. Makes me feel better."

"Fine," he sighed. "My arms are going numb. Do you think your grandfather was lying about not having the evidence?"

"No," she answered. "I think he was telling the truth, but I think I know what this key goes to, and Pops wouldn't even think about it. The evidence could be stashed inside right under his nose."

"Where are we talking about?" Eric asked.

"I'll tell you when we get there. I don't need you trying to ditch or kill me. If I'm the only one that knows, then I'm safer."

"Still don't trust me?"

"What do you think?" Maya asked. "Take the next left up here. That trail will lead us to the back of Pops's property."

Eric was huffing and puffing a little bit, but Maya wanted to make good time. She glanced at her watch. It was 0830. Pops should be leaving for work in about a half hour unless Josh had called him about her. Then he might have left earlier.

"We're not too far away," Maya said. "Do you need a break?"

"No, I'm good," Eric said. "Just years of smoking have caught up with me. Bad habit, I know."

"It is, but I guess we all have something," she said, thinking about her drinking.

They continued walking in silence for a while. Juniper appeared happy and the day was still cool, so Maya wasn't too worried about her. When they got to the outskirts of Pops's ranch, Maya would get her some more water. She didn't want her getting sick or having a dry nose, making it more difficult to do her job.

"Can I ask you something?" Eric said.

"Maybe. Depends on what it is."

"It's personal, but I want to know you better."

"Why?" Maya said.

Eric shrugged. "I knew Zoey well and saw you when you were a baby. I guess I'm just curious."

"You can ask me, but it doesn't mean I'm going to answer."

"I understand. When I shot Harold Conner, you went over to see if he needed medical attention."

"Right," Maya said, not sure where he was headed with this.

"You went pale. Like you saw a ghost. What happened?"

Maya debated how much she wanted to reveal to Eric. It was only a matter of time before she arrested

him. He thought she was helping and that they were
working together, but she was like him, she supposed.
Once she got what she needed, she was done with him.
She decided to keep her flashbacks to herself.

"Why does it matter?" she asked. "Seeing someone
dead is never easy and Harold did try to grab me, so I
think my reaction is normal. The ranch is about another
half mile. Let's hike in silence."

Much to her relief, Eric did.

They came down a mountainside and Maya could
see the ranch in the distance. From afar it appeared so
peaceful. The barn was older and had been updated
when her grandparents bought it. It had a great hay-
loft that she used to love to escape to, especially in the
summertime.

Two horses, Daisy and Velvet, were out in the pasture. Daisy was retired, but Velvet, Daisy's last foal, was
young and still green. Pops had been trying to convince
Maya to help him get some rides in on Velvet, but so
far, she'd declined. It had been a long time since she had
ridden, and she didn't know if she was up for starting a
young horse. They were often unpredictable. Although
Pops had offered to help her and be her ground person.
He hadn't been able to ride since he injured his leg at
the beginning of the summer.

"The horses are out on the pasture for the day," Maya
said. "That means Pops has just about left or is close to
leaving. He likes to turn them out in the morning before
he heads out so that they can graze all day. Let's wait
here and make sure he's gone."

"Okay," Eric agreed.

Maya didn't like that he was following her plan so
easily. Maybe she should turn her cell phone back on and

let Josh know where she was. She was about ready to do that when Pops's garage door opened, and he pulled out in his patrol vehicle. He headed down his driveway, a swirl of dust behind the SUV. The engine gunned when he reached the road and then he was gone.

"Let's go," Maya said, indicating to Eric that he still needed to stay in front of her. Juniper strained on the leash, ready to go as well.

Eric took the lead and said over his shoulder, "Where should I go?"

"The barn," she said.

As they came out of the tree line, both mares lifted their heads and turned in their direction. They spooked and took off with their tails up in the air. They galloped for a few hundred feet and then turned around, staring and snorting at the odd trio heading their way.

"Let's go a little bit wide," Maya said. "I don't want to scare the horses to the point that they go through a fence. Pops is already going to be mad enough at me."

Eric followed Maya's directions and they made it down onto the property. Guilt washed over her as they walked by the round pen to the front of the barn. Not only was she not keeping Pops up to date on what was going on, but she was going to break into his house as well. Although she knew where the spare key was hidden. Did that count as breaking in?

"Stop here," Maya said. "I need to grab the spare key out of the barn."

"I'll come with you," Eric said.

"No, you won't. Juniper is going to watch and guard you. If you flee, she'll apprehend you. If you come after me, she'll also apprehend you. Got it?"

"Got it."

She turned to her dog and told her to watch and guard. Juniper wagged her tail and then locked her eyes on Eric. Maya knew the dog was secretly hoping he would run. She'd love nothing more than to take a good bite.

Maya headed into the barn. The sweet aroma of fresh-cut hay filled the space. She wasn't sure if it was first cutting or second cutting, but the hay bales that were stored in the extra stall were a lush green. It had been a good hay season this year. She went to the tack room, pausing to make sure she didn't hear Juniper growling or any other indications that she'd latched onto someone.

Maya opened the door to the tack room where the saddles all sat on their racks and the bridles hung in a perfect row. The smell of leather mixed with saddle soap and oil permeated the room. She went to a shelf that had shoeing supplies. Pops didn't do his own farrier work anymore, but he kept extra shoes and nails just in case one of the horses lost a shoe. The nails were in a jar and so was the spare key to the house.

Opening the jar, Maya finagled the key out and went back outside. Juniper was staring at Eric, still hoping he would run. She was like a statue.

"Good girl," Maya praised her. "Relax."

Juniper gave a little whine, obviously disappointed that she didn't get to have any fun. Maya couldn't explain to the dog that sometimes not biting a person was actually a good thing.

"This way," she said, heading to the back door. They climbed up the stairs and Maya pointed at the side of the back porch. "Stand there and don't try anything."

Eric did as he was told, which continued to unsettle

Maya because it meant either he was telling the truth and didn't want to hurt her or he was waiting to get the evidence and would then try something. The back door gave an eerie creak as Maya opened it up.

"You go first," she said to Eric.

He complied again. Maya stepped into the mudroom behind Eric. Juniper was still by her side with her gaze locked onto Eric.

Juniper let out a low growl, feeling Maya's tension. Maya didn't mind that at all.

She said, "Go straight ahead, through the door and take a left. We're headed to the living room."

Eric followed her instructions and they all headed farther into the house. The living room had large picture windows that looked out over the meadow where the horses grazed. They had settled back down and were eating. The mountain peaks sat regally in the distance, a nice clear day in Colorado.

Maya scanned the living room and her eyes landed on what she thought her key belonged to. A large hope chest sat off by a rocking chair. She had sat with Nana as a child in that rocking chair. She'd been consoled there, read to and loved. But it was the chest next to the chair that held Maya's interest. She moved Eric off to the side where she could see him while opening up the wooden chest.

"Stay here," she told him.

"You think everything is in that chest?" Eric asked.

"I don't know."

"You don't know? We hiked all this way, you've kept me cuffed, and you don't know?"

"It's the only thing I can think of," Maya said. "Juniper, watch and guard."

Juniper sat down on her haunches and locked her gaze onto Eric again. Maya could tell she was still hoping Eric would give her an excuse to have some fun and bite.

"She won't just bite me, will she?" Eric asked.

"Don't move and don't stare at her. If you do that, I think you'll be fine."

"So why is this the only thing you can think of for the evidence?" Eric asked.

"When I was growing up, I was fascinated by this chest and what could be inside," Maya answered. "Nana caught me trying to pry it open once with a screwdriver and was furious. Usually when I got in trouble, I could tell it amused her, but this time was different. She sent me to my room and when I came down later, she explained to me that this hope chest had belonged to my mother and was very special to her. I was to never touch it again. I didn't understand because usually Nana was good about showing me things of my mom's. When I moved out and enlisted and had a home on base, I asked Nana if I could have it. A piece of home. But Nana said no. I never understood, but if it's holding the evidence, that could be why."

"Let's see what's in it then," Eric said.

Maya headed over to the wooden chest and first tried to open it without a key. It was definitely locked. For the first time in years, she unclasped the chain around her neck and then put the key in the lock. She started to turn it, and at first it was sticky. Maya fiddled with the key, wondering if she was completely wrong about this whole thing, but then she heard a click.

Chapter Thirty-Eight

Maya's hands shook as the key turned the old lock. She heard a final click and the clasp on the front released. She pulled the key out and put her necklace back on, rubbing it again for good luck.

Taking a deep breath, Maya lifted the lid to the wooden chest. The old hinges creaked and groaned in protest at being moved after all these years.

She stared inside.

Nothing.

There was absolutely nothing except a musty smell.

"Is it there?" Eric inched closer. Juniper growled and stood up.

Maya sat back, disappointment filling her. "No. There's nothing. It's completely empty."

"What?"

"You heard me," she said, standing. "There's nothing in there."

She'd been so certain that the evidence would be there. Why would Nana give her this necklace and be so stern about this hope chest unless there was a good reason? There had to be something Maya was missing.

She crouched back down and felt for panels or any kind of hidden compartment. Even a special button to release. There was nothing. As she pushed on the wood, her fingers grazed a rough spot. She leaned over more and peered inside. There were numbers etched into the bottom. They weren't big, but Maya could make them out.

They were latitude and longitude numbers.

She stood back up and went to find a piece of paper. "Stay here. Don't move. I don't want to have to pry a Malinois off your arm. She's so excited to bite that she probably won't release well."

"What did you find?" Eric asked. "Come on. You can tell me."

Maya ignored Eric and went to the small reading nook off the living room. It had once held all her childhood books and had a window seat where she'd loved to read and dream. Pops now had his desk in there. Maya found a piece of paper and then rummaged through the desk drawers until she found a local map.

She went back into the living room where Eric was looking a little nervous with Juniper guarding him. Maya figured it was good for him. She wrote down the numbers and then unfolded the map. Finding the area where the coordinates matched, Maya saw a familiar area—Deer Valley Pass.

"Son of a…" she muttered. She'd just been up in that area looking for the booby traps.

"What?" Eric asked.

"I don't think we should have been thinking about where my mom stashed the evidence. We should have been thinking about Nana. She loved to camp and would take me every summer up to this area to explore. There's even an old mine we would hike into a little bit. I'm guessing my mom gave the evidence to her for safekeeping and Nana moved it. Wait here, I need to get some supplies together."

"I don't suppose I can get these cuffs off?" Eric asked. "They're not very comfortable."

"We'll see," Maya said.

"What about Juniper? Are you going to call her off?"

"Not until we're ready to go."

"You can trust me, I swear."

"People who swear something like that are usually lying."

She went into the kitchen and grabbed some non-perishable food and water bottles from the cabinets, along with a first aid kit. Maya knew where Pops kept extra backpacks and she snatched one of them, putting everything inside. She opened up the kitchen drawer that held the extra keys and took the set out that went to Pops's old Chevrolet truck. She shoved them in her pocket and went back in the living room, where Juniper remained staring at Eric. Maya swore the dog was grinning as Eric stood there uncomfortably.

"Okay, let's get going," she said. "I think we're getting closer to maybe finding this."

And getting justice for my mother and Nana. I know where you left everything, Nana. Very smart.

"So now where are we going?"

"It's a pretty good distance away from here, so we're going to borrow Pops's truck. Follow me."

"I don't suppose you're going to undo these cuffs?"

"No," Maya said. "I feel better having your hands behind your back, and you owe me after your last escape. Let's go, the truck is parked out under the barn overhang."

They headed out the back door and Maya locked up the

house, now feeling very guilty for not only breaking and entering, but also for stealing Pops's prized possession. He had bought the Chevy when it was brand-new, after coming home from Vietnam. Maya knew he had many great memories with that truck thanks to pictures she'd seen of Pops and Nana's wedding day where they were driving off in it, a happy couple with a bright future ahead of them. How could they have known where life would take them and the ups and downs they would go through?

If anything happened to the truck, Maya would never live it down. Pops hadn't talked to her for several months when she missed Nana's funeral. If she wrecked this truck, it would probably take several more months before he spoke to her again.

Maya unlocked the passenger door. The truck was a single cab and had a bench seat that three people could squeeze into. She told Juniper to hop in first, wanting her in between her and Eric. Eric gave her an unhappy look and then crawled in next to Juniper, his hands still behind his back. Maya didn't know when she'd cut the cuffs off, or if she would. She still didn't know who to believe. The only people she trusted right now were Josh and Pops.

After climbing in the driver's side, Maya fired up the old beast. It started right away. She peered down at the gearshift. It had been a while since she'd driven a manual transmission, but she figured it was like riding a bike. It should come back to her pretty quickly. Pops had taught her how to drive with the manual first. He had said you never knew when you'd have to drive a stick shift and it was a skill everyone should have. Maya was grateful for that now.

She put the truck into first and worked to find the

timing between the gas pedal and releasing the clutch. The truck lurched forward and then smoothed out.

"This is going to be a fun ride," Eric said.

"It could be a little bumpy," Maya said.

She headed down the driveway, hoping that Pops wouldn't come home for any reason, and felt better when she got to the main road and headed west. With the truck it would still take them about thirty minutes to get to Deer Valley Pass. They had time to talk, and Maya had more questions.

"Tell me, if we find the evidence," she said, "what's going to happen to it? Are you going to kill me and take it?"

"I told you, I'm not here to kill you, but I would like to have the evidence and get it into the right hands."

She shifted gears and ground them a little bit but managed to find third and get the truck up to a little higher speed. Juniper stared out the front window, enjoying being next to Maya and not in her special compartment, but every now and then Juniper would glance at Eric. Maya saw him scoot closer to the door.

"By right hands, who do you mean? Do you mean destroy it? Or do you want to use it to buy your ticket to freedom?"

"I'd like to make a deal with the FBI and clear my name of the wrongful charges."

"What about the charges that are true? Will you be willing to pay for those crimes or are you going to try to plead out and cooperate as a witness?"

"I wouldn't mind trying to work out a deal," Eric said. "I'm a cop. I wouldn't survive in prison. We could take bets on how fast I would be shanked or beaten to death."

"And I understand that, but I want justice for everyone who's been harmed in this—especially my mother and grandmother."

He stared out the window and then turned and faced her. "I want justice for them too. I can tell it's eating you up, but no matter what happens, you need to move forward with your life."

"Is that your way of telling me that you're going to make sure I don't get any of the evidence?"

"Maybe," Eric said.

"That actually feels like the truth," Maya said. "And in that case, I'm leaving the cuffs on."

She shifted the truck and pushed down on the accelerator. They had to get to the evidence before anyone else figured out where it was.

Chapter Thirty-Nine

They parked at Deer Valley Pass trailhead. Maya considered hiding the truck in a grove of evergreens, but she didn't want to scratch it up. It wasn't like the old vehicle was in mint condition or anything. In fact, some of the letters to *Chevrolet* were missing and spelled *Chev let* on the back. But she didn't want anything serious to happen like a tree branch falling on it, so she parked in a normal location, risking someone seeing the truck and calling it in to Pops or Josh. Even if that happened, the response time would be a little while, giving Maya, Juniper and Eric a head start on their search.

Maya felt like she was starting to get the answers she needed, except for one thing—who killed Nana and why did they stage it to look like a suicide? It had to have been because of the evidence that was so desperately wanted, but if so, was Eric the killer? Or was it someone like Abigail and Blake? Or were they all in on it together? Was Eric actually at the scene or did someone set him up? If Maya could get a few more answers then as far as she was concerned, Eric Torres could rot in prison along with everyone else involved.

She stepped out of the truck. Juniper stayed put, taking her middle seat duties very seriously and staring at

Eric. Maya walked around and opened Eric's door. Juniper decided to not wait and came flying out, stepping on Eric on the way.

"Thanks a lot," he muttered.

"Guess she didn't want to wait," Maya said.

Eric shuffled his way out and stretched his legs. His arms were probably cramping, but she didn't care. There were ways to slip out of those restraints and he probably knew them. Maya wanted to see if he left them on. If he did, then in her mind, that might mean he was more trustworthy.

"The mine entrance is up the trail about a mile," she said.

They walked in silence and in the usual order—Eric first, followed by Maya and Juniper. The trail came around a bend, and from what she remembered, the mine entrance should have been straight ahead of them. But there was nothing.

She came to a stop and pulled out her map. Eric stopped too and turned around. Juniper kept her eyes on him, still daring him to make a move.

"The entrance should be right here," Maya said. "Just a little way in front of us."

She put the map down and studied the landscape when it finally hit her. A rockslide had come down either in the winter from an avalanche or this spring with the snowmelt runoff. The rocks had cascaded down and covered the mine entrance.

"Looks like there was a rockslide and it covered up the entrance," Maya said. "The evidence could be lost forever if that's where it's at."

"Is there another way in?" Eric asked.

"Possibly," she said, studying her map. "We'll need

to hike up and around to the backside of this mountain to find out. But even if there is another entrance, the mine could be very unstable. I'm not sure it would be safe."

"There's only one way to find out," Eric said. "Let's keep going and check it out."

"Okay," Maya agreed. "But if the mine doesn't look safe, we're not going in there."

He shrugged. "Let's see what we're getting into first."

"The next part of the trail is going to be a bit more difficult."

"That's great," he said, sarcastically. "Having my hands free to help balance would be great too."

"I'll think about it," Maya said, knowing there was no way she was going to let him loose if she could help it. Before they started again, she gave Juniper some water. She took a drink herself and offered some to Eric. Then they were on their way.

The trail started to climb and had more obstacles including rocks and shallow holes. A few times Eric slipped in front of her, but he caught his balance. Maya was beginning to wonder if she maybe should let him go free when she caught sight of something shiny. The sun had glinted just right.

"Stop," she said. "Juniper, sit. Stay."

"What now?" asked Eric.

"Stay where you are. Let me check out the trail ahead of us. Juniper, guard."

Maya stepped by Eric, not happy to have him behind her, but she didn't need a booby trap to go off right now. And at least Juniper was there to help guard him. While the person making them didn't create the deadliest traps in the world, they could still do some serious damage. And she supposed if they caught you in the right spot, they *could* be deadly.

Maya got down on her hands and knees and studied the trip wire. It stretched across the trail, but it also looked like this booby trap was getting more sophisticated. She followed the wire back to the bushes and continued to try to figure out how she could disarm it. She noticed a white card in the bushes that had fallen on the ground. At first, she thought it was a credit card, but when Maya picked it up and brushed it off, she saw it was a student ID. She stuck it in her pocket wondering if the marijuana stash Juniper had found could possibly be from the same person.

At least now she had a good idea who was setting these traps.

"Can we just carefully step over this wire?" Eric asked. "Or is there something I don't know?"

"The person setting these is getting more sophisticated," Maya said. "I wouldn't step over it. There could be another wire or something else that might catch us off guard. It may take me a little bit, but I think I can disarm this."

"I can help if you want," Eric said. "You can tell me what to do."

"No, it's okay, I'll figure it out."

Maya followed the course of the wires. This time, the person had outdone themselves and created several layers, more than just a simple wire to disarm. Maya was glad they'd stopped before they set off the trap.

She was about ready to start disarming the trap, when she heard a rock rolling down the mountainside. Someone was out there. Was it another hiker? Or had someone seen the truck and followed them? Or could it even be the booby-trapper? Maya didn't want to take any chances, so she scrambled back over to Eric.

He'd heard the person too. Maya took him and Juniper and pulled them all behind some bushes as she pulled her gun from its holster. They weren't concealed very well, but it was better than nothing. She didn't hear anything more and was beginning to think she was overreacting. Although Juniper was also tense. She sensed someone there too.

"Quiet," Maya told her dog. She didn't want Juniper to give away their position. Juniper listened, but her ears stayed pointed straight up and she quivered with excitement.

A figure came out of the shadows and around the corner. Maya strained to see who it was. If it was a hiker, she had to warn them about the trap. If it was Abigail or Blake, then the trap might just be the best thing that happened.

Chapter Forty

Still holding her gun, Maya waited, barely breathing. Eric also stayed quiet. Juniper kept her eyes on the trail. The person changed course, stepping off the path and cutting through an area with grass. Maya caught glimpses of someone in dark clothing walking through the trees below them. Were they trying to come around and surprise them?

Eric mouthed, *Cut my arms loose, I can help.*

Maya shook her head. She had no doubt that this could be an ambush and she had Eric under control—for now. There was always a possibility that somehow Eric had gotten a message to Abigail or Blake. They might be here, tracking and hunting them. Maya could at least have the upper hand with Eric if he stayed handcuffed. She stayed low and kept scanning the area where she heard a rock roll down the mountainside.

Suddenly, the sound of a wire snapping echoed off the mountainsides. She heard a cry of pain from the person and then some four-letter words.

She knew that voice.

She stepped out from behind the bush. Juniper was right by her side; she recognized that voice too. Maya debated having Juniper watch and guard, but she figured with Eric cuffed, Juniper could easily catch him.

They headed toward the location of the four-letter words. Maya slipped a little on pine needles that littered the ground as she navigated downhill. She caught a glimpse of a dark blue shirt. The sun gleamed off the person's name tag. She kept her gun drawn just in case he wasn't alone, but when Maya found the victim, it was exactly who she thought it would be.

"What are you doing here?" she asked.

"Trying to help you," Josh said.

Maya holstered her gun and Juniper wagged her tail. Josh sat on the ground, a wooden stake impaled in his thigh. Juniper went over to him and started licking his face.

"Thanks, Juniper," he said.

Fear struck Maya for a moment seeing Josh injured. She couldn't move. The thought that she would lose another person she loved paralyzed her. Then her training overrode her fear and she kicked into action.

Maya crouched down and said, "I don't need saving, but you might with this booby trap stuck in your leg. I thought you were Abigail or Blake coming after us. I could have shot you. Why didn't you stay on the trail? What are you doing here?"

"I thought I heard you and then everything was quiet. I wanted to try a different vantage point and make sure I wasn't walking into a trap in case someone had kidnapped you. Abigail never showed up at the sheriff's office this morning. We can't find her or Blake, so I thought maybe they had taken you along with your felon friend. Son of a bitch, this hurts."

Maya absorbed what Josh had just said. The more

she found out, the more she realized Eric was actually telling the truth.

She inspected where the stake went into Josh's leg. There was a chance that it had gone into his femoral artery. With any luck it hadn't, but she thought he was starting to look pale.

"He's not my friend, but Eric is here. He didn't kidnap me, though. I went with him voluntarily. He has on flex-cuffs, because I didn't know if he might be working with Blake and Abigail too. He swears he isn't…and I can't believe I'm saying this, but I'm starting to believe him," Maya answered. "I'm worried more about you, though. The stake that impaled you could have nicked your femoral artery. How do you feel? Dizzy? Cold?"

"Right now, I'm fine. In fact, I'm pissed off to have wood sticking out of my leg, so I don't think I'm bleeding out or dying anytime soon."

"The stake could be the only thing keeping you from bleeding out."

Maya took off her backpack. She still had the first aid kit in there. She pulled out gauze and wrapped Josh's leg to keep the area around the wound as clean as possible and try to stabilize the stake so it wouldn't move. Then she took out a tourniquet and wrapped it around his leg above the wound. She pulled down hard to make sure it was applied right.

Josh cried out in pain, but Maya knew it had to be tight even if it was painful. If the stake shifted or moved, he could bleed out in minutes. The tourniquet might be all that kept that from happening.

"Sorry about that. I need to borrow your radio and call this in," Maya said.

Josh nodded and she grabbed his mic off his shoulder. She pushed the button, hoping they had radio service. Much to her relief, after calling in, she heard the dispatcher answer.

"This is FS 28," Maya repeated, using her badge number. "I have an officer down and need a helicopter to get him out. He needs immediate medical attention. Best landing zone is near the Deer Valley Trail in the meadow." She let go of the button, waiting.

"You really think I need a medevac?" Josh asked.

"You want to walk out of here?"

"No."

"Then yes, I think you do. It's too far to the trailhead to meet an ambulance. Why didn't you listen to me?" Maya asked, feeling annoyed now. "You wouldn't be in this predicament if you had just stuck to the plan."

"Plan? What plan? I woke up to an empty house and had text messages that you were with a wanted felon. You really think I was just going to go to work and not do anything? Say good morning to your grandfather and tell him that you were with an armed and dangerous man, but it was okay because you texted me that you were fine?"

"You have a point, but I had things under control."

The radio crackled and dispatch got back to Maya, letting her know that they received her message, and they would be sending the chopper in. She broke out in a sweat. This all brought back memories from a few months ago. When she'd helped her friend Doug get into a medevac chopper, it was the last time she saw him. She didn't know what she'd do without Josh.

I really am in love with him. Nothing can happen to him. It would be all my fault.

"Damn it," Maya muttered to herself.

"What?" Josh asked.

"Nothing. I just wish you'd listened to me, that's all. How'd you find me anyway? My phone is off."

"I know," Josh said. "That was annoying. I tried to ping it, but since it was turned off, I knew I would have to contact the phone company, but going through them would take too long."

"I thought you might do something like that, and I didn't want to run down the battery in case I needed it," Maya said.

"I had your messages and I showed Pops. He'd just received a call from his neighbor that after he left, Daisy and Velvet were spooking. The neighbor thought it could be a mountain lion and hiked out to see what was going on. Instead, he saw you and a stranger entering Pops's house and stealing his truck. What we didn't know is if Eric was making you do this or not. We went back to the house and found the hope chest opened up. Your grandfather and I saw the numbers and looked up the coordinates. I told him I would look for you here while he worked on getting some extra deputies to come in and try to find Abigail and Blake."

"And he agreed to that?" Maya said. "I'm surprised that he didn't want to come with you."

"I think he did, but he knows his limitations from his injury. I can walk if you help me a little bit."

Maya heard someone else approaching them and drew her gun. Eric came out from behind the bushes.

"I hate to interrupt this lovers' quarrel, but I'm going to," Eric said. "I've been listening in. We need to get out of here. Your boyfriend may have been followed. Abigail would have been smart enough to do that. Not to mention you just radioed in your location. She would for sure be listening in on the radio chatter. Blake too."

"Great," Josh said, "Advice from the felon."

Maya ignored Josh. She knew Eric was probably right. "I need to get him to where the helicopter will meet us. That's my first priority."

"Then undo my hands and let me help," Eric said, turning around and holding out his hands toward Maya.

"Don't trust him," Josh said.

"I know, but you're a big guy. I don't know if I can get you down the trail by myself."

"I can walk," Josh said, starting to stand. When he was about halfway up, his leg gave out and he sat back down. Juniper went over to him again and started licking his face. Josh ruffled her fur in appreciation.

"Who knows what that stake hit? There's no way you're walking out of here on your own," Maya said. She hated to let Eric be free, but she needed the help. She was strong and she had helped move people in battle, but a big guy like Josh was starting to push her limits. She didn't want to admit that, but she had to. "Juniper is with us. If Eric tries anything, she'll bite him."

Maya pulled her knife out of her backpack and flipped the blade open. She went over to Eric and started cutting the plastic cuffs. They each popped off and Eric moved his arms around, shaking them out.

"That feels a lot better," he said. "Now, let's get your boyfriend to where he can be picked up."

"Stop calling him my boyfriend. To you he's the deputy sheriff of this county," Maya said, feeling annoyed.

"Got it," Eric said, going over to Josh. "Then let's get the deputy sheriff to where he can get medical attention."

Maya and Eric got on each side of Josh and helped get him to his feet. They started the slow descent back down the trail with Juniper by Maya's side. Josh put as much weight as he could on his leg. It took a little bit, but they finally came out of the tree line and back into the open meadow.

Maya could hear the helicopter in the distance, the sound of the blades echoing off the mountains. She and Eric carefully helped Josh sit back down on the ground. Maya took Josh's vitals and checked the tourniquet. Everything seemed to be holding in place and Josh's vitals were good. She was just worried about the stake moving around or coming loose—she didn't want further damage done.

The chopper was getting closer. Eric looked at both Maya and Josh.

"Sorry to do this," he said. "But I'm outta here."

Then he sprinted off.

Juniper was ready to go after him, but Maya called her off. Reluctantly, Juniper listened and came back. Maya praised her. As much as she wanted her dog to go after Eric, she couldn't leave Josh. That would leave him extremely vulnerable. As frustrating as it was, they would track Eric later. Maya figured he would run when the cuffs were off, but she still felt like he had played her. She would figure out how to get him. Someday, she'd be the one to arrest Eric Torres.

"I'm going to kill that guy," Maya said. "This is the second time he's done that to me."

"Is there anyone else out there?" Josh asked, sitting up. "Do you think he set an ambush for us?"

Maya peered around. If there was someone, their best bet would be to come from the direction of the willows that ran alongside a stream. She and Josh were easy targets.

"I don't see anyone," she said.

"We're in the worst place possible—a wide open space," Josh said.

"Next time, don't get hurt and we can stay hidden."

"Next time, wake me up when you decide to run off with a wanted felon," Josh said.

Maya shook her head. "You're infuriating."

"Like you can talk."

"I know," she said. "I'm trying to be better, but I'm not good at relying on others."

"How did that work in the military?"

Maya hesitated. She had to be honest with Josh. "I relied on my Marine brothers and sisters there. A lot of them didn't come home alive. They came home in a C-130 with flags over their caskets. I swore after that I would take care of myself and not put anyone else I cared for in danger. I feel like all I've done is buried friends and loved ones. I thought it would be better to just worry about me. Plus, it's easier to push you away than it is to admit that I love you."

"You love me?"

"Yes. I do…" Maya was quiet for a minute and Juniper gave out a small whine. She reached out and petted Juniper. "I've never felt like this about anyone, but I can't love you."

"Why not?"

"Because I can't lose you too. What if something happens to you?"

Josh reached up and placed his hand on her cheek. She took her hand and covered his.

"You're not going to lose me," he said. "I'll always be here for you."

"Just don't lie to me about that."

"I won't," Josh said.

Maya was about ready to say more when Juniper stood up. She started barking and growling in the direction of the willows.

Chapter Forty-One

Eric fled, running as fast as he could. He looked back over his shoulder, certain that Juniper would be after him, but Maya had called her off. Relief swept over him. Maybe she was starting to trust him. Maybe she was starting to realize that he wasn't here to hurt her, but he desperately needed that evidence.

After listening to Josh, though, he knew that Abigail and Blake wouldn't be far away. They might even be here. Maya, Juniper and Josh would be sitting ducks at their location. Eric didn't think that Abigail would shoot down a helicopter, although who knew. She'd become desperate and had done things that shocked even him. If she thought making a helicopter crash would give her a chance to find the evidence first and get away, she might just do it.

Eric made it across the meadow to the willows that ran along a creek. Even though it was September, the bugs were still out and as he approached the water, mosquitoes started buzzing him. He swatted at them but knew he'd have to tune them out. It didn't matter how many swarmed him.

Abigail was somewhere around here. She had to be. Eric needed to stay hidden but flush her out. How he was going to do that was beyond him. He had to think like her.

As he went along the creek bed, trying to stay out of the water, he hoped he wouldn't run into any moose that might be bedded down for the afternoon. That would be his luck and make the mosquitoes swarming him seem like nothing.

The creek curved around, and as Eric came around a small bend, he saw someone downstream about fifty yards hiding in the bushes.

Blake Conner.

Maya pulled her Glock and Josh pulled his Sig Sauer. She held onto Juniper's leash, since she didn't know what Juniper was barking and growling at. Moose often hung out in the willows, and while they were beautiful animals, they had a habit of charging. A bull moose had even killed a resident in Pinecone Junction last year near downtown. The last thing Maya needed was Juniper tangling with a moose. Then they'd all need the medevac chopper. Not to mention their pistols would only piss a moose off.

Juniper continued to lunge and hit the leash as Maya tried to stay as low as possible. While they didn't have anything to hide behind like a boulder or a bush, the grass was tall from the summer rain and helped hide them a little bit. She strained to see why Juniper was barking.

The willows started to sway and move. Out came Blake Conner, gun drawn. He was scanning the meadow in front of him. Maya knew it would only take seconds before he located them with Juniper barking.

"Quiet. Down," Maya said.

Juniper looked like she wanted to argue and then, much to Maya's relief, she dropped to the ground. It was too late, though. Blake had seen them, and he had a clear shot. The only saving grace was that he had a handgun and the range was too far away, but with Josh's injury, there was no way they could move and get to cover.

"You and Juniper need to get out of here," Josh said. "Leave me. I'll take care of myself."

"I'm not leaving you," Maya said.

The sound of the chopper echoing off the mountains grew louder and louder. They were getting closer. Maya didn't want more casualties. She might have to call dispatch and tell them to have the chopper wait. She peered through the grass again. Blake was headed her way. She had to react.

"Hang on to her leash unless you hear a gunshot. Then let go," Maya told Josh.

She leapt to her feet. Juniper followed suit, right by Maya's side.

Josh grabbed the leash and followed Maya's order. She held her gun straight out in front of her in a high ready position, ready to fire.

Maya's finger remained on the side of her gun, like she had been taught. You didn't put it on the trigger until you were certain you were going to pull it. Blake kept coming their way, his gun aimed at them. He hadn't fired either. He wasn't new to firearms; he knew he didn't have a good shot, but he had probably heard the call over the radio to dispatch and understood that Josh was injured and not able to move fast. She and Juniper had to stop him.

"Stop and put your weapon down," Maya yelled. "Or I'll send the dog."

Blake only smiled and kept coming toward them. Maya took a deep breath.

"If he comes any closer, take him out," Josh said.

"I will. I'm going to give him one more chance." She yelled out her instructions again for Blake to drop the weapon. He continued forward, closing the gap fast.

She moved her finger to the trigger, pulling it halfway back when Blake dropped to the ground. She took her finger off the trigger in surprise. The rifle shot echoed off the mountains as the sound traveled slower than the bullet. Maya turned toward the boom of the rifle and then dropped down to the ground. Josh clung to Juniper, who had heard the shot and was ready to go bite someone.

"Juniper, down," Maya said.

Juniper dropped down. Her golden eyes stared at Maya, begging to do her job.

"Where the hell did that rifle shot come from?" Josh asked.

"I don't know," Maya said. "But that's not good. That rifle has a better range, and I don't know if the shooter would take out the medevac or not. I wish I had binoculars so I could see who's out there and their location."

The sound of chopper blades cutting through the mountain air came closer. Maya could see the helicopter as it popped up over the tree line. The pilot would be looking for them and with the way they were on the ground, it would make it harder to spot them.

Maya strained, trying to see who was out there. She finally saw a person coming down the hill in their direction, holding a long gun.

Abigail.

Since she'd shot Blake, Maya guessed that it meant Abigail was at a breaking point. She needed to get rid of everyone who could be a witness against her. Did that include Eric? Maya had begun to believe him, but she still thought there was a possibility that he and Abigail were working together.

"Can you see who it is?" Josh asked, unable to turn because of his injury.

"It's Abigail. She took out Blake."

"Does she know we're here?"

"I don't know," Maya said, her words lost by the noise of the chopper.

The grass was now starting to flatten down from the wind created by the helicopter. Sticks and dirt scattered and blew around. Maya had to either help the pilot land or get them to leave. She saw Abigail stop on the hill and aim the rifle toward the helicopter. Maya was about ready to stand up and wave the pilot off when she saw Eric come flying out of the willows near Abigail. He tackled her and pushed her to the ground.

They rolled around, each trying to gain control, and then Abigail managed to punch Eric in the face. She stood and took off towards the tree line, with Eric in pursuit.

"What's happening?" Josh yelled over the sound of the helicopter.

"Eric surprised Abigail and they fought each other. She got away and took off."

"Take Juniper and go after them," Josh said. "Backup should be here any minute. Deputy Wilson was only a few miles away."

"I'm going to stay with you until I know you're safely out of here," Maya yelled back.

Juniper lay down and flattened her ears. Maya knew the last time a medevac chopper had landed, Juniper had been injured and was airlifted out. She was probably worried the same thing was happening today. Maya petted her and reassured her that they were okay. Then she stood and waved at the pilot. He saw her and placed the skids down on the ground.

Two flight nurses came out of the helicopter with a carry litter for Josh. Before they reached them, Maya leaned over and gave Josh a slow, tender kiss. "You better be okay," she said.

"I'll be fine." The flight nurses arrived and went to work lifting Josh on the litter and starting an IV. Before they picked him up, he reached out and took Maya's hand. "I love you too," Josh said. "I didn't know if you felt the same way, but we'll talk more, after you catch Eric and Abigail. You just come home, got it?"

Maya hesitated, not really sure how to answer, and then she said, "Got it. And always. I'll always come home."

"Find those two and make them pay for what they've done."

"You know it," she said.

The nurses loaded Josh in the chopper and closed the doors. Maya stood back so that she didn't have debris thrown at her from the downwash.

The bird lifted off and she felt like she could breathe again when it flew over the trees, out of sight and danger from a rifle shot. As the noise of the helicopter dissipated, she turned and stared in the direction of where Eric had tackled Abigail.

There were no signs of them.

Maya looked down at Juniper. "You ready to find some bad guys? Maybe this time I won't have to call you off a bite."

Juniper wagged her tail and started dancing up and down with her front paws.

"Let's go do this," Maya said.

Chapter Forty-Two

Maya was ready to head in the direction Eric and Abigail had fled after their fight, but she realized that Blake's body was still over near the willow bushes. She needed to check on him and make sure he really was deceased. If he wasn't, she'd have to get more medical help. Although from what Maya saw, the shot was good.

Juniper followed Maya and changed direction toward Blake. When they were near, Juniper stuck her nose up in the air, taking in the scent. She wasn't trained to find human remains, but that didn't mean the dog didn't smell the change in odor.

Blake was lying in the grass, his face pale, and his eyes had no life in them. The rifle was a large caliber and he probably hadn't felt a thing once the bullet hit him. The shot was spot on target wise, center mass like all law enforcement was taught. If you hit someone in the central nervous system, they were dead. Maya took note of that. She had to be careful with Abigail.

Checking for a pulse, she confirmed that Blake was deceased. They would have to come back for him later. Right now, the two people who could answer her questions about her mother and grandmother were on the run.

Maya wanted to catch up with them. The odor would

be fresh, and the day was still with very little wind—ideal conditions for Juniper to track.

"Okay, girl," Maya said. "This is what you've been waiting for. Let's go. Go find 'em."

Juniper's eyes locked with her for a moment. Maya swore Juniper smiled and then she put her nose down and started working. Maya only had a rough estimate of where Abigail and Eric had fought since she'd watched from a distance.

Since the day was still with no wind, they might have to get closer to the source of the odor for Juniper to catch the scents of Eric and Abigail. There was a chance Juniper would remember Eric's scent too. Maya stayed out of her way and let the dog work.

Juniper paused and stuck her nose down into the dirt. Excitement rose in Maya as she watched her dog work back and forth, pinpointing the scent exactly. Maya was ready when Juniper took off.

The track was on.

Maya pushed herself to keep up with Juniper, but the track didn't stay on a trail. Rather, it went through rough terrain. She slipped a few times but managed to catch her balance. There were fallen trees and rocks, but Juniper navigated through them, and Maya did the same.

Eventually, she realized they were heading back to the trail where the booby trap had been. She hoped they wouldn't run into any more issues with the traps, but it went both ways—a booby trap could get Abigail and Eric too.

They arrived back on the trail and Juniper slowed, air scenting for a moment and then taking off again. She had her head down, following the footsteps with her nose. Juniper never wavered and they went past the point where Josh had been injured. Maya pushed thoughts of Josh out of her head. She couldn't get distracted right now, but she also didn't know what she'd do if she lost him.

The trail dipped and went up and down. Maya vaguely remembered hiking back in here with Nana. If she remembered right, the path would eventually lead to a clearing with a waterfall that probably was part of the water source for the creek along the willows.

Feeling her chest tighten from the exertion of running with Juniper, Maya gulped in air. Juniper, on the other hand, seemed just fine and wasn't slowing down. They jogged on for what seemed like forever when Juniper slowed and lifted her head. The clearing should be just around the next bend. Juniper air scented and gave a low, guttural growl.

Maya shortened the leash and stood next to her dog, catching her breath. Based on Juniper's reaction, they would need to proceed with caution.

"Okay, let's go find 'em," Maya said, releasing slack in the leash.

They moved forward, and as they came around the turn, Maya saw Eric and Abigail facing each other in a standoff.

Eric had his gun drawn and had possession of Abigail's rifle. He may have grabbed it when they were fighting, but now he held the gun steady and was calm and cool. Maya didn't know if that was good or bad.

Abigail's face was bloodied and bruised. Eric was yelling at Abigail, but Maya couldn't make out what he was saying. She needed to better assess the situation before she let Juniper go. Juniper could only apprehend one person and Maya could take the other, but she had to plan it carefully.

She would like to have both Eric and Abigail alive so that she had a better chance of figuring out the truth about Nana's and her mother's deaths.

"Quiet," Maya whispered to Juniper, using the command for her dog to go stealth. She had trained different scenarios with Juniper, including keeping her quiet so they could have an easier time sneaking up on someone.

They slipped behind some large fir trees that provided good cover closer to Eric and Abigail. It gave Maya a better chance to listen. She pulled out her phone, turning it on. She hoped she'd left it in silent mode so that it wouldn't make any noise. Much to her relief, it was quiet. Maya pressed the app for the voice recorder and hit record, hoping the phone would work at this distance. The more evidence she had to put Eric and Abigail away for their crimes, the better. Maya carefully put her arm through the branches and found a good spot on the fir tree where the phone could sit and record.

"Admit it," Eric said, his gun straight out in front of him pointed directly at Abigail. "Admit that you framed me for the murders. That you're dirty."

Abigail laughed. "Why? Why admit it out here? There're only trees as your witness. Plus no one will believe you. You're as dirty as me."

"Maybe I am, but there is a difference. I have a conscience and I want to hear you say it for once in your life."

"Do you? You were doing corrupt shit before I was. I just figured out how to work the system better than you. You're jealous," Abigail said.

"No, I'm not jealous. I just finally want to move on

with my life. I don't want to look over my shoulder all the time and wonder if I'm going to get gunned down because I know too much or didn't do what some judge or lawyer wanted me to do so they could make more money. I want out of this mess and your confession is one step towards that."

"My confession is nothing," Abigail said, "but if it makes you feel better, then hell yeah, I framed you for murdering those asshole cops and that judge. You feel better now?"

Maya leaned back against another tree. She had one answer now. Juniper looked up at her, wanting to know if she should wait. Maya used her hand command, asking the dog to stay. Juniper went back to staring through the trees.

"So," Abigail said, "you know where that stupid whore stashed the evidence?"

Anger flashed through Maya at hearing someone refer to her mother that way, but she pushed it down.

I have to stay calm, wait this out and find the right moment to make my move. You're a Marine. Act like it. Use your head and your training.

Maya went back to listening. Eric had a pretty good idea where the evidence was, but would he tell Abigail?

"Maybe I do, maybe I don't," Eric answered.

"I'll kill you," Abigail spat back at him.

"Go ahead. Then you'll never know where the evidence is stashed. You can keep killing people, but until that evidence is gone, you'll never be free," Eric said. "But I guess if I'm going to serve life in prison for murder, then what's one more?"

"What do you mean?" Abigail asked.

"I mean I'm done with this. With you. I'm tired of

you and I'm ready to end this," Eric said, moving his finger to the trigger.

Maya couldn't let him kill Abigail. Not until she knew exactly what had happened to her mother and grandmother. She rushed out from behind the tree. Juniper flew out in front of her, and Maya yelled, "Drop the gun!"

Eric turned, surprise showing on his face.

"Don't do it," Maya pleaded. She kept an eye on Abigail, not trusting her. "I need to know more. I have questions I need her to answer. Please don't shoot her."

Abigail smiled, and Maya could see she was missing some teeth. Eric must have caught her with his fists at some point, but he also had scratches and a black eye starting to form. Abigail wouldn't go down without a fight.

"Officer Thompson," she said. "I'm so glad you're here. Please tell this psycho to put his gun down."

"I heard everything," Maya said. "I heard what you said, so don't try to play games. Juniper hasn't had a bite for a while. She's itching for one."

"So scary," Abigail said. Her eyes darkened and even though she smiled, this time it wasn't friendly. Her pleasant demeanor was replaced with coldness.

Maya turned back to Eric. "Please don't shoot her. Let me arrest her and have her pay for her crimes. I heard everything. I'll testify on your behalf. I promise."

Eric's eyes flicked back and forth between Maya and Abigail.

"Fine," he said, lowering the gun.

Chapter Forty-Three

Relief swept over Maya when Eric put his gun in a low ready position. She still needed him to set it all the way down.

"Place your gun on the ground," Maya said.

"I'd rather keep it until you have her in cuffs. I don't trust her, and neither should you," he said.

"You two know I'm here? I can hear you," Abigail piped up. "Come and get me, Maya, I'm ready to turn myself in."

Maya knew better than to trust either of them, but at this point, if she was going to place trust in one over the other, it was now Eric.

"I don't want to approach her with my back to you while you're still holding a gun," Maya said. "Please put it down."

Eric hesitated and then slowly set his gun on the ground. "Okay, I understand, but watch yourself."

Juniper stayed by Maya's side, and she unclipped the leash. Juniper was her best bet for backup and protection. Maya turned her attention to Abigail. "I need you to put your hands behind your head."

"You think I don't know the drill? I've been doing this job since before you were born. Yeah, I've done things I shouldn't have, but I paved the way so little snots like you could have things easier. You should be thanking me, not arresting me."

Maya took a deep breath. Abigail wasn't going to make this easy. "I appreciate what you've done, but we need to end this now."

"You don't have any idea what 'this' is. You think this ends with me? Think again," Abigail said. "You're just like your stupid mother, who was nothing better than a low-life drug addict. You're no better than her."

"You're right. I am just like my mother because we're both resilient," Maya said, still working on approaching Abigail so she could get a handhold on her and cuff her. "My mother was strong. She overcame her addiction and she gathered evidence that will put you away for life. She was smart and kind. She was raising me as a young single mother, so if I'm like her, then I'm good with that. It's a compliment."

Maya stepped toward Abigail. Juniper stayed with her, her eyes locked on Abigail, waiting for her to make a move against her handler.

"When I killed your mother, I enjoyed every minute of it. I was even kind. I gave her what she wanted, one last high on her way out. I could see it in her eyes, she loved it when I shot her up with heroin."

Maya hoped her phone was still recording. She worked to detach herself from what Abigail was saying, but it felt like she was getting stabbed and old wounds were ripping open. She was getting her answers, but also paying a price. Maya had to keep Abigail talking.

"You're wrong about my mother enjoying the heroin," Maya said. "I was there, remember? You failed. You couldn't find me, and you couldn't kill me because you're worthless too. I was hidden right in front of you. You opened the closet door, but you didn't see me, but I remember my mother fighting you every step of the way. She fought to stay alive, and you had to give her heroin to subdue her. She didn't want it and she certainly didn't enjoy it. She just knew she had to sacrifice herself for me. She's nothing like you," Maya said, glancing to see what Eric was doing.

He had stayed in place and was listening in. She could tell that given the right moment, he would go after the gun again. Could she trust him or was this an ambush? She hoped she could rely on him, but she had to get Abigail under control. She needed some more answers.

"So why did you kill my grandmother so many years later?" Maya asked. This was her chance to get a confession.

"What makes you think I did that?" Abigail said.

"Don't you want to take credit for it? Another notch in your belt?"

Abigail laughed. "Once you were grown up, your grandmother was sticking her nose into places it didn't belong. Imagine my surprise when I heard that she was cooperating with an FBI agent in the Montana office about evidence her daughter had that could blow open that asshole's investigation."

"So you killed her and made it look like a suicide?"

"Why not? It's fun to be creative killing people. With your mother's death I didn't have to be so imaginative. She had a history that would make investigators think her addiction caught up with her. You know how it is. If it's a prostitute and drug addict that dies, no one gives a shit, but an elderly lady who goes to the town sewing circle and is the sheriff's wife? That would make people investigate more. I couldn't have that. Suicide made more sense. I even made her write her own note. She made me swear I wouldn't hurt you if she cooperated. I let her believe that. The FBI agent was a problem, but funny thing happened. His brakes failed driving here as he came over a mountain pass. Drove off the road and down a steep embankment. He didn't make it. Too bad."

Maya started shaking. Nana had tried to protect her 'til the end. Nana had always promised she would keep Maya safe. If only she had been home, maybe she could have done something. Maybe she could have saved Nana. Maya didn't know about the FBI agent, but that had to have been what triggered Nana to move the evidence from the hope chest.

Stay in the zone, soldier. You can do this. As hard as it is, get the answers. Get justice.

"I suppose that makes sense," Maya said, trying to play along and shove down emotions. "You screwed up, though. You used the same gun on Nana that you used on my mother."

"Did I screw up? From what I remember, the investigators suspected your grandmother killed your mother and then couldn't live with it. I may have helped them think about it that way. They called me to get some files on your mother. I was able to help them focus their investigation. Case closed. Everything was perfect until you had to go and stick your nose into things."

"No," Maya said, stepping up to Abigail. "Everything wasn't perfect for you because my mother had given the evidence to my grandmother for safekeeping. And when that FBI agent died on his way here because his brakes failed on a mountain pass, my grandmother knew what you needed, and she took it from you. You'll never get that evidence. It's over—put your hands behind your head and get down on your knees."

Abigail smiled at Maya. "I'll never surrender."

"Maya!" Eric yelled as Abigail pulled out a knife she'd hidden in her palm. Abigail drew her arm back, ready to slice at Maya's neck, when Maya saw brown fur fly by her face.

Juniper latched onto Abigail's arm and shook it, knocking her down to the ground. Maya rushed in to help her dog, who had a great grip with her back teeth. Nothing was going to get her dog off Abigail. Juniper had been waiting all day for this.

Abigail tried to stab Juniper, but Maya blocked her and grabbed Abigail's arm, twisting it so that she had to drop the knife. Eric jumped in and helped Maya pin down Abigail's arm. Juniper pulled and shook Abigail with her whole body.

Abigail went limp. Juniper had managed to shake her so hard that Abigail had hit her head on a rock and was knocked out cold. The knife fell out of her hand and Maya grabbed it. Juniper continued to shake and bite.

"Good girl," Maya praised.

"If you call off your dog, I'll help you cuff her," Eric said, stepping back before Juniper decided he was next.

Maya nodded and told Juniper to release. Juniper rolled her eyes toward Maya, not wanting to let go.

"It's okay, girl," Maya said. "Out."

Juniper finally came off the bite but stayed over Abigail, ready to strike again. Maya and Eric rolled her over and put cuffs on her. Maya picked up the knife and thought about everything that Abigail had said about her mother.

She fingered the knife, knowing from her training in the Marines that if she stabbed Abigail in the right place, she could kill her instantly. Or she could just slit her throat. It wouldn't bring back Nana and her mother, but it might make her feel better. At the very least, it's what Abigail deserved. Her hand started shaking.

"Don't do it," Eric said. "Put the knife down."

Maya continued trembling, wanting nothing more than to stab Abigail over and over. She wanted to make Abigail pay for all the pain she'd caused. Her grandmother and mother had given their own lives to protect Maya. It seemed only fair to end this by killing Abigail.

"Maya, you're better than this," Eric said. "This isn't you. You're not like me and you're especially not like Abigail, but if you do this, then she wins."

Tears started streaming down Maya's face. "She took everything from me. Everything. I've waited for this moment my whole life. I was a scared kid when she took my mother, but I'm not a scared little girl anymore."

"I know," Eric said. "You're amazing and strong. You're nothing like her and she'll pay for it in prison. She's screwed over so many people that there will be a lineup of prisoners waiting for her. Even though she'll be kept in isolation, at some point they'll get their revenge and it'll be worse than anything you could do to her. Please, give me the knife."

Maya knew he was right. Killing Abigail wasn't what Nana or her mother would want. But she wasn't going to hand the knife to Eric. Not until he explained a few things. Maya took some deep breaths and Juniper came over, pushing into her leg. Somehow Juniper always knew how to help Maya calm her emotions.

"I'm not giving you anything yet. I still need some

answers from you," she said, stepping away from Abigail before she was tempted again to do something rash.

"What do you want to know?" he asked.

"I know Abigail planted evidence, but I also know you were there the night my mother died. And probably when Nana died too. Why were you there? Why didn't you stop Abigail? You're just as guilty as her."

Chapter Forty-Four

Eric went over to a rock, sat down and put his head in his hands, rubbing his face. Maya thought he had aged right in front of her. The arrogant man who had led her on chases through the forest and messed with her was no longer there. Instead, he was just someone who looked defeated.

"Tell me the truth. Please," she pleaded. "I understand everything else. I believe you about Abigail, but I don't understand you. You were watching me. You could have killed me, but you didn't. What's the deal with you?"

"There's more to the story," Eric finally said. "First, I need to know, are you going to arrest me too?"

"Yes," Maya said. "You're still a wanted felon. I can help clear you of the murders, but there's other crimes you should do time for."

Eric stood back up and took in the waterfall. "I know I should go to prison. I understand where you're coming from, but if I serve time, there's no one to protect you."

"Protect me? Why would I need that?"

Eric sat back down. "When your mother decided she wanted to go home, she made a deal with Abigail and made me swear that I would protect you if anything happened to her. I agreed and then helped her buy a bus ticket so she could take you home. But as you know, Abigail killed Zoey and she wants to kill you too."

"We have Abigail handcuffed, though. She's going to prison, so I don't need your help."

"Abigail still has her loyal people and she could easily talk her way out of prison, especially with the lawyers she knows. You may never be out of danger and I'll certainly be killed if I go to prison."

"I just… I don't know what to say. I still don't understand why you didn't try to stop Abigail. Why didn't you keep her from killing my mother and Nana?"

"I wish I *had*. If I could go back in time, I would," Eric said. "I showed up at your house that night because I was under the illusion that I could convince your mom to come with me. I realized she was in danger on her own and I thought I could help her. I told her Abigail was coming for her. Zoey talked to the wrong people and didn't keep her end of the bargain, but she wouldn't listen. She believed that she could still get Abigail and the others arrested and stay safe. I came back later to try again to convince her to leave and saw the house in flames and I knew I was too late. I saw you sitting with your grandfather. You were wrapped in a blanket and snuggled up with him. I knew you'd be okay and that I'd held up my promise to protect you, so I went home."

Stunned, Maya didn't know what to say. His story matched her memories. She remembered hearing her mother yelling that she wasn't going with him. Maya had been too young to understand.

"What about Nana?" she asked. "How did she get caught up in this so many years later?"

"Your grandmother called me out of the blue. I was

still working at the department. I couldn't leave because Abigail had blackmail on me too. When your grandmother called, I was shocked. She told me that Zoey had confided in her and told her everything about what happened up in Montana. That she and her husband had raised you and you were a Marine and deployed to Afghanistan. She said she'd read an article in the paper about a couple agents with the FBI and some other agencies that were looking into the corruption in our town from the police force on up to the judges. She told me that she had the evidence from Zoey. You were safe in Afghanistan, at least from all of this, and she wanted to do something with what Zoey had gathered. I agreed to meet with her, get the evidence and take it to the right people. I didn't want her involved."

"Then what happened?" Maya asked.

"It was my fault. I can't even say how sorry I am," Eric said, staring at the ground. "I made the mistake of talking where someone overheard me. I'm sure whoever it was ran as fast as they could and told Abigail. I arrived that night and waited out by the trees like your grandmother told me to. She didn't show, so I finally went to the house. Knocked on the door. No answer. I went inside and saw her. I knew then that I would be framed for her murder too. I'm so sorry. Maybe if I had stayed this would all be over."

"Or maybe you'd also be dead," Maya said.

"Maybe, but I went back to my job and pretended that nothing had happened. Then I heard about a year later that Zoey's case and your grandmother's case had been reopened. There were DNA samples being run. I knew I had to leave and come here and protect you.

I'd failed Zoey and your Nana, but I wasn't going to let Abigail hurt you."

"How did you find out that I'd sent in the DNA?" she asked.

"I still have a couple of reliable contacts in the department. They called me."

"What about Kendra?"

"What about her?"

"Did you kill her?" Maya asked.

"No, I didn't. She was working for Abigail and was supposed to get close to you and gather information. I think as she got to know you, she felt guilty about everything she was doing. She started to realize you were kind of a friend. I was trying to get her to give me information, and I thought I could force her into it, but realized I was crossing a line I didn't want to. When I left her, she was alive. I'm guessing Abigail, Blake or Harold found her."

"We tried to find her family to notify them and couldn't locate anyone. Her father was killed in prison. Do you know of anyone?"

"No." Eric shook his head. "That's why she was in the system and perfect for Abigail to control. I thought when she joined the Air Force she was going to get out of our town and out of Abigail's reach, but when she discharged, unfortunately she came back home. Abigail found her right away."

"Thank you," Maya said.

"For what?" he asked.

"For telling me the truth. For the first time in my life everything that happened makes sense."

Juniper's ears perked up and she turned and faced the trail. There were sirens in the distance.

"My backup is finally here. He was supposed to be here a while ago. New guy, maybe he got lost," Maya said.

"Before he gets here, can I ask you something?" Eric said.

"You can. I don't know if I'll answer," Maya said.

"Fair enough. What's going on between you and the deputy sheriff?"

"Why do you care?"

"I still take my promise to Zoey seriously. I just want to make sure you're okay and he's a good guy."

"It's complicated."

"I understand, but—are you happy with him?"

Maya hesitated. She didn't owe him anything, but for some reason she decided to give him the truth.

"Very happy," she said.

"I'm glad. That's all I need to know."

Chapter Forty-Five

Maya and Eric stood there staring at each other. Juniper made sure she remained between them.

"What do you say?" Eric asked. "Will you let me go? Now that you know everything."

"I'm sorry," Maya said. "You still have felony warrants out. I need to arrest you."

"I appreciate that," Eric said. "I can tell in the end you'll always do the right thing."

"I try, although I was ready to stab Abigail. Thank you for stopping me."

Eric took a step back. "You're welcome," he said. Then he took another step. "I'm sorry, Maya. I'm a cop. I won't survive prison either. Abigail isn't the only one with a list of felons who want revenge."

"Please don't run," Maya said. "Turn yourself in. Make a deal. I'll vouch for you. My phone is still recording over there. It has Abigail's confession."

"I can't. I'm sorry. I need to go."

"Then I have one last question," Maya said. "It's about something you said earlier."

"What's that?" Eric asked.

"You said your involvement in all of this cost you your family."

"It did."

"You said children. How many do you have?"

"Three," he said. "Two daughters and a son. They don't want to have anything to do with me. I can't say I blame them, but I do dream that someday, I might be able to reconcile with them. My ex-wife left me and moved to Alaska when they were young. I haven't seen them since. She took custody and I didn't blame her, so I didn't reach out, but I want to change that. It's one of many big regrets I have. Another reason prison just doesn't work."

Maya shook her head. "Maybe they would actually be more willing to connect with you if you did the right thing."

"Maybe, maybe not. For now, I need to stay on the run. Like Abigail said, this whole thing is bigger than just her."

"Don't you want the evidence?" Maya asked. "Don't you want to know if it is stashed in the mine?"

"I do, but I think you're at a point to find it and do what needs to be done."

"If you run, I'll send Juniper after you," Maya threatened.

"Then I'll have to take my chances," Eric said.

"I mean it," Maya said. "I'll send Juniper to get you."

"You really do, don't you?"

"Yes."

"Then go ahead, arrest me." Eric turned around and put his arms behind his back. Maya had Juniper guard while she cuffed him.

Maya took Eric back over to where Abigail was just as Deputy Wilson came up the path they had originally hiked in on, looking out of breath.

"I'm so sorry, Officer Thompson," he said. "I took a wrong turn on the way here."

"Didn't you grow up around here?" Maya asked.

"Yeah, I did, but I get lost easily," he said.

"You'll have to work on directions if you're going to be a deputy. You can make up for it by helping me take Abigail Harper and Eric Torres to the parking lot. I'll let you book them into jail tonight."

"Yes, ma'am. I'm so sorry. I'm going to be in so much trouble."

"No," Maya said. "You're not. Unless you keep calling me ma'am. Then I'll have a talk with your boss."

"Thanks."

"Just don't do it again. Let's get these two down the trail and off to jail where they belong. Then I have one more thing to do."

By the time Maya helped Deputy Wilson take Eric and Abigail to the parking lot, she was exhausted. Eric went with another deputy who had just arrived, and Abigail went with Deputy Wilson to the local jail, where she would receive medical care. They would both be held there until the FBI arrived. The crimes had crossed state lines and several had occurred on national forests, so now Lucas would be working with the feds. Maya drove the old Chevy truck with Juniper by her side and her mind raced at all the information Eric had told her. She'd listened to the recording on the way down the mountain to town and it had turned out perfectly. Every word from Abigail was picked up.

Maya had called the hospital and Josh was fine. The stake had missed his artery by millimeters. He was resting and doing well. She really wanted to see him, but instead she called Pops and, after apologizing, asked if he wanted to go for a drive back up to Deer Valley Pass. Maya knew where the evidence was stashed. She also called Lucas and asked him to join them.

Pops and Lucas met her at the Deer Valley Pass trailhead. Pops agreed to ride with Maya in the truck and Lucas would follow them. Juniper sat between Maya and Pops.

"Don't get used to this," Maya said to her.

Juniper let out a yip and then curled up on the seat. Pops petted Juniper and then they rode in silence for most of the drive. As they got closer to Deer Valley, Pops spoke up. "Did you hear that Eric Torres escaped?"

"What?" Maya said, almost driving off the road. Juniper lost her balance and fell into her, giving her an indignant look as Maya straightened the truck. "How the hell did that happen?"

"The deputy taking him in said he was stopped at some railroad tracks. Before he knew what was happening, Eric had the handcuffs off and kicked out the back window. He took off and we haven't been able to find him."

"Why didn't you call me? I could have tried tracking him."

"You're tired, Juniper is tired and I feel like we have the most important person in custody—Abigail. We put out a BOLO for him and deputies are out looking for him now. We'll find him. I'm curious to see who this evidence convicts, but I'm really curious to see if she's the one in charge. She's not saying anything right now," Pops said.

"Me too," said Maya. "She'll probably lawyer up."

"Probably. Where do you think it is?" Pops asked. "I

mean, if you're going to break and enter and steal my truck, I hope you at least know where it is."

"I thought it was the mine, but when I was up by the waterfall, I remembered a fire tower up the hill. Nana took me there once to see it. It's not in use anymore, and in fact the road to it is closed for the year. But a perk of being a Forest Service employee is that I have a key. I think Nana took the evidence there."

"Did you tell Torres about this?"

"No," Maya said. "It's my secret. Well, ours now. If he comes back to this area and goes to the old mine, he might just think that the evidence was gone or destroyed. I'm pretty sure that mine is flooded now anyway. He won't make it too far in there."

Pops smiled. "That's my girl."

Maya stopped at the brown gate that closed the access road to the fire tower. She unlatched the lock with her key and then hopped back in the truck and drove to the fire tower parking area. Not too many years ago, a Forest Service employee would live up there for the summer. "I'll go with Lucas and check it out," she said.

"I'll stay here with Juniper. Call me if you need anything."

"Okay," Maya said.

Lucas stepped out of his vehicle and joined her. Maya really wanted to go through all the evidence, but if she wanted a court conviction to stick, she needed to have Lucas properly collect and document everything for chain of custody. They stared at the steps in front of them.

"How many stairs am I climbing tonight?" Lucas asked.

"I'm not sure. A lot."

"I thought I was over this PT shit when I left the Marines," Lucas said.

"Well, you know what they say, 'Once a Marine, always a Marine.'"

"Yeah, whatever."

Maya and Lucas began the climb up. Her legs were burning by the time she reached the top. Luckily, her key worked in the door. She walked in and saw that the place had been shut down for the winter. Since no one stayed here to watch for fires anymore, tourists were allowed up in the summer.

Nana had brought her here on their last camping trip before Maya left for boot camp and shown her a special compartment where extra equipment and supplies could be stored. She'd been friends with the volunteer here for many years.

Maya went over to the compartment door and opened it. She peered down inside and saw a black duffel bag with the initials *Z.T.* embroidered on the end. She smiled.

"Thanks, Nana, thanks, Mom," she said as she stepped aside so Lucas could photograph the bag and wiggle it out of the tight space to lug back down the stairs. They made the trek back down the stairs and he held the bag up for Pops to see and then put it in his vehicle. He would take it to the sheriff's office to log the evidence with Miranda and hold it securely until the FBI arrived.

She opened the driver's door and climbed back in.

"I can't believe it was there," Pops said.

"I know. I can't believe it either."

"Let's go celebrate. Maybe dinner?"

"Agreed," Maya said. "Then I better go visit Josh. I haven't seen him since he was flown out of the meadow."

"I hope you can take tomorrow off," Pops said. "Maybe spend a little time with Josh."

Maya shrugged. "I need to work for a little bit. I have an arrest to make. I know who made the booby traps."

Eric stood on a ridge in the distance, watching through binoculars. His truck was parked at a pull-off about a half mile away. He'd picked it up from where he'd left it before meeting with Maya. He'd gone into the mine just far enough to know that if there was a duffel bag full of evidence in there, it was long gone. Then he'd thought about the coordinates Maya had.

He'd found a map and looked at them himself. Sure enough, she had duped him. The coordinates went to a fire tower, not the mine. But they were all in the same area.

He was proud of her, and now he watched as Maya came down the stairs of the fire tower, with the other investigator who had the duffel bag in hand. He had to give it to her. She was tenacious.

He'd wanted to clear his name. Pull out some of the stuff he knew Zoey had on him. She hadn't really wanted to get him into trouble, but she had wanted to make sure he kept his promise to keep Maya safe.

Eric peered up at the sky and said, "Hope you're happy with what I did and what I told her, Zoey. You should be proud. She's a lot like you—a fighter."

He hiked back to his truck and headed out of town. He'd watch the news and see the fallout from all of this. He knew he could never head home again, so instead, he just drove west, destination unknown.

Chapter Forty-Six

The next day, Maya pulled up to the hospital in her patrol vehicle. Juniper was back in her compartment and not happy about it. She much preferred the front seat of Pops's truck. Maya let her stick her head through the door that opened to the cab to try to make up for being back in the patrol vehicle.

"Behave yourself. No jumping and don't mention to Josh that you dug another hole in the yard," she said to Juniper. "I think he's in a lot of pain still. He'll see the hole soon enough."

Juniper whined and gave her a slurp.

"Okay then," Maya said.

She knew that Josh had refused any type of narcotic painkiller. He didn't want to be tempted into using again, so he'd insisted on Tylenol. Maya understood, but Tylenol didn't kill the pain he was in. She was looking forward to having him back home, though. She'd stayed at the house without him, and it felt odd. She still felt like a guest.

Josh came out in a wheelchair, and he stood with the help of crutches. Maya helped him into the front seat. Then she climbed into the driver's seat and headed away from the hospital.

"I'll be glad if I never see that place again," Josh said.

"Me too," Maya said.

Juniper gave a bark in agreement and stuck her head back through to say hi to Josh. He rubbed her face and she made happy grunting noises in between trying to lick him.

"How'd your arrest go this morning?" Josh asked.

"It actually went well for an arrest," Maya said. "But it was tough since I arrested a juvenile."

When she had been disarming the booby trap, she'd found a high school ID belonging to Ethan, the son of Daryl, the hardware store owner. Maya did some more digging and discovered that the kid had a history of problems in school, including sending death threats and smoking marijuana. Miranda had called Maya and left a message that the drug paraphernalia Juniper found did have a fingerprint that matched Ethan.

"Did the kid admit to doing it?" Josh asked.

"At first, he totally denied it, but then I showed him the ID I'd found along with the fingerprint on the marijuana, and he knew he was busted. I feel for Daryl and his wife. They seem like good parents. They moved up here hoping it would help their son, but he needs more help than a change in location. I suspect Daryl knew it was his son when I went in the store to question him, but he was probably trying to protect him."

"That's tough. Hopefully, they can get the kid the support he needs."

"I hope so," Maya said. "I'm glad to have that case wrapped up, but I hate seeing someone so young getting into that type of trouble."

"I agree," Josh said. "Any news on the other case? Has the FBI made arrests yet?"

"I heard from one of the agents that they were going to do some warrants and arrests today. The evidence was overwhelming and made several cases open and shut. My mom had photographs, voice recordings and even some physical evidence with DNA and finger-prints. Some of the judges were about ready to retire. Same with some of the lawyers. I can't believe they were still involved in all these activities," Maya said. "It's crazy. But the FBI was happy to have everything I handed over. Lucas did give me one item from the bag, though. He didn't think it would help with the case and he thought I'd want it."

"What's that?" Josh asked.

"A picture of me and my mother. I was probably about eighteen months old. I need to have it framed. Maybe I can get a copy made and give it to Pops."

"That's great. I'm glad he let you have that."

"Me too. I went to my cabin and loaded up the dog run. I'm bringing it to your place and setting it up some-where outside of your nice yard."

"Does that mean Juniper did more landscaping work?" Josh asked.

"You could say that," Maya said, thinking about the holes she'd found this morning. She'd gone back inside to get more coffee, and in minutes, Juniper had dug another hole. Maya thought Juniper had looked quite pleased with herself. She would pop her head out of the holes like a prairie dog.

"Do I want to see it?" Josh asked.

"Probably not. I'll be buying you some trees if you really want to plant them or at least filling in holes and buying you sod," Maya said, deciding to change the sub-ject. "Did you hear that Eric Torres escaped?"

"I did. How are you doing with that?"

"I'm okay. I'm going to find him, though. I don't care what it takes, but I also feel like the more Lucas goes through the evidence, what little he can share with me points to Abigail being the ringleader in all of this. At least she's sitting in jail with no bail. The feds and the state investigators are talking with prosecutors trying to determine how to move forward and how they want to charge her. I think it will be a while before they get that all figured out."

"That's right where she deserves to be," Josh said. "What's going on with your grandfather and the investigation?"

"The sheriff's committee decided to put him on paid leave. Doc Clark talked to him and said the DA is planning to have him arrested soon. I'm so nervous for Pops, and I know that means you'll have more on your plate."

"We'll figure it out if it happens," Josh said. "I already called my dad. He's licensed here in Colorado. He said he'd come out and represent your grandfather if need be. I'm anxious about taking over, but I've decided I'm up for the challenge."

"That's fantastic," Maya said. "And I'd love to meet your dad. Actually, I'd love to meet your whole family."

"You say that now. Keep that in mind when they all descend here. My mother called me about five times yesterday."

"I'm sure she was just worried," Maya said. "They can't be that bad."

"I love them very much, but there's more than one reason I moved out of state."

Maya laughed and said, "Now I'm intrigued." She

pulled into Josh's driveway and parked. "I'll get Juniper out after I get you settled in the house."

She helped Josh inside and took him to the living room, where she had a surprise. She'd managed to buy some furniture for his living room online and have it shipped up to his house. She hoped he'd like it.

"What do you think?" Maya asked. "Now you can watch the Bears in comfort."

A grin spread across Josh's face. "It's fantastic. Thank you. You didn't need to do this."

"I wanted to and you're not charging me rent and Juniper is redoing your landscaping, so I figured it was the least I could do."

"Well, thank you."

"Let's get you settled," Maya said, helping Josh over to the love seat.

He sat down and she went out to get Juniper. Juniper came flying out of the vehicle and ran up the steps to the front door, where she jumped up and down. Maya followed her and made her settle. She had Juniper's bed in the living room too and had worked with her on staying in place. So far it had gone pretty well. She got Juniper settled and then sat down next to Josh, snuggling into him.

"Is this okay?" Maya asked. "I don't want to hurt you."

"It's great. You're not hurting me."

"I have a question for you, though," Maya said.

"Shoot. What is it?"

"Your bed is more comfortable. Mind if I sleep there? I do come with a Malinois that sometimes wakes up early, although she's not really a morning dog. She does snore, though."

At the mention of her name, Juniper picked her head up, tilted it and stared at them. She sighed and then put her head back down and went back to sleep.

"I don't mind at all," Josh said, with a smile.

"I mean, once you get healed."

"I think having you with me will help me heal up better," Josh said.

"Okay, then," Maya said. She leaned over and kissed him.

"I could definitely get used to this," Josh said.

"I still don't know what 'this' is," Maya said. "I mean, are we having a fling? Something more serious? I come with a lot of baggage and…"

"Maya, stop," Josh cut her off. "We both have baggage. We both have a past. We've both had traumas, but we should know that when we find something special that we shouldn't hold back. We don't know what tomorrow is going to bring, but I do want tomorrow to be with you."

"I feel the same way," Maya said.

"You up for giving this a go? I know it means you'll have to talk to your boss and I know it means that we may not be able to work on investigations together, but I'd like to come home at night and be with you and Juniper."

"I'm definitely up for giving this a go," Maya said. She took a deep breath and uttered the words she'd had a hard time saying. "I love you, Josh Colten."

* * * * *

Acknowledgments

I'm so grateful for everyone who's helped me on this book. To say I appreciate all they've done is an understatement. My first thanks is to all the readers out there. I appreciate each and every one of you. You've made this dream possible.

One of the things I've enjoyed most about writing fiction is the number of people I've met who agree to discuss and answer questions about their professions. I'm always humbled and honored at what so many experts are willing to share. As always, any mistakes are mine and mine alone. In addition to that, as a writer, I love taking some fictional liberties with the jobs portrayed in this book. Please know that in real life the professionals are remarkable people who work hard to keep our public lands and streets safe. They put their lives on the line every day to protect others. Thank you!

Special thanks goes to Forest Service Law Enforcement Officer Chris Magallon. Thank you for answering my questions about your fascinating job and for keeping our forests safe. When I first connected with Officer Magallon, he was still working his K-9 Ice. I recently learned that Ice crossed the rainbow bridge. Thank you,

Ice, for your service and may you now have all the steak dinners you want.

A big thank-you to retired chief of police Dave Lewandowski. I appreciate your expertise and willingness to continue sharing your stories and knowledge with me. Dave's wife Jamie has also given me so much encouragement and I can't thank her enough. Another good friend that has been willing to read parts of my book and share his expertise is MSgt Dr. James A. Burghard, USA/USCG/USAF, Retired. Thank you so much for continuing to help me. A big thank-you to his beautiful wife, Marie Burghard, who I'm lucky enough to call my best friend. Your support and inspiration mean the world to me. One last expert who has answered numerous questions is retired sergeant Patrick O'Donnell. Patrick has a great Facebook group and podcast called *Cops and Writers*. Check them out, even if you're not a writer. They are both fantastic and informative resources.

I've been so lucky to work for Sherlock Hounds Detection Canines since 2005. Along the way, I've met some amazing trainers who continue to push me to be a better handler. They've also been willing to answer questions about the areas of K-9 handling where I have less experience. Thank you to Mackey Kelly of Canis Major Dog Training and Lanie DeLong of Blue Dog K-9. I also want to thank my business partner Beth Kelly for giving me such a great opportunity to work dogs and for being such a great friend.

To become a better writer, you need honest feedback and encouragement. My critique group, Broad Horizons, has been there for me and helped me along during this journey. I couldn't have done this without you! Beta readers are also important and help make a book better. Thank you to Anne Hunsinger and Brooke Terpening for taking the time to read this book and give me some great feedback.

Thank you to my "team" that has helped make my publishing dreams come true—especially my agent Ella Marie Shupe. Thanks for believing in these books and characters and finding a home for them with such a great publisher. I am very thankful for my editor Mackenzie Walton who has helped make each book better. The entire team at Carina Press is fantastic and I appreciate all of you. Thank you so much!

Another friend who has helped me tremendously is fellow K-9 author Margaret Mizushima. Thank you, Margaret, for being such an amazing mentor and friend as well as giving me your feedback and answering all my questions.

My family has always encouraged my love of writing. A big thank-you to my husband who has been by my side through this whole journey. I love you so much and your support means the world to me. And to my parents who have always believed, thank you and love you both. My aunt June and uncle Maury deserve so much thanks for always having faith in me and being such great fans. I love you both very much. You are an amazing "Ant" and "Unc." My brother and his family have also been very supportive during this journey. I appreciate your love and inspiration.

My final thank-you goes to the wonderful dogs I've worked over the years and to all the K-9s currently on the job. Dogs are the most amazing animals. There's a reason they are called our "best friend." Thanks to dogs, our world is a better place.

About the Author

Award-winning author Kathleen Donnelly is a K-9 handler for a private narcotics detection company based in Colorado. She enjoys using her K-9 experience to craft realism into her fictional stories. Kathleen loves the beauty of the mountains, which inspired her choice of setting for her series. She lives near the Colorado foothills with her husband and her four-legged coworkers.

Visit Kathleen on her website at www.kathleendonnelly.com, on Facebook at Facebook.com/authorkathleendonnelly, follow her on Twitter @katk9writer or find her on Instagram @authorkathleendonnelly.

A small-town sheriff running from her past learns to love again in the first book in K-9 Defenders, a suspenseful new romance series from award-winning author Sandra Owens.

Read on for an excerpt from In His Protection *by Sandra Owens, out now from Carina Press!*

Chapter One

"Damn, you shot the sheriff."

Tristan Church glared at his brother while considering putting his ass on the ground. For one, stating the obvious while Tristan tried to convince himself that he was having a nightmare. That he had not, in fact, shot the sheriff. For another, he seriously wanted to wipe that smirk off his brother's face.

But he'd have to take Kade down some other time. At the moment, he had to accept that he wasn't in the middle of a nightmare, that he actually had shot the sheriff. He was never going to hear the end of it. Even his dog was giving him the side-eye. Fuzz cozied up to the sheriff as if too embarrassed by his person to be seen with him. *Traitor.*

"The hell, Chief. You shot me," Sheriff Skylar Morgan yelled, glaring at him as red paint dripped down her arm. "You can't tell the difference between me and the bad guy? You have your eyes checked lately?"

He narrowed said eyes. "I had the bank robber in my sights, *Sheriff.* You jumped in front of him." Skye was the bane of his existence. She was their county sheriff, and he was the city police chief. They bashed heads over everything, mostly because she was more stubborn than Old Man Earl's goat. He wanted her out of his life, and he wanted to lock his lips on hers and kiss that sass right out of her mouth. He wasn't sure which he wanted more, but he was sure about one thing. He'd go to his grave before admitting he liked her sass.

"If a hostage jumps in front of the bad guy, you gonna shoot him, too?" She poked a finger into his chest, leaving a red fingerprint on his T-shirt.

She had him there, and that chafed. He leaned down, putting his face inches from hers. "No, I only like shooting sheriffs."

And as hard as he'd tried to forget he knew her intimately, knew her soft sighs and the feel of her fingernails scraping down his back, he hadn't been able to. A year later, he still had erotic dreams of her. Not as many as he used to, but they still happened. He shook his head to rid it of images of a naked Skye under him.

"Let's try this again," Kade said, then smirked at Tristan with entirely too much amusement in his eyes. "Try not to shoot the sheriff this time, brother."

"When did you say your leave was up? Tomorrow, right?" His brother was Delta Force, stationed at Fort Bragg. He was also downright annoying.

"You trying to get rid of me?" Kade slapped him on the back. "If I didn't know you loved me, my feelings would be hurt."

"Since when do you have feelings?" he muttered, turning his back on Kade's laughter so his brother wouldn't see his grin.

Kade gave a sharp whistle. "All right, people, let's give this drill another go."

"Don't shoot me this time," Skye said as she passed him.

Tristan wondered if the only way to shut her up *was* to kiss her.

"I'd never shoot you, even accidently, beautiful Skylar." Kade winked at her, then monkeyed his way up the ladder to his tower.

Tristan lost his grin. Kade was the only person in the world besides him and Skye who knew about that night. His brother also knew how to annoy him, and since that was one of Kade's favorite things to do, he flirted with Skye whenever Tristan was around.

The law enforcement officers—some Skye's people and some his—took their places. A few years ago, Tristan had talked Kade into conducting training drills with his officers. After the drill was over, they'd have target practice. Five months ago, Skye had showed up with her deputies and crashed the party. Tristan still didn't know how she'd learned of the drills.

Since Marsville's squirrely mayor considered himself an expert with a weapon, and since Luther would love playing cops and robbers, and since he was as likely to shoot himself in the foot, or God help them, one of them, the drills and especially target practice were top secret. Every one of Tristan's officers had been sworn to secrecy, and the location was out in the boondocks on two acres he had bought for next to nothing.

No one was supposed to know about this place outside of his police force and his brothers, but Tristan had a sneaking suspicion Kade was the one who'd tipped Skye off. It would be just like him to do that, then sit back and enjoy the hell out of the fireworks that exploded anytime Tristan and Skye were within spitting distance of each other. His brother denied it, of course, but Kade loved stirring shit up.

From his lookout tower, enabling him to see everything going on below, Kade blew his whistle, signaling the drill was starting. Tristan kept eyes on Skye as they moved through the obstacle course he, Kade, and their baby brother, Parker, had built to simulate a few of Marsville's downtown buildings.

Parker, being an artist, had insisted on accuracy, thus all the storefronts looked just like the real ones, the only difference being there weren't any roofs. That had been Kade's idea, so he could see what was going on inside the businesses from his "boss tower" when they drilled.

Tristan let Skye take the lead. He inwardly snorted. *Let her* his ass. She'd taken the lead, no *let her* about it, but he was enjoying the view. Skylar Morgan was easy on the eyes from her front and her back. She was tall, but still a head shorter than him, a body he could drool over if he allowed himself—and he had once— light brown hair that she kept in a tight bun low on her neck when in uniform, and blue eyes that had a hint of violet in them. Funny, though, how those eyes turned icy blue when they landed on him. But stored in his memory bank was how dark they'd turned when he was buried deep inside her and she'd screamed his name.

He could almost hate her for that night because she'd slipped right inside his mind and stolen any interest he might have had for any other woman after her. He wasn't a manwhore, but he wasn't a monk either. Or, he hadn't been before Skye. He wasn't liking his new monk status so much.

If he'd known who she was the night he'd met "first names only" Skye at Beam Me Up, Marsville's honky-tonk bar, he would have steered clear of her. Hell, if he'd known how miserable she'd make him, he'd have run far, far away.

Who was he kidding? He'd have done exactly what he had...followed her to her motel room. A man in a trance. Over the past year, he'd decided that Skylar Morgan was a witch and had slipped enchantment powder in his drink when he wasn't paying attention to what her sneaky hand was doing. He wanted her to unchant him.

The only reason he'd been at Beam Me Up that night was because the Watters brothers had been causing more trouble than usual. He'd stopped in to see if they were at the bar, and if so, put a stop to their shenanigans before things got out of hand, as often happened with those boys. They hadn't been there, but the beautiful woman sitting at the bar had drawn his attention, and since he knew every living soul in Marsville but had never seen her before, he thought she was just passing through. Why not join her, see if she was interested in a little playtime, and then she'd be gone the next day.

After a bit of small talk and a lot of chemistry sizzling in the air between them, "first names only" Skye let him know she was interested. Only one problem, she was back a month later. The new sheriff in town. And when Luther introduced her to the existing chief of police, Tristan got his first glimpse of how icy blue her eyes could turn. He tried not to take it personally when she acted like they'd never met, but he had.

Then there was her name. She preferred Skylar, and that was what everyone called her. But she'd told him that night her name was Skye, so she'd forever be Skye to him. Added fun...fire flamed to life, melting some of that ice in her eyes, every time he called her Skye, and he knew why. His calling her Skye was a reminder of the night they'd spent together, and try as she might to hide it, he saw desire in those flames. He just didn't know what to do about it.

"Much better, people," Kade called from his tower. "Except for you, Chief. You daydreaming over there?"

Tristan blinked, then scowled at Skye when she snorted. When he was satisfied she'd seen his scowl, he turned it on his asswipe brother. "No, I am not. I was observing."

"Uh-huh," Kade said, the laughter in his voice downright annoying. "That's enough training for today, people. You did good. Trade your paintball guns for real ones and let's annihilate some targets."

When they'd built their fake town, they'd included a changing room with lockers for their weapons. Because Tristan had one female officer and hoped to have more eventually, they'd added a wall between the two dressing rooms, giving any women training with them privacy. Skye and Vee, his officer, disappeared behind the wall. Tristan tried not to imagine Skye peeling off her paint-splattered T-shirt. He failed.

"She's really gotten under your skin, brother," Kade said, coming up next to him.

Tristan didn't have to ask who *she* was. "You're seeing things that aren't there."

"Right, keep on lying to yourself."

He glared at his brother, then stomped away. If he wanted to lie to himself, that was his business. He was halfway to his car when he realized Fuzz wasn't following. His dog was in love with Skye and would jump ship to the sheriff's department given half a chance. Tristan gave a sharp whistle, and a minute later, the German shepherd trotted his way.

"I know she's pretty, but you need to remember who feeds you, bud." Not that he blamed Fuzz for his fascination with the sheriff. At all.

Don't miss In His Protection *by Sandra Owens,*
available wherever books are sold.
www.Harlequin.com